Judith could not help looking back.

She managed to meet his gaze steadily, amusement at her own folly bringing a soft curve to her lips and an added sparkle to eyes already bright with an awareness she could not deny.

To her astonishment Oliver's expression sobered and a dark flush stained his neck. Then he laughed.

'Marry, angel,' he said, somewhat unsteadily, 'but you do have the most unsettling effect upon a man.'

Dear Reader

We welcome back both Louisa Gray, with an intriguing Regency, and Sarah Westleigh, who has moved to Tudor times to explore the death threats to Elizabeth, both gripping reads.

We introduce a new American author, Kate Kingsley, where Danielle is ostracised by New Orleans and ends on the high seas, and have a second Patricia Potter story for you, set in New Mexico 1846, where Tristan Hampton has a hidden enemy.

June is bursting out with goodies indeed!

The Editor

Sarah Westleigh has enjoyed a varied life. Working as a local government officer in London, she qualified as a chartered quantity surveyor. She assisted her husband in his chartered accountancy practice, at the same time managing an employment agency. Moving to Devon, she finally found time to write, publishing short stories and articles, before discovering historical novels.

Recent titles by the same author:

A MOST EXCEPTIONAL QUEST
HERITAGE OF LOVE
LOYAL HEARTS

ESCAPE TO DESTINY

Sarah Westleigh

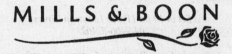

MILLS & BOON

MILLS & BOON LIMITED
ETON HOUSE, 18–24 PARADISE ROAD
RICHMOND, SURREY, TW9 1SR

First published in Great Britain 1994
by Mills & Boon Limited

© Sarah Westleigh 1994

Australian copyright 1994   Philippine copyright 1994
This edition 1994

ISBN 0 263 78254 9

Set in 10 on 11½ pt Linotron Times
04-9406-82102

Typeset in Great Britain by Centracet, Cambridge
Printed in Great Britain by
BPC Paperbacks Ltd
A member of
The British Printing Company Ltd

CHAPTER ONE

JUDITH hated Sark. Yet she loved it, too. Loved its inaccessible, rugged coastline and the security of the closely knit community of those who had come with the Seigneur to recolonise and defend for Queen Elizabeth this tiny, abandoned island. No enemy could now use it as a stepping stone in an attempt to deprive the English Crown of the other, larger islands off the coast of Normandy, the only remaining continental possessions brought to it by William the Conqueror.

But she hated the sense of confinement, of being cut off from everything beyond its meagre limits. On a clear day you could see Guernsey from where she stood on the cliffs of Longue Pointe, the southern bastion of Le Grand Bay. After the recent sudden storm the larger island stood out, dark against a sheet of brilliance reflecting the newly emerged, glaring sun, with the smaller islands of Herm and Jethou strung like jewels between, the nearby Ile des Marchands, divided from Sark only by a narrow passage, completing the chain. Somewhere beyond the distant, glassy horizon lay a new world of untold riches, but she would never see it.

The ground was wet and Judith shifted her stance, lifting her skirts clear of the sodden turf. The tidal race was on, sending white-capped waves scurrying through the passage between the rocky headland and the Ile des Marchands.

She hated storms, but now it had passed safely over she could enjoy watching its aftermath. Shielding her eyes against the brightness, she scanned the scene. No ships had come to grief locally, it seemed, but something was being tumbled in the boiling water coursing through the passage. If it wasn't smashed to pieces first, whatever it was would either be swept past the island altogether or, more likely, be caught by the wind and current and washed ashore at the foot of the cliffs below. Without further thought she clutched her shawl about her, lifted her skirts still higher and began a scrambling descent of the nearest, precipitate access to the shore.

Her father enjoyed the benefit of half the value of all flotsam and jetsam collected from the shores of Beauregard. Anything the sea brought in might prove valuable.

Halfway down she paused to regain her breath and to take another look, brushing her heavy brown hair back impatiently as the wind whipped it about her face. She had guessed correctly. The flotsam was being washed towards the rocks. It was nearer now, and so was she, she could see it quite clearly——

Shocked, she froze to make sure her eyes had not deceived her. But no, it was a dark head she had glimpsed, and pale limbs working desperately to bring their owner towards the tiny haven.

She gave a gasp of concern, not fear, for what threat could such a creature pose now, even were he proved later to be enemy or pirate? Quickening her pace, she continued her scramble down the path, regardless of brambles and furze and any damage to her gown. Coming to the plateau at the top of the low but almost sheer cliff at the head of the inlet, which guarded access to the valley leading up to Beauregard, she ran round its rim to the rough steps hewn from the rock by her brothers, finally erupting on the shore in a tangle of skirts to pick herself up, breathless and filthy with mud.

He would be dashed against the rocks at the foot of the towering Longue Pointe within minutes. She sped down the shingle and round the small inner bay, then leapt from stone to stone, light and agile on her feet, knowing every inch of the shore. He was being swept into shallower water, but appeared too exhausted now to help himself.

There was a large flat rock among the welter of smaller ones, exposed at low tide but now sunk beneath the surface of the water. If she could reach that, she could edge along it and prevent his being smashed to death, possibly even haul him to safety.

She plunged deeper into the sea, wading out up to her waist before she reached the rock and scrambled up. The sea covered it only by a foot or so, though soaking spray plumed up with every pounding breaker. She inched along the treacherous surface, seeing the body being washed nearer with every swelling wave. But the man — for it was a man — was defying nature to keep himself afloat. At last the waves delivered him at her feet. Judith bent down and grasped his upper arm.

'Give me your hand.'

He coughed and spluttered, ejecting water from his mouth and throat. Shook wet hair from his face, opened a bemused, bleary eye which focused uncertainly on her face. His mouth quirked into a smile.

'Marry! A blessed angel!' he gasped, and gave her the sinewy hand she had requested.

Judith ignored the effect of that jaunty smile, concentrating instead on towing him towards shallow water without scraping him against the barnacle-encrusted rocks. Her footing was none too secure, for seaweed clung with tenacious slipperiness to every surface. But, somehow, she managed, assisted by his instinctive efforts to save himself.

She jumped down from the rock into the deep water again. Taking a new grip under his arms, she half towed, half dragged him over the ring of small rocks fringing the shingle, then struggled to drag him from the water, for the first time in her life thanking God for her stature and for the hard work which had toned and strengthened her muscles.

Having effected her rescue, the fact that his long, sparely fleshed, muscular body was entirely naked could no longer be ignored. She felt the hot blood begin to creep up her neck and was thankful when, with a groan of agony, he shook off her hands and rolled over on his front, clenching his fists and burying his face in his arms.

She immediately forgot to be embarrassed. Horrified, she gazed at his back. His skin had been bruised and grazed all over by contact with rocks, but his buffeting in the sea did not account for the ugly weals or the oozing wounds where the skin had been torn from the bunched muscles by leaden-tipped tails.

'Who did that?' she gasped.

But he merely gave a breathless, groaning grunt and shook his head.

'Come' she said urgently, 'let me help you up the beach. You must move, or you will be overtaken by the tide!'

Making a supreme effort, he raised himself to hands and knees and crawled up the shingle.

'That will be far enough,' she said at last.

At her words he collapsed to the ground and lapsed into unconsciousness. Sheer willpower had brought him thus far. His entire body shook convulsively, and she knew he had been in the sea too long. He needed to be wrapped up and set by a fire; he would not survive left naked in the open.

She had thrown off her shawl before entering the water. Retrieving it, she covered him as best she could, careful not to drag it over his damaged skin, though he was mercifully unaware of her actions. He would feel his agony again only when he regained consciousness.

Surveying his position, she decided he would be safe enough while she went for help. After a last, anxious scrutiny of the tousled head her eyes seemed drawn to the long, moisture-beaded limbs left uncovered by her shawl. The sprinkling of dark hair on thighs and shins, pasted to the flesh, glistened in the warming, westering sun. He was very beautiful.

Shaking herself mentally, she turned towards the rough-hewn steps and the direct path up the valley to her home.

Out of breath, she panted into the communal chamber of the long, low, stone building recently completed by Pierre Le Grand to house his family.

'Mother!'

A woman, bent over the fire stirring a pot of broth hanging on a hook above the flames, straightened and turned, wiping a flushed face with the back of a work-worn hand. She gave a dismayed gasp.

'Mistress Judith!'

Judith's cry had not been addressed to old Marie, but to another woman sitting spinning near by. Ester Le Grand's eyes focused on her daughter's bedraggled appearance and filled with apprehension.

'Look at the state of you, child! What's amiss?'

'Where is Papa?' asked Judith, ignoring both her mother's and their servant's concern. 'Is he in the byre?'

Her younger sister, Genette, just emerging from

childhood and promising to be as fragile and dainty as
Judith was strong and blooming, spoke from her seat
by the small window.

'All the men have gone to the other side of the
island. Didn't you hear the alarm? The reports were
loud enough!'

'Alarm? They've fired the warning signal shots? No,
I didn't hear them. I was down in the bay. Do you
know what the danger is?'

'Not yet. The boys will be back to let us know.' Ester
Le Grand swept over to feel her elder daughter's
sodden gown. 'You are soaked to the skin, Judith! Get
those clothes off at once!'

'I will, but, Genette, will you go and see if you can
find the boys? I need their help. I've just rescued a
man from the sea, and I cannot bring him up alone.
We'll need a litter, and ropes——'

'A man? What kind of a man?' asked her mother
sharply.

'I don't know. Genette, *please* go!' urged Judith.

'But I want to hear——'

'There's nought to hear!' interrupted Judith
impatiently. 'Anyway you'll discover everything there
is to know later! But if we don't get him up here into
the warm, and fast, he'll die.'

Ester Le Grand made an imperative gesture. 'Do as
your sister asks, Genette. Bring Jasper, too, if he can
be spared.' And, as Genette petulantly dumped the
sewing in her hand and flounced from the house, Ester
returned her attention to Judith. 'Now, wench, get out
of those wet things while I fetch you something dry to
wear!'

Judith stripped off her gown and petticoats and stood
shivering, the linen cloth she had used to dry her skin
draped about her, while she waited for her mother to

return. Reaction, a strange excitement and a certain coolness in the air after the storm rendered even the warm room helpless to dispel her shivers.

'Come nearer the fire,' ordered Marie, a solid, dumpy figure whose physical shortcomings emphasised the slender grace of her absent mistress. An old servant, who had come with the family from Jersey, she had taken charge of the household and all those in it many years since. She continued stirring her pot while frowning at Judith. 'What does he look like, this fellow you've rescued?'

'I don't know. Dark-haired. You'll see for yourself soon.'

Judith's reply was brusque, for how could she describe the beautiful stranger without increasing the *frisson* of anticipation already gripping her?

'Now, tell me the tale,' ordered Ester on her return, dumping on a nearby bench the things she had brought from the far bedchamber which her two daughters shared.

Judith complied as she dressed.

'An Englishman, you say?' murmured Ester as Judith fell silent.

'I believe so. He must have understood me although I spoke in our dialect, not pure French, but he replied in English,' said Judith as she laced dry shoes on her feet and straightened up.

'You're sure he isn't Spanish?'

Her mother's anxiety mirrored that in Marie's eyes. Although England was not at war with either France or Spain, attack from either or both was a constant concern. Even a lone Spaniard was to be feared, for he could herald the advent of more. And the island was already in a state of alarm over something.

'He spoke in English,' reiterated Judith. 'You'd

better dry those clothes, especially the shoes. The ones
I'm wearing will get wet too, I shouldn't be surprised;
the ground is running with water after the downpour.'

''Tis as well this homespun is tough,' grunted Marie
as she draped the gown before the fire. ''Tis disgraceful
the way you mistreat your clothes, Mistress Judith, you
should be learning to become a young lady——'

'Oh, do be quiet, Marie! Why should I wish to
behave like a young lady, cooped up here on Sark?'

'Never let your father hear you speak so!' Ester's
tone was sharp. 'He came here because he desired the
prestige of holding property. Without it, despite all his
qualifications, he could not truly call himself a gentleman. It is an investment in the future. And he has done
well, the Seigneur has rewarded him generously for his
legal advice and organisational help, granting him
subtenancies and extra rights. It is not our place to
question his decisions, however unwelcome we might
find them!'

'I know all that.' She also knew that her mother
regretted the softer life to be enjoyed in St Helier. She
sighed. 'I am merely being realistic, Maman.'

'Your father is doing his best to arrange a suitable
marriage for you, Judith. When he does, you will
regret your hoydenish ways——'

'Master Perrier will not care,' muttered Judith
rebelliously.

Ester broke off the argument as Judith's brothers
burst into the room. Both had quivers of bolts slung
from their waists and knives sheathed at their hips, and
carried hunting crossbows and heavy staves. Not much
with which to defend the shores against cannon and
invasion, but their father, plus the other tenement
holders themselves or one of their men, had been given
a musket and trained to use it. The obligation laid

upon the colonisers to defend the island for Queen Elizabeth was taken most seriously.

Judith, who had only just covered herself decently, greeted their arrival with relief. Edward, the eldest, had grown no taller than his father, but was decidedly more brawny. Josué, two years younger and, at eighteen, still growing, was shorter and slighter but surprisingly strong. They would manage a litter between them, with her to help. She was as tall as Edward. She must, she supposed, take after that remote ancestor who had given the family its name. Her above-average height for a woman had already cost her one advantageous alliance.

But she wouldn't think of that now!

'Jasper is not with you?' she asked anxiously, feeling that another helping hand, especially that of her father's able foreman, would not come amiss.

'Nay. He remained to defend the landing. There's a Spanish carrack lying off the other shore.' Edward lifted heavy brows and gave her a look. 'We would rather be there, too, but Father sent us back with a message, we met Genette and she said the matter here was urgent.'

''Tis a matter of life and death! We must be quick if we are to save this man. You must make up a litter, while I find a blanket and go to Penna for salve. I'll meet you down in the bay, bring rope as well, be as quick as you can!'

'Do you think he's a Spaniard, off the carrack?'

'Why so much alarm over a Spanish merchantman?' cried Judith, avoiding the question as she disappeared from sight in search of a blanket.

'But carracks are armed, it's off their normal course and looking as though it might try to land troops at

Eperquerie,' Edward shouted after her. He lowered his voice as she reappeared. 'Could he be off it?'

'I suppose so,' admitted Judith, folding the blanket smaller and rolling it into a bundle to go beneath her arm, 'though as I keep telling Mother, he's no Spaniard, I think he's English. And he's taken a dozen or so strokes of the lash.'

'A dozen?' scoffed Edward with a shrug. 'He could've got those for anything. I've heard of men surviving a hundred and more——'

Judith shivered anew, afraid to image what his back would have been like then, thankful when her mother cut Edward short.

'We don't want to hear any bestial tales from you!' said Ester sternly, giving a meaningful nod in Genette's direction. Genette was listening with avid interest.

'He's no rough seaman to be whipped for dis-obedience, either!' put in Judith hoarsely.

'And carracks don't carry galley slaves. Poor fellow!' exclaimed Josué. 'Come along, Edward, don't waste time! Whoever he is and however he came by his stripes, he needs our help!'

They all departed together, though while the boys went to look for rope and suitable stakes and strong cloth to make the litter, Judith made for the original shelter of bracken, stone and furze the family and all its dependants had inhabited until the house was completed. Their erstwhile nurse, now married to Jasper Sidney, still lived in it. Since Judith had emerged from childhood Penna had become a friend, despite the ten years difference in their ages.

The old shelter still seemed like home. Penna looked up from her sewing, a glad smile lighting her round face, as Judith greeted the children playing in one corner of the room. From his advanced age of five, her

youngest brother, Samuel, the only member of the Le
Grand family born on Sark, was lording it over Penna's
two children.

'Judith! Have you news?'

'There is a Spanish carrack lying off to the east,
Jasper is still over there.' Judith repositioned the
blanket under her arm. 'But I've come on a different
errand. I need some of your salve, as much as you've
got.'

'You've hurt yourself?' frowned Penna.

'Not for me. I've found a half-drowned man down in
the bay, his back is lacerated and needs dressing. The
boys are making a litter to bring him up, but I'd like to
plaster his wounds with the salve before they move
him.'

Penna went swiftly to fetch a jar from a shelf.

'Will this be enough? I've some more in the store-
room; I made enough to last the winter while the
marigolds were at their best.'

'This will be enough for now,' said Judith, inspecting
the contents, 'but he will probably need more. His
entire back is raw, and he has a lot of other grazes.
He'll most likely develop a fever, too. He's very weak.'

Penna eyed her young friend thoughtfully. 'The sea
water will have cleansed the wounds, and will help
them to heal,' she advised slowly. 'You seem concerned.' She paused, cocking her head on one side
enquiringly. 'Is he young? Good to look upon?'

Judith's colour mounted, betraying her. 'Not over-
young, though comely enough,' she muttered awkwardly. 'But I would feel concern for any man——'

'Not if he were elderly, ill-formed and had an evil
face with broken, stinking teeth, I'll be bound! Or
happened to be a haughty, hateful Spaniard,' Penna

added, her own distaste putting a grim note into her voice.

'Not all Spaniards can be so worthy of our dislike ——'

'Those I have seen support the tales others tell of their overweening, cruel pride — and as for their Inquisition. . .'

Judith shuddered. 'This man has suffered the lash, and I do not think he is a common sailor to warrant such punishment for some neglect of duty or insubordination. . .'

'Then go to him quickly! Do not allow my teasing to delay you longer! Here, take this flask of wine!' Penna thrust the leathern container in Judith's hand and pushed her towards the door. 'I would come with you, but must stay with the children. Be careful, my dear.'

'I will.'

Judith made the promise, wondering what Penna had meant by it. Careful of the path? Careful of the man? Careful of what? she asked herself as slung the long strap of the flask over her shoulder and began the descent, conscious that she had been ready to talk in order to delay her return, despite her sense of urgency. He had been naked, she had seen him, he knew it, and she was nervous of facing him again.

With the blanket and salve to carry she had to tread warily, to concentrate more on her footing even on the easier path. She glanced downwards a couple of times when it gave her a view, but he was too near the face of the cliff for her to glimpse his figure until she reached its edge. He lay sprawled just as she had left him.

So it came as a shock when she scrambled down the last steps to the shore and looked round to find him crouched defensively, her shawl twisted about his hips, a large stone held threateningly in his hand.

Gone was the exhausted lethargy, the quirky, heart-wrenching smile. His features held taut alertness, his chin thrust forward belligerently. Judith was uncomfortably aware of every tensed muscle in his strong, quivering body. He reminded her of a nervous animal at bay.

When he saw who it was his tension slackened, but his eyes lifted to scan the cliff above her head, wary of new danger.

'You are quite safe,' said Judith quietly. 'I am alone.' He continued to eye her doubtfully and she smiled, holding out her burden. 'I came to put salve on your wounds, and brought a blanket and wine for your comfort. My brothers are bringing a litter. I imagine the climb would prove too stiff for you at present.'

'I thought you might be French,' he said. 'Where am I?'

'On the island of Sark. We are of Norman descent, come recently from Jersey, but owe allegiance to the English queen. We speak a French dialect, though most people here can speak pure French if necessary and a few of us speak English. You are safe here.' She had spoken in his tongue to reassure him.

'Praise God! And no Spanish have landed?'

She shook her head. 'Not to my knowledge. There is a carrack off the other coast; our men have gone to defend the island against attack. Though should a landing party come in peace we can scarcely deny the men hospitality.'

He groaned. 'Would that it had capsised and gone to the bottom!'

Though intrigued, Judith ignored this. She could satisfy her curiosity later. 'Would you like some wine? And may I treat your wounds?' she asked.

The smile emerged. He sank back to sit on a stone,

his knees drawn up and clasped to his chest. His shuddering had scarcely abated at all, his teeth chattered and his speech came with difficulty. 'Aye,' he murmured, 'to both. I will not deny that my back is accursedly painful. Is there skin yet left on it?'

Judith handed him the wine-skin, feeling heat glow throughout her body. Determined not to show her awareness, she squatted at his side and inspected his wounds anew. Having drunk, he lowered his crisp brown curls, almost dry now, so that his forehead rested on his knees. She longed to reach out and stroke his hair, tenderness for a strong man weakened by adversity bringing tears to her eyes. But she knew he would not appreciate such maudlin solicitude.

So she spoke briskly. 'Plenty. You suffered no more than a dozen or so strokes of the lash, though the damage is bad enough, and made worse by your flirting with the rocks. Spread the blanket over your knees for warmth, then I will smear the salve on.'

He complied, and Judith prepared to anoint his wounds.

'This may sting,' she warned.

'I'm ready.'

Her fingers were trembling. She had tended her brothers' scrapes and scratches often enough — but this was different. Never before had she touched a strange man in this intimate way, and a man who, despite his present sorry state, exuded some magnetic power she found herself unable to resist. She longed to caress, to comfort him. The temptation was almost irresistible. She had never in her life felt like this before and caution — yes, Penna, I do see what you meant! — made her hesitate before commencing her task.

When she did finally lay a salve-laden finger on his

back a deep shudder ran through him and a groan was wrenched from his throat.

'My apologies,' she muttered.

'Marry, but 'tis nothing! Carry on,' he gasped.

Only the fact that he remained upright convinced her that he had not fainted again. Apart from the convulsive shivering and an occasional uncontrollable flinch he remained completely immobile while she worked. As she neared the end of her task, her own jangled senses once more under control, she heard the first sounds of approach from the path.

"Tis my brothers,' she reassured her patient. 'You *are* English?' she added, wishing to be able to reassure them in their turn.

'Aye,' he stated flatly.

The two lads arrived at the top of the cliff and looked over the edge at the pair twenty feet below. 'Do you want the litter down there, Judith?' shouted Edward, eyeing her companion with unconcealed curiosity.

The stranger climbed to his feet and stood a moment, swaying in the breeze. The worst of his shivering and shaking seemed to be over. The wine had warmed him, no doubt. He had his voice under better control, too.

'Marry,' he exclaimed lightly, 'but I doubt my legs will carry me up to the path. I have never felt so devilishly weak. Did he call you Judith?'

'Aye, sir, for that is my name.'

'Strange!' he murmured, sinking down into an exhausted squat.

'Bring the litter here!' called Judith, not certain whether she had heard him correctly. Her name was quite ordinary.

The boys scrambled down the uneven, twisting steps to join them, dragging the litter behind. Judith wondered how the injured man would fare, being carried

up such tricky terrain. Lightly laden, her brothers could
negotiate it with agile ease, as she had done. With a
man tied between the poles, they would find the ascent
more onerous.

Greetings were little more than a nod. The boys
spread the litter and the man stretched out on it, face
down.

'You will have to bear the blanket over you,' Judith
explained quietly. 'It will warm you and ease the
pressure of the ropes.'

He nodded. His fingers grasped fists full of shingle as
the excruciating operation of tying him on proceeded,
but he made no complaint.

Edward and Josué lifted one end of the litter each
and carried it to the foot of the cliff.

'Hold on,' advised Edward briskly as he prepared to
climb the first steps, taking the head end of the litter
with him. 'You'll be almost vertical while we climb up
here. Judith, help Josué to lift him.'

Judith sprang to assist her younger brother, adding
her strength to his as they heaved the litter and its
burden after Edward, who was moving up one step at
a time. Eventually they reached the top of the cliff,
where everyone rested thankfully before beginning the
ascent to the house. The stranger, breathing heavily,
once more buried his face in his arms.

The remainder of the journey seemed simple by
comparison: a steady climb beside fertile fields which
had already yielded their harvest.

Back at the farmhouse, Ester, Marie and Penna took
over the arrangements, instructing that the stranger be
placed in the bed normally shared by Edward and
Josué. The boys would sleep in the store-room for a
few nights.

'What is your name?' demanded Ester without

ceremony, peeling away the blanket and inspecting the man's wounds with practised eyes.

'Oliver,' he murmured, 'Oliver Burnett.'

'Where are you from?'

'Plymouth.'

Judith exclaimed. An unmarried maid, she should not, by rights, have been in the room, but no one had sent her away. 'Fancy, Maman! Your father wed a lady from Plymouth!'

'Aye.'

Everyone was too busy to pursue the topic further. Satisfied that their patient was friend and not enemy, the women fussed around cleansing and treating his wounds until certain that they had done their best for him. Then they fed him some broth, gave him more wine to drink, and left him to sleep.

Speculation as to what he had been doing aboard a Spanish carrack kept the conversation going long after Penna had departed to see to her children.

Pierre Le Grand returned soon after sunset to find his wife and daughters gathered around the fire. A solidly built, sprightly man in his mid-forties, his square face framed by a brown beard still untouched by grey, he greeted his family with a reassuring smile.

Edward and Josué, with little Samuel trotting at their heels, came panting in from the fields, where the older lads had been practising their archery on wild game. The right of chase over his own land was one of the special privileges granted to Pierre by Helier de Carteret.

'You never know, might have to use these on the Spaniards,' Edward had grinned as they'd departed with their bows.

'Is the danger over?' asked Ester anxiously.

Her husband shrugged. 'A small party of Spaniards

landed earlier, but they came in peace. A watch has been set to warn of any further invasion, but the rest of us have returned to our homes.'

'What did they want?'

'Shelter to anchor and repair storm damage, they said, but I suspect that to be merely an excuse. They are searching for a man who fell overboard in the storm; he or his body may have been washed ashore——'

'Did they say who he was?' demanded Judith anxiously.

'No. But he must have been important or they wouldn't expend so much effort to find him.'

The women exchanged glances. Josué spoke up.

'He's here, Father, but we cannot hand him over. They had been torturing him.'

'Here!' Pierre's amazed expression turned to one of anxiety. 'The officer is being entertained at Le Manoir at present; some of the soldiers have gone to the ale house. Does anyone else know he is here?'

Judith shook her head. 'No, Papa. Not unless Edward or Josué have told——'

'Of course we haven't!' interjected Edward.

'Will they search the island?'

'Probably, my dear.' Pierre patted his wife's shoulder and sighed, leaning his musket in a dark corner. Winding up the length of slow match he carried, he thrust it into his pocket. 'Helier will have to allow some sort of an enquiry, at least a search of the shore. I'd better take a look at this fellow.'

'He's asleep. I'll show you.'

Judith stood up to lead the way through the store-room to the solar, where her parents and Samuel slept. Oliver Burnett had been placed in the central private chamber, and her own and Genette's lay beyond that.

She had scarcely begun to cross the windowless store when the dogs began to bark in the yard.

'Strangers!' grunted her father, and turned back.

Judith remained where she was, hovering, her heart thudding. She was not left long in suspense. The outside door was flung back on its hinges, letting in the last of the daylight and a draught which threatened to extinguish the single candle already lit.

Two men swaggered in, surveying the assembled family haughtily. Soldiers off the carrack. Dressed in knee-length hose, thick, protective leather jerkins and metal helmets, each carried a sword and other martial clutter at his hip. One had an arquebus over his shoulder and held a glowing slow match in his hand.

'In the name of His Most Catholic Majesty, King Philip of Spain,' cried the leading man, in bad French, 'we come to search your house!'

'Your king has no jurisdiction on this island!' asserted Pierre, speaking fluently in the same language.

'Spaniards are masters of the world!' proclaimed the man loftily.

He reeked of wine. The fumes carried to Judith, hovering in the dimness of the store. Neither of these men was the officer, who was still no doubt enjoying Helier de Carteret's hospitality at Le Manoir. These were dangerous underlings, bold in their cups.

'What is it that you seek?' Pierre still spoke in reasonable tones, attempting to quieten the drunken belligerency of the soldiers.

'A damned heretical spy!'

Pierre shrugged. 'There is no spy here.'

'And no stranger has sought your hospitality?'

'No, curse you!'

Edward's aggressiveness was a little overdone. The soldier eyed him calculatingly. For the first time he

noticed Genette, standing slightly behind her brother.
The man's eyes devoured her budding figure and took
on a dangerous, hungry glitter.

'We shall see!' he sneered. 'But all in good time.
First, we shall enjoy a little pleasant entertainment.
Come here, maid!' he coaxed in a thick, slurred voice.
'I've a mind for a kiss!'

He took a step forward. Genette gave a scream of
terror and fled to her father's protective arms. Pierre
pushed her behind him, but it was Edward, young and
spoiling for a fight, who leapt to his sister's defence.

'Cursed Spanish upstarts!' he roared. 'Pillage and
rapine are all you're good for!' and leapt at the man,
wielding his staff, which had been near at hand.

He caught the fellow a resounding blow to his head,
though it did not do much harm, glancing off the
conical iron helmet, but it dazed the soldier enough to
make him stagger to a stop.

No one noticed the arquebusier behind him swinging
his weapon from his shoulder and putting his match to
the vent. The gun went off with a stunning and
deafening report. The man was practised and expert,
and so had it pointing in the right direction at the
crucial moment. Edward fell to the floor, blood pumping from his chest.

Josué gave a cry of grief and anger, snatched up his
own staff and went in to the attack. But one sweep of
the still smoking arquebus and Josué lay on the floor,
nursing a broken arm. Judith heard the bone snap.

The man who had fired, who now seemed to be in
control, roared an order in Spanish. He extinguished
his glowing match, dropped his own now useless fire-
arm to the floor and drew his sword. 'We search now!'
he told the distracted Pierre, showing ruthless disregard

of the havoc he had just wrought. 'Where are your other rooms?'

Ester and Marie, uttering anguished cries, had rushed forward to tend the stricken boys. Pierre, holding the sobbing Genette, gestured helplessly with his hand. 'A store-room and bedchambers, through there,' he muttered.

Firelight and the single candle illuminated the living quarters, but beyond lay nothing but dim, fading daylight. 'The candle! Hand me the candle!' roared the soldier.

Judith roused herself from her shocked stupor. Edward was dead, she knew it, his eyes were open, staring. And all because of that wretched man she had saved from the beach! A shiver of revulsion shook her. The Spaniards would have passed them by had he not escaped their clutches. . .yet if she allowed them to find him it would not bring Edward back to life.

Swiftly she sped through her parents' room to the chamber where the Englishman lay and closed the door behind her. He was awake, roused by the sound of conflict, sitting on the edge of the bed framed between parted curtains, flushed, alert and defensive, one of Edward's spare knives in his hand. As she appeared, he pulled the linen sheet over his lap.

'What's amiss? Spaniards?'

'Quiet. Not now. Get back in bed, cover yourself and don't make a sound.'

While she hissed her urgent instructions Judith was stripping off her clothes. The stranger, observing her determined, purposeful expression, obediently swung his legs back on the bed, turned on his face and pulled up the covers, wincing as he did so. But his feverish, puzzled, considering gaze remained fixed on Judith as she disrobed. And the knife remained clenched in his fist.

She hesitated before throwing off her body-smock, but it would look strange if she wore it in bed. With a final, defiant gesture, she tore that off, too, and tossed all her clothes over the bump made by his heels. The soldiers had finished searching the store. They would be in here soon. She turned back the covers and took a deep breath.

'Move over, hide your head,' she hissed, and slipped into the bed beside him.

CHAPTER TWO

SHE could feel the tension in his muscles, hear his breathing, shallow and controlled. He had done what she asked without question. Judith held her own body rigid, fighting her fear. The clammy dampness of sweat gathered on her spine, occasioned as much by the consciousness of his body heat as by fear. But there was no time to analyse her feelings, to acknowledge embarrassment, even, for the soldiers were already approaching. She heard the clink of armour and weapons, the growling, heartless voices in her parents' solar.

Her father appeared powerless to stop the search. Genette's high-pitched, hysterical crying rasped at her raw nerves, the only sound to penetrate from the communal room.

She stiffened still more, clasping the bedcovers as though they were a lifeline as the door crashed back. A dark figure, partially lit by the flame of the light he carried, loomed in the doorway, his shadow leaping and towering to mask the man behind him.

He gave an exclamation and said something in Spanish which brought forth a lewd chuckle from his companion.

Judith watched the flaring candle's progress, staring at it like a startled rabbit. Then she reared up on one elbow, her back to Oliver Burnett, hoping that in the shadowy light behind the partially drawn curtains the extra height of her body would hide the slight mound of his. She had not drawn them close, knowing they

27

would only be flung back, an invitation to closer
scrutiny. It took no acting at all for her to show terror.

'What is happening?' she gasped, speaking in the
local dialect. 'I was woken by a report—who are you?'

The arquebusier frowned, not understanding her,
and did not answer. He gestured his companion
through to the last bedchamber, handing him the
candle, obviously telling him to continue the search.
The other man demurred, reluctant to leave such a
prize as Judith to his fellow.

Judith willed him to go, for she would feel marginally
safer without his presence. The arquebusier had, after
all, saved Genette even though he had killed Edward
and injured Josué. She drew a shuddering breath,
praying that after a brief look they would go away.
They were out for drunken mischief more than anything, and surely they'd already caused enough of that
to satisfy the most inebriated appetite. Except perhaps
their appetite for women. A deep shudder shook her.

At her back she could feel Oliver Burnett's taut,
burning body. He was running a fever, she had seen it
in his flushed cheeks and glittering eyes. He shifted
slightly, as though unable to prevent the restless movement, and she moved too, to cover any disturbance.
For a moment heated flesh touched her cool thigh. A
new shiver ran through her, a *frisson* which had nothing
to do with fear. But the lecherous Spaniard, returning
from the far bedchamber, caught the sound of her
indrawn breath and gave a ribald laugh, finding satisfaction in what he imagined to be her fear of him.

He took a step towards the bed but, before he could
reach her or the other man had a chance to intervene,
even if he intended to, which was doubtful, a voice she
scarcely recognised spoke harshly from the doorway.

No one had noticed Pierre Le Grand approach.

Believing him cowed, the Spaniards had dismissed him
as a threat. He faced them now, his musket poised,
primed and ready. Behind him stood old Marie, her
eyes popping, a flaring candle held in her shaking hand.

'Drop your swords,' Pierre commanded. He aimed
his heavy weapon at the pair, holding his smouldering
match threateningly over the vent. His gaze rested
briefly on the bare shoulders and partially exposed
swell of his daughter's breasts and she heard the harsh
intake of his breath. When he went on his voice shook
with anger. 'I want no more violence,' he said, vio-
lently, 'but unless you leave my house immediately I
will set fire to this musket. Lay down your arms!'

The leader shrugged. He obviously understood pure
French better than he spoke it. 'We are finished here,'
he announced haughtily. 'We were about to sheathe
our swords and go.'

'Then do so. But no tricks. We settlers are here to
defend this island against intruders such as you. I shall
be no more afraid to fire this musket than you were.'

The Spaniard eyed the wavering weapon, smiled
sourly, carefully sheathed his sword, motioned to his
companion to do the same, and bowed with insolent
arrogance. '*Madre de Dios*! If we wished to take your
paltry island you would be unable to prevent us!'

Pierre took a firmer grip on his weapon. 'Out!' he
commanded furiously.

The two Spaniards swaggered from the room without
further demur, though the lewd one could not resist a
final leer in Judith's direction. Hardly had Marie closed
the door behind them than Judith was out of the bed
and throwing on her clothes.

'My thanks, angel,' whispered a voice from behind
her.

Judith glanced sharply over her shoulder. His eyes,

brilliant with fever, rested upon her. She hurriedly covered her shift with a petticoat.

'I am no angel,' she retorted sharply, remembering to keep her voice low.

'Must be,' he muttered thickly. 'Judith. . .safe on the Judith. . .'

He was rambling. Thank God he had not spoken while the soldiers were present! She pulled her gown over her head, slipped bare feet into her shoes and prepared to leave him.

First, though, she laid a hand on his burning brow. He still held the knife clutched in his hand and she left it there. She could not deny him the means to defend himself.

'Please be quiet,' she urged, 'your life depends upon it.'

A faint smile touched his cracking lips. 'Angel,' he muttered again.

Judith gave up, leaving the room in a fit of exasperation. Stupid man! To lose command of his senses now, of all times!

She closed the door firmly behind her, crossed her parents' solar to the store. Closed that door behind her, too. If Oliver Burnett should cry out his voice should be inaudible beyond it.

The soldiers were still there. She'd heard some kind of commotion, dogs barking, hens squawking, heralding the arrival of a horse by the sound of the hooves, which had set her heart beating all the faster. Now she listened to discover what had caused it. Once again she hovered in the store-room, peering round the half-closed door to see what was going on.

Helier de Carteret had come! He and a Spanish captain of soldiery stood in the centre of the room, the Seigneur protesting forcibly at the death of Edward

and the wounding of Josué, who lay by the fire, pale
and shocked, wrapped in a blanket. His arm had been
roughly splinted. Edward's body lay on the far side of
the room, shrouded in a linen sheet.

'The Queen shall hear of this,' thundered de
Carteret, every inch the outraged lord despite his
simple country dress and the plain but costly sword at
his hip. 'She will protest to King Philip! I allowed you
and your men to land on this island I am sworn to
defend for Her Majesty so that you could search its
shores. This is a clear breach of the peace between our
nations!'

The Spanish captain, resplendent in a jewelled doublet, his hand resting lightly on the ornate hilt of his
sword, did not appear unduly alarmed. 'Such breaches
are all too frequent,' he intoned haughtily, his French
decidedly better than that of his underlings. 'Your
pirates harass our treasure ships in the New World,
they steal our gold and silver, our pearls and our
precious jewels, but what does the heretical Elizabeth
do to stop them? Nothing!'

'After your despicable betrayal of John Hawkins at
St Juan de Ulloa, promising safe harbour and then
bringing in soldiers from Vera Cruz to take his ships—
who can blame our merchants for seeking their
revenge?' demanded de Carteret.

'Heretics to a man,' snapped the captain. 'We but
sought to save their souls!'

'By torture, burnings and hangings? How many
good, pious men, followers of the Lord Jesus, are still
languishing in prison, or serving as slaves aboard your
galleys and galleasses?' thundered an austerely dressed
man who had entered the room in the wake of de
Carteret.

Cosmé Brevint, a fiery Huguenot refugee, had been

chosen by the Seigneur to minister to his French-
speaking people because so few understood English,
and so few English priests could communicate effectively in French.

'You Spaniards believe you own the world, and your
Romanist Pope Pius only encourages your fanciful
claims!' Brevint went on scornfully, his slight frame
quivering with passion. 'Someone must teach you that
you do not, and that each man's soul is his own, under
Jesus, who alone can save it!'

'Certainly, you cannot come ashore here letting off
arquebuses and killing my people!' Helier took up the
attack equally forcefully. 'The sound of that shot has
brought almost every man on the island to this farm.
You will do well to depart at once!'

'In our own good time,' replied the Spaniard dis-
tantly. 'Be careful, sirs, for, like your queen and your
compatriots, you are heretics all!'

'Pshaw! Here, we are Presbyterian; we do not recognise the authority of Rome!'

'The Holy Inquisition——'

'Can destroy our bodies but can neither destroy nor
save our souls! Be on your way, sir!'

Brevint nodded sagely, endorsing his patron's words.
'God's truth in Jesus will prevail!' he proclaimed
fervently.

The captain spoke rapidly in Spanish to the two
soldiers, both now considerably more sober than when
they arrived. Ignoring the islanders' impatience, they
replied at some length before taking up positions at his
back.

'My men tell me they were provoked,' said the
Spanish captain stiffly, abandoning the religious
argument.

'My sons were provoked!' burst our Pierre angrily.

'That man there,' he pointed, 'threatened to molest my younger daughter! The poor child is weeping still!'

Genette renewed her sobs as though to confirm her father's words.

Judith felt it safe to creep into the room. 'I was in bed,' she told the Seigneur, her voice shaking. 'They threatened to molest me, too.'

'Soldiers,' said their captain frostily, 'will be soldiers, wherever they are, whatever the circumstances. These men will be disciplined.'

'An you ordered this search, then you are as culpable as they!' De Carteret was not a man to be easily appeased, nor one to overlook a breach of faith or honour. 'You gave me your word, Captain!'

'They exceeded their orders,' admitted their commander. He threw the men a hostile glance, resenting the uncomfortable situation in which they had placed him. 'Drunken scum! Come!'

He spun on his heel and stalked towards the door. The arquebusier picked up his weapon as the two soldiers followed. Judith decided she would not like to be in their shoes when their captain vented his pent-up wrath.

Everyone jumped and stood for an instant in startled silence while the booming sound of several cannon echoed over the island. The Spanish captain was the first to react. He flung open the outer door and strode through.

'That pestilential pirate must be attacking our ship again!' he roared. 'To the landing immediately, or we shall fail to embark before the ship makes sail! I require your horse, Seigneur! Follow me!' he added in Spanish, waving the foot soldiers forward.

Mounted on Helier's horse, he set off into the

lingering dusk at a brisk canter, the two soldiers
following as fast as they could on foot.

Helier de Carteret gave a bark of bitter laughter.
'Not so much as a "by your leave"! I suppose it would
be too much to hope that the privateer they say has
been chasing them for the past two days will sink the
carrack, with all hands!'

An even more reverberating salvo echoed over the
island.

'An answer from the carrack!' guessed Helier. 'So it
isn't sunk, more's the pity! That pursuit, and the storm,
explain its presence here in our waters, by the way.
But I must follow, and see all the accursed Spaniards
leave my fief!'

'They will be unwise to draw anchor before the next
slack water,' muttered the tenement holder from Dos
d'Ane, one of those who had come with the Seigneur.
'The firing has ceased. The privateer will have stood
well off. She'll not want to risk being swept on to
rocks.'

'But the Spaniards will be in no doubt that she's
there, waiting for them. She won't want to sail in these
waters in the dark, I'll warrant. She'll not weigh anchor
until full tide in the morning. Mayhap we'll see some
action! Curse that bastard for taking my mount!' de
Carteret added angrily.

Riding horses were in short supply on the island.
The Seigneur eventually set off on the back of Pierre's
cart-horse.

Those who had gathered in the yard dispersed, most
to round up the rest of the Spaniards, to see them
returned to their ship and to make sure they did not
come ashore again. One or two, including Cosmé
Brevint, remained to comfort Pierre and his family,

while Jasper went home to make sure Penna and the children were safe.

Judith could not stop herself from shaking. Now the danger was over, reaction set in. The family had joined the Pastor in praying for Edward's soul. Little Sammy, eyelids drooping, stood cradled in old Marie's arms. Josué lay sleeping by the fire, his forehead cool to her touch. Penna must have administered a sedative. No one noticed when she picked up a candle, slipped from the crowded room and went through to where Oliver Burnett lay.

He had thrown back the covers to his hips to prevent the cloth from searing his wounds and lay on his face, his limbs moving restlessly, his head tossing on the pillow. Inarticulate mutterings came from his dry lips.

The knife lay exposed on the bed beside him, dangerously close to his body. Judith put down the candle, picked up the weapon and sheathed it, then wet a cloth with water from a jug left by the bed earlier. Tenderly, she bathed the sweat from his forehead and neck, moistened his lips. Concern over his condition, the fact of having something to do, cured most of her own shakes.

Their spring water was pure and clear, fit to drink without boiling. She leaned nearer and spoke distinctly.

'Master Burnett! Can you hear me?'

His mutterings stopped, so she assumed he could.

'You must drink. I have a cup here, and a straw. Lift your head and suck.'

For a moment she thought he had not understood, but then he raised himself on his forearms and took the straw into his mouth.

He drained the cup. The sweat had already beaded his brow again. Judith mopped it up as he dropped back to a prone position.

'England,' he said distinctly. 'Must sail to England. Where's the *Mermaid*?'

'The *Mermaid*?'

'My brigantine. . .'

His voice tailed off. She thought he said 'Judith' but wasn't sure, for he had sunk back into incoherence.

So he had a ship. He did not look like a sailor. At least, like no sailor she had ever met. She studied his restless, fevered face for deeply encrusted, weather-beaten lines, his long, tapering hands for signs of hardening against salt water and rope-burns, and could find none.

Yet he was sunburned enough for little white lines to radiate from his eyes. And his hands did not have the soft appearance of being complete strangers to work. . .

She took one between her own capable, roughened palms, stroking and soothing. Not a hand belonging to an indolent gentleman, she decided. A strong hand, which could undertake hard work if necessary, though not often called upon to do so. Like his entire body, which was honed to a degree of fitness which had saved his life but showed no evidence of punishing, unrelenting toil.

A new fit of shuddering overtook him and his fingers closed convulsively on hers, steel bands which bruised even her hardened flesh. But she let him hang on while the spasm lasted, and when his grip loosened she released her hand only in order to work her fingers back to life and moisten the cooling cloth again.

She prayed he would not die. Although he had been the indirect cause of Edward's death she could not hold it against him. He had arrived in great distress, and no charitable person could have done other than take him in. Edward, once convinced of the need, had given

unquestioning support. But he had always been of a
fiery nature, and had over-reacted to the Spaniards,
particularly to the threat to Genette. Had he kept his
head he would probably still be alive. His temper had
thrown a lighted match into the powder keg of the
soldiers' inebriation and caused an explosion. No, in
fairness Edward's death could not be laid at Master
Burnett's door.

Though the present state of her jumbled emotions
could be! She had never before met a man who could
so bring her entire body to throbbing life. Just the sight
of him set her senses into a spin. And a touch sent
strange sensations streaking along her nerves.

It was really quite ridiculous. But the thought of his
recovering and sailing out of her life left her feeling
bereft. Yet she knew nothing about him except his
name!

One other thing, to be exact. He came from
Plymouth, where her maternal grandmother had been
born.

Lucas Balliene, a Jersey merchant importing goods
to the islands, had met Catherine Gilbert on one of his
trips to the mainland. Had wooed and won her. Their
daughter, Ester, had married Pierre Le Grand.

As though on cue, Ester entered the chamber, her
eyes red-rimmed from weeping.

'Judith,' she admonished, scandalised. 'You should
not be here, alone ——'

'What harm can it do, Maman? He is barely conscious, and I am but cooling his brow. He needs
someone to be with him.'

'Marie and I will take turns, if it seems necessary.
Dear lord! He is almost uncovered!'

'Only because his back is painful. I know he should

be kept warm, but it would cause him great discomfort to have the covers drawn up again.'

'His back would be better bound. Fetch that old linen sheet. We will tear it into strips.'

Judith did as bidden, returning from the store to find her mother gently smearing on more salve. Oliver Burnett shifted restlessly under her touch, muttering to himself.

'We must lift him up,' said Ester doubtfully. 'I will call your father——'

'There is no need to trouble Papa,' put in Judith swiftly. She did not wish to face her father again until she had had time to forget the wanton picture she had presented earlier. 'I will tell him to lift himself—thank goodness you taught us all to speak English, Maman!'

'Your father learned it in London, when he trained at the Temple, and my mother taught me. We both thought it useful knowledge. One never knows. . .'

'It will be useful now. Although I believe Master Burnett speaks French I am sure he will respond better to his native tongue.'

She leaned close again, laying a hand on a sound part of his shoulder. 'Master Burnett. Would you like more water?'

'Water!' he gasped, rasping dry lips with an equally dry tongue. Then again, 'Water!'

'Lift yourself up. See, I have the cup and straw.'

As he heaved upon his forearms, roused from his stupor by the promise of relief from a dreadful thirst, Judith spoke again.

'While you are drinking, my mother will bind your wounds. Then you will be able to bear the bedcovers over you to keep you warm.'

'Too hot,' he muttered.

'But you must keep them over you!'

'We should have done this before,' remarked Ester grimly, working swiftly so as not to tax the injured man's strength for too long. 'He would have been more comfortable.'

'What happened?' croaked the patient suddenly. He had already drained the cup.

'The Spaniards have gone back to their carrack. Someone attacked it with cannon. A pirate ship mayhap.'

Oliver lifted his head, a sudden flare of interest making his eyes more brilliant then ever. 'Which pirate ship? What was it named?'

'I know no more. I will try to find out tomorrow.'

'The *Sea Hawk*,' he murmured. 'Was it was called *Sea Hawk*?'

Ester had almost finished winding the strips of linen about his torso. She tucked in the end and straightened.

'You know of this pirate ship?' she demanded.

'Privateer,' he corrected. 'Aye.'

The effort had been too great. His few moments of lucidity passed. As he flopped back to the mattress and Ester carefully covered his body, his feverish mutterings began again.

Judith remained by his side for a while longer, replacing the covers whenever he threw them off. Ester seemed to have forgotten her scruples over allowing her daughter to be alone with the sick man. She departed to order the rest of the household. Sammy was already in bed, but the events of the evening had left their mark. It was not long before he woke screaming.

Having settled him again, Ester ordered Judith to bed.

'Marie will sit with Master Burnett for a couple of hours. Then I will take over. I'll call you for the final

watch,' she promised, eyeing her daughter's reluctant
face with a mixture of exasperation and understanding.
'I cannot believe any harm can come from that. But he
is an attractive young man, Judith, so do not lose your
heart to him. He comes from a different world.'

'I know that, Maman.' Judith flushed painfully. 'But
I found him. I feel responsible.'

'And he will be grateful to you. Do not mistake
gratitude for affection, Judith.'

'I am too tall, too — too solidly built to attract any
man's affection,' Judith muttered despondently.

Ester took her daughter into what was intended to
be a comforting embrace. The top of her head came up
to Judith's nose, which made Judith feel even bigger
and more awkward.

'No, you are not, my love. Only to a little whisk like
that fool from Guernsey! You have nothing to be
ashamed of, my child.' She smoothed Judith's tumbled
hair from her high, smooth forehead. 'Thick wavy hair,
nice grey eyes — your nose is not bad, and your mouth
is well-shaped.'

Judith shifted impatiently. 'But my face is too broad
and I suffer from freckles!' she protested.

Ester laughed. 'Quite the end of the world, I agree!
Nay, child,' she continued more seriously, 'you look
well enough. Simon Perrier is smitten. Your father is
negotiating the match — '

'But I have no wish to marry Simon Perrier! He has
not two words to say for himself and is. . .is not
attractive to me!' That was putting it mildly. 'And to
live in La Sablonnerie! 'Twould be worse than here!
Think, Maman! I would have to cross La Coupée every
time I wished to visit you or any of my friends on Great
Sark!'

'La Coupée is perfectly safe except in a gale, Judith.

Little Sark has good, productive land and the Perriers are prospering. Simon is a decent young man farming land which will be his one day. You could do far worse.'

'I will not wed with Simon Perrier, Maman! Now were it Philippe de Carteret——'

'Show sense, Judith! He is not yet twenty years of age, far too young for a man in his position to wed! Besides, when the time comes he will choose within his own class, the daughter of an important Jersey or Guernsey family.'

Judith had had a crush on the Seigneur's son for the past year, a crush which was fast disappearing with the advent of Oliver Burnett. However, mention of it had served to distract Ester's attention from her new and far more disturbing regard for the older stranger.

He was undoubtedly taller than her. Heavier, too, despite his slender build. He must be all muscle, she thought admiringly, remembering the weight they had lifted up those tricky steps.

Which reminded her of Edward. And Josué. The quick tears sprang to her eyes as she released herself from her mother's embrace.

'How is Josué, Maman?'

'Sleeping quietly, thank God. His arm will mend. Penna did her best, but I will send for Jean Quesle to set it properly tomorrow.'

'And. . .Edward?'

Judith was almost afraid to ask. Ester swallowed.

'He will be buried tomorrow. Pastor Brevint is available and there seems no point in delay. Now, get yourself off to bed, Judith. You will wake Genette if you do not hurry!'

Judith took a last look at the restless figure on the bed and retreated to her bedchamber. Genette, who had tiptoed through earlier, had sunk into a deep sleep, emotionally exhausted. She did not stir as Judith crept in beside her.

But Judith found it difficult to settle. The events of the day kept running round and round in her head like a dog in a spit. Only they kept shooting off at tangents, idle, disconnected thoughts and images which all seemed to end with that of a quirky smile on an exhausted, undaunted face.

CHAPTER THREE

SHE seemed barely to have dropped off when a gentle hand shook her shoulder.

'Judith!'

'Mmm?'

Judith stirred sleepily, then shot upright as memory returned. 'What is it?'

'Shush!' Her mother put a finger to her lips, the gesture shifting the shadows cast by the rush light she carried. 'Your turn to sit with Master Burnett.'

'Oh!' Fully awake on the instant, Judith slid from the bed and began to don her clothes. 'How is he?' she demanded.

'Much the same. I'll go back. Come when you are ready.'

Since she was quite used to dressing in the dark of a winter's morning Judith needed no light to complete her toilet. She sponged her face to freshen herself and ran a bristle brush over her hair to remove the worst of the tangles. She had long ago become resigned to her looks and vanity was not one of her vices. Normally she was far too busy to bother about her appearance. Yet now, for the first time in years, she wished she had a light, a mirror, and a more becoming gown to wear.

Ester went back to her bed and Judith was once more alone with the patient, still wondering at her mother's allowing her to tend the stranger. But in his condition he could scarcely pose any threat and her reputation was solid enough to withstand a few raised brows should anyone outside the family discover the

43

freedom she had been allowed. Some of the more
puritanical souls might mutter under their breaths, but
Le Sieur Le Grand's family, like that of the Seigneur,
was above overt criticism. In any case Ester had taken
the precaution of leaving the communicating door
open.

Oliver Burnett still moved restlessly. His forehead
felt burning hot. His fever had risen during the night.
She leant over to mop his brow and met his fevered,
glassy stare. She need not have worried over her
appearance, she mused wryly. Oliver Burnett had lost
all trace of lucidity. She could not rouse him to drink
and had to content herself with moistening his lips.

She sighed and sat back uneasily on the hard chair,
wondering whether she should suggest the surgeon
bleed him when he came to set Josué's arm. Pro-
fessional attention seemed necessary. Perhaps he
would do it out of charity for a man in dire need, or
perhaps her father would pay the modest fee he would
charge. She herself had no money, or she would gladly
have met the cost.

Gradually, the sky began to lighten. High water
would be about now, she thought, and wondered what
had become of the Spanish carrack. Had it sailed at
midnight? Or prudently waited until dawn?

The raucous crowing of their cock usually awoke the
household and that morning was no exception. Hens
began to cluck, dogs to bark and one of the cows
lowed, asking to be milked. People began to stir.

Genette came through, and as she did so she cocked
her head, listening to the sound of distant cannon-fire.

'It sounds a long way off,' she remarked, moving
nearer the bed and eyeing their guest with more
interest than Judith felt necessary. 'I suppose they're
out at sea by now. I'm glad they've gone.' She appeared

quite unperturbed by the sounds. All signs of the previous evening's distress had gone as she leant over the patient and trailed a cool finger across his forehead. 'Is he better?'

'No.' Judith's reply was short. 'I expect they sailed at slack water, as was suggested. The privateer must have lain in wait. You'd better feed the hens for me.'

'That's your job.' Genette grinned cheekily. 'I'll stay here and bathe his fevered brow if you like.'

'I do not like!' Judith did not find Genette's suggestion at all amusing. 'Mother entrusted his care to me! Please, Genette, don't be difficult! Nursing a stranger is no task for a young girl like you! Feed the hens before you do the milking, there's a dear; it won't take you long.'

''Tis no task for you, either, Judith. You're only a couple of years older than me!' protested Genette. She swallowed and a quiver entered her voice. 'And I don't feel up to farm work. I am still upset by what happened. Poor Edward!'

She stifled a heart-wrenching sob.

'If you hadn't panicked he wouldn't have acted so rashly. Maybe he would still be alive,' Judith retorted tartly.

Realising that her sister had not been impressed by her histrionics, Genette rounded on her. 'Are you blaming me for his death? It's not fair! You brought *him* here!'

She pointed dramatically at the bed. Judith sighed, exasperated but resigned.

'The Spaniards would have come anyway. They did not know he was here, they were just searching about. And no, I'm not blaming you, it was as much Edward's own fault for overreacting.'

'Thank you!'

'What is done is done,' went on Judith sombrely, 'it
cannot be helped now. But without him and me and
Josué to help, the others will be hard pressed to attend
to the animals before the funeral. So pull yourself
together, Genette, and behave like a grown-up if you
want to be treated as one!'

Sometimes her sister irritated her beyond endurance.
Judith would never admit to jealousy, but Genette's
dainty, taking ways set resentful emotions loose which
she found it difficult to control. She did not want her
sister nursing Master Burnett.

As soon as it was fully light Ester dispatched Jasper
Sidney to fetch the surgeon. Jean Quesle arrived with
his wife, Rémy, who acted as midwife to the little
colony. Like the pastor, they were Huguenot refugees,
grateful to Helier de Carteret for his patronage. Judith
knew the island was lucky to have the services of so
skilled a man. Many a town with far more inhabitants
than the two hundreds or so people who lived on Sark
had only an apothecary to tend their ills. The Quesles
made a scant living, but accepted relative poverty as
being more bearable than persecution. And on Sark no
one would starve.

When the surgeon arrived Judith moistened Oliver's
lips once again before leaving him to join the others in
the kitchen. He would come to no harm alone for a
few minutes. With the doors open between, she would
hear should he need her.

Having admonished Ester for not calling him to
attend Josué the previous evening, Jean Quesle reset
the young man's arm, shaking his head over the double
fracture.

'The arm will mend, but may not be quite straight,'
he told them regretfully. 'Be thankful that 'twas your

left which took the blow, Josué. You will still have a strong right arm to work for you.'

White-lipped, Josué had borne his pain stoically. 'I am thankful that I am not dead, like my brother. Those bastards!' he choked.

'You will miss Edward,' agreed Quesle, 'but do not mourn for him. He died an honourable death, and as Pastor Brevint will tell you, we must believe he is happier now. Recover quickly, for you are now your father's eldest son; your responsibilities have grown overnight!'

'Master Quesle!' Judith stopped him as he began to pack his implements. 'Will you examine someone for me? I feel sure my father will pay for your services——'

'Indeed he will,' agreed Ester quickly. 'I was about to ask you myself.' Pierre was not present. He had gone to recover his horse and to organise the funeral. 'It is the man from the Spanish ship. My daughter rescued him from the sea yesterday.'

Quesle lifted heavy brows. 'The man for whom they were searching? He was here?'

'Yes, and he is very sick,' put in Judith before he could ask any embarrassing questions. 'He is through here.'

The surgeon examined the patient, congratulated the ladies on the care they had already given, re-dressed the wounds on the man's back and cupped him.

'The fever should break within twenty-four hours,' he told them. 'Keep him under constant observation until then. Call me if you are anxious, but he has a strong constitution. He should recover quickly from his ordeal.'

'You will all wish to attend Edward's funeral,' remarked Rémy Quesle in her quiet voice as her

husband prepared to leave. 'I can remain with Master
Burnett while you are absent, if you would wish me to
do so.'

'That would be most kind, Mistress Quesle.'

Ester accepted the offer without hesitation.

Judith breathed a sigh of relief. The question of who
would watch over Oliver had been worrying her. Old
Marie, Penna—everybody would want to pay Edward
their last respects. The capable Rémy Quesle's offer
seemed like the answer to a prayer.

Edward's body, sewn into a shroud, was loaded on
the cart. Josué, because of his injury, and Marie,
because of her age, rode in it too. Black ribbons had
been tied to a whip propped up beside the driver's seat
and the horse's back draped with a black cloth. Jasper
led the animal while everyone else plodded along
behind. As the soberly dressed cortège wended its way
along the narrow, rutted tracks more and more of their
friends joined the mourners making for the piece of
land near Le Manoir set aside for church and burial
ground.

The church had not yet been built, so they still
worshipped in each others' houses, Cosmé Brevint
holding several services in various parts of the island
each Sabbath. Unlike in England itself, no fine was
imposed for non-attendance, but few wished to avoid
the weekly duty. There were no recusants on Sark.

Progressing along the Grand Chemin, they passed
by the lane leading to Helier's mill, only recently
completed, standing tall and stark against the skyline,
visible from almost every corner of the island. Its sails
turned steadily in the wind. The urgent need for a
means to grind corn had taken precedence over the
desire for a permanent place to worship.

Edward was laid to rest without fuss but with due

ceremony. The party returned to Beauregard, the older women crowding into the cart. Pierre walked with downcast head, his shoulders slumped. Judith could sense his disappointment. He had been working hard to provide a worthwhile legacy for his sons. Now the eldest, the one most like himself, who would have inherited the sub-fief, while his younger brothers held tenements under him, had gone. Josué would inherit now. But perhaps the thing her father would grieve for most was the loss of a strong pair of hands.

One should not be sad when someone died, she reminded herself. Yet it seemed impossible not to be. She would miss Edward.

Pierre had broached a cask of sack smuggled in from Spain, and offered drinks to all those who had accompanied them back to the house. Judith took the opportunity to slip through to see how Oliver Burnett did.

Rémy looked up as Judith entered and smiled reassuringly into the girl's anxious face. She rose from the chair, a sturdy figure in serviceable brown. 'He is quieter now. He's a fine-looking fellow.'

'Yes. I'm glad he did not drown.'

'I wonder why he was flogged.'

'So do I. He's not been able to speak much yet.'

'Hardly surprising. How fortunate for him that you spotted him when you did.'

Judith found she could smile. 'I thought he was some valuable piece of lost cargo being washed ashore!'

'A man such as this one must be of more value than any salvage!'

'Oh, yes.'

Judith's fervent reply brought an understanding gleam to Rémy's eyes. 'So you will tend him well,' she observed softly.

'Until he leaves. He is anxious to leave. We are

taking it in turns to sit with him.' Judith quickly sought
to allay any suspicion that she alone was concerned for
the stranger, or that she held out any hopes in his
direction. 'But I can take over now, if you would like
to take a beaker of sack with the others.'

'Is Master Quesle with them?'

'Aye, I believe he came especially to escort you
home.'

Rémy smiled, and Judith realised yet again how
devoted the couple were to each other. They had not
been wed above two years, had married just before
their flight from France. Rémy was no beauty, and her
solid figure, though a mite shorter, was less shapely,
heavier than her own. Yet Rémy had attracted the
good doctor, a fine-looking man in his prime.

The other woman touched her cheek with caressing
fingers. 'You are quite beautiful, Judith. Has no one
told you so before this?'

'No! And really, Mistress Quesle, I think you exag-
gerate! You are trying to be kind——'

'Not at all. If you want him, you can get him.'

Judith did not know what to believe. She was so
used to thinking herself ordinary, if not downright
plain, that she could not take the other woman's
assertion seriously.

'I—I don't!' she protested. 'I scarcely know him! I
know nothing of his circumstances, even whether he is
married!' A rush of confusion made itself plain in her
burning cheeks. 'Really, Mistress Quesle, how can you
believe. . .?'

Rémy laughed. 'I do wish you would stop deceiving
yourself, my dear. No unattached girl with your spirit
could help admiring—wanting such a man!'

'Well, he'll be leaving as soon as he is able and will
scarcely have time for dalliance!'

'Make the most of his convalescence,' advised Rémy with another smile. 'A man is at his most vulnerable when he is recovering from an illness.'

Shocked, Judith stared at the other woman. 'Is that how you. . .?' Words failed her. She could not complete the question.

Mistress Quesle laughed outright. 'No, my dear Judith, it is not! But a woman — even the most beautiful of women — must use some artifice to catch her man — unless, of course, she is content to wed where her family wills and suffer forever the attentions of a husband for whom she has no feeling.'

'I have been told that affection grows——'

'And so it may! But why risk the reverse? No, my dear, I know my opinions are not shared by most, but I have seen too many women brought to childbed by men they despise, perhaps loathe, or even actively hate, but cannot deny, to counsel blind reliance on the choice of others. Such a choice has probably been dictated by some financial consideration, almost certainly to seal an advantageous alliance. Wed for love, my dear, affection perhaps, but otherwise not at all.'

With that, Rémy gave Judith a swift kiss on the forehead and departed.

Judith stared after her, her thoughts in turmoil. So much of what Mistress Quesle had said agreed with her own ideas. But she could not bring herself to believe that catching a man when he was vulnerable could lead to lasting happiness. She wished the surgeon's wife had not put the idea into her head. Such deviousness went right against her own basic instincts.

And the advice was completely opposed to that of her mother and Penna! They had warned her to beware of becoming attached to a man who could have no lasting place in her life!

But all three had so easily recognised the attraction she felt. Was she really so transparent?

When she approached the bed again she felt awkward, embarrassed. Was she devoting too much time to the man? Yet when she looked on his flushed, uneasy features, the spots of burning colour emphasising the prominence of his cheekbones, saw the way his rumpled hair hung over his forehead in a sticky, damp thatch, how the untrimmed beard made his strong jaw look even more pointed than it was, her knees went weak and she was overcome with such tenderness that her hand shook as she applied more moisture to his lips and wiped the sweat from his brow.

Penna came to relieve her soon after and the vigil continued. Judith left the bedside with reluctance.

When her mother woke her the next morning Judith saw streaks of daylight through the window, heard the noise from the farmyard and knew she had been allowed to oversleep.

'You did not call me!' she protested.

'There was no need. He is better, his fever has gone. He needs no one to sit with him now. Come, you too, Genette! 'Tis time to get up!'

Judith dressed quickly, her bubbling happiness somewhat dampened by apprehension. She was unused to pretence or deceit, but Master Burnett must not suspect the attraction she felt for him. It would be difficult to disguise her real feelings, but hide them she must.

So although Genette danced through with apparently artless enthusiasm to greet their guest, Judith followed more slowly. Not even her mother's perception would have penetrated the steady front of neighbourly concern she presented to the man lying in the bed.

'Marry!' he exclaimed. 'An angel *and* a sprite come

to bid me good morrow!' He winced as he attempted
to move and stifled an oath. 'It seems my back is still
raw. I must remain like a beached fish, flat on my belly!
By my troth! 'Tis as well the storm came when it did!
Else I would have lost even more skin from my back!'

'Why were they flogging you?' asked Judith quietly,
her heart sinking. He had likened Genette to a sprite.

He gave a comical grimace. 'Do they need an
excuse?' he wondered wryly. 'Nay, but they had
decided I was an heretic, and sought to save my soul.
Had I remained, I was destined for a bench in a galley
at best, a hangman's noose or the flames at worst. The
idea did not appeal to me. Drowning seemed preferable. So, when all hands were occupied in saving the
ship, I took the opportunity to leave it.'

His hands had been tied to the whipping post. He'd
retained enough presence of mind to sag, to pretend
he'd lost his senses.

'Cut him down,' the Inquisitor had ordered a soldier
set to guard him. 'Throw him back in the hold.'

Everyone, including the soldiers on board, were
desperately engaged in lowering sail. Despite the weakness induced by hunger and pain it had been easy
enough to take his guard by surprise, to wrestle his
knife from him, slit his throat and jump overboard
before anyone else realised what was happening. By
the time the first arquebusier had let off a shot he was
well out of range and, in the sheeting rain, out of sight.
But he did not think such details were fit for feminine
ears.

'How clever, how brave of you!' exclaimed Genette
admiringly.

The little one was regarding him with starry eyes.
His angel was guarding her expression, busying herself
about tidying the bed. Even as he tried to read her face

she moved to the foot. Without uncomfortably craning his neck he could no longer see her.

'You were fortunate to be so near the island.'

Her quiet alto voice floated melodiously over him. He wished he could see her quite lovely, unruffled features. Mayhap, with a little effort. . .

The expression he caught on her face as he struggled painfully over to sit up was far from unruffled. Startled surprise was followed quickly by confusion, in turn replaced equally speedily by one of calm enquiry. But she could not disguise the surge of blood flushing her cheeks.

'You are feeling stronger, sir?'

The hint of self-consciousness in her expression pleased him. He remembered the delicious feel of her body as she lay beside him. He had been too astonished and, in truth, too weak, to respond normally to her nearness then, even had danger not been imminent and self-preservation uppermost in his mind. He had lain there feeling completely impotent, afraid for himself, afraid for her, unable to see and able to do absolutely nothing but sweat and leave their survival to the quick wits of a young girl. His only comfort had been the cold steel in his hand. He had determined to sell her virtue and his own life dearly. Afterwards the sense of her presence had remained with him, returning even in his fevered imagination: infinitely calming, infinitely exciting.

Her confusion at facing him, her reaction to sight of his bandaged torso, told him her impulsive action had been out of character, dictated by the emergency. She had probably never been in the same bed as a man before. He suppressed a smile.

But she had not been unaware of him. His eyes gleamed as he eyed her flushed face. Her immediate

recovery of composure told him she would not fall
easily into his arms. She would offer a sturdy challenge.
But the conquest would be all the more satisfactory
when it came. He felt better by the moment and a grin
spread over his face as he spoke.

'My strength is returning, and will do so the more
quickly if you will stop fussing and tell me how you
found and saved me. And I do not believe I have yet
thanked you for twice saving my life. I am yours to
command — once this deuced weakness has left me and
I am capable of being useful!'

Judith's colour, which had begun to subside, rose
again. His tone had been teasing, yet beneath the
lightness she detected a determination not to let her
withdraw into the remoteness of mere acquaintance.
He wanted to acknowledge his debt and redeem it in
friendship and possibly service. Though what service
he could render her she could not begin to imagine.
Maybe he would try to trade on her sympathy and
demand more of her than she would be willing to give.
Well, she had been warned. She must accept his
gratitude for what it was worth. No more and no less.

'No thanks are due, sir,' she said stiffly. 'I would
have pulled a cask of wine or a bale of silk from the
water as readily! And as for the Spaniards — your safety
was ours. Had you been discovered they would not
have spared us. . .'

'They threatened me with. . .with. . .and they killed
Edward,' put in Genette, ignoring Judith's frowning
remonstrance.

'Your brother, the one who helped to carry me up?'
enquired Oliver quickly. 'I cannot tell you how sorry I
am — I would I had not caused your family sorrow ——'

'You did not!' Judith declared stoutly. 'Genette
should not have mentioned it! Not yet, anyway.' He

would have had to find out sooner or later. 'They were
drunk and out to make trouble. Edward reacted too
recklessly. It would have happened were you here or
not.'

'I had to know.'

'But not until you were stronger.'

He shrugged, and winced. 'But for me they might
not have dropped anchor off Sark.'

This was irrefutable. Judith did not attempt to deny
it. 'But you had to attempt escape. You could not
foretell the consequences.'

'You are generous, angel. I hope the rest of your
family is as forgiving.'

'Why do you call her "angel"?' demanded Genette.
'Her name is Judith, and you should be more
respectful!'

'If you insist.' He grinned unrepentantly and
repeated his former words. 'You are generous —
Mistress Judith.' He returned his amused attention to
the younger sister. 'You, I gather, are Mistress
Genette. I am pleased to make your acquaintance,
Mistress Genette.'

He bowed from the waist as he sat, and only Judith
noticed another slight wince as he moved.

Genette, overcome at meeting laughing green eyes,
blushed in delicious confusion.

'Marie, our elderly maid, and Mistress Sidney, who
is wed to my father's foreman, will be here shortly to
make you more comfortable and bring you something
to eat,' said Judith evenly. 'Come, Genette, we have
work to do!'

She herded her reluctant sister before her as she left
the room. Turning to close the door and so afford him
privacy, she could not help looking back. She met the
battery of those green eyes and knew precisely why

Genette had reacted so strongly. But she managed to meet his gaze steadily, amusement at her own folly bringing a soft curve to her lips and an added sparkle to eyes already bright with an awareness she could not deny.

To her astonishment his expression sobered and a dark flush stained his neck. Then he laughed.

'Marry, angel,' he said, somewhat unsteadily. 'But you do have the most unsettling effect upon a man!'

Judith closed the door quickly.

'Well, come on, then,' urged Genette moodily from the store-room where she had decided to stand and wait. 'You are such a puritan, Judith. What harm would there have been —— ?'

'I am prudent, not puritan, as you very well know!' exclaimed Judith angrily. 'It would be unwise for either of us to remain in Master Burnett's bedchamber now he is recovering, and especially alone. I assume you have no wish to lose your reputation and mar your chances of making a good marriage?'

'Do not concern yourself over *my* prospects, sister,' said Genette airily. '*I* shall have no difficulty in finding a suitable husband.'

Unfortunately, Judith knew she was right.

Equally unfortunately, both girls had to pass through the invalid's room to reach their own. Normally they retired before their brothers and emerged after they had risen. In any case, a certain amount of intimacy in the family did no harm and the bed curtains were normally drawn. But for young girls to pass through the bedchamber of a stranger was a different matter and posed a problem. Ester solved it by unearthing a screen from some recess of the store.

Josué soon joined Oliver at night, glad to share his bed with the visitor rather than continue to sleep on

the floor in kitchen or store. Apart from an ache and
the awkwardness of his splinted arm he had recovered
from his ordeal with surprising resilience.

It was not long before Oliver was testing his legs
about the bedchamber. Judith could scarcely tear her
eyes away from him. Instead of finishing below the
knee the borrowed over-stock and baggy Venetian
breeches ended above, though happily the nether-hose
covering his feet reached high enough to meet them.
His torso was still swathed in bandages. Even moving
unsteadily he was tall and lithe and quite breathtaking.

'Fever is very weakening,' Ester reminded him when
he was forced to sit down after a turn or two. 'In
another day or so you will be back to normal. How
does your back feel?'

'Much less sore, I thank you, though ——' he shifted
his shoulders uneasily ' — I fancy the bandage is stuck.'

'Then I will remove it. Judith, bring warm water and
a cloth.'

Judith held the bowl while her mother worked at
soaking the linen from healing scabs. He would always
bear the scars of his ordeal. She hated those responsible
with an intensity she had seldom felt over anything
before.

'There,' said Ester when she had finished. 'I believe
the wounds will be better left uncovered now. Be
careful how you treat them.'

'I can assure you of that,' he said wryly.

'You should be able to wear this shirt.' She handed
him one of Edward's working garments, plain apart
from some smocking at the shoulders. 'Mayhap you
would like to sit by the fire for a while, and sup with us
later.'

'You have been most kind to me, Mistress Le Grand,

and my presence has brought you nothing but sorrow.
I can but assure you of my deepest gratitude.'

He reached out, took her mother's dainty hand in
his long fingers and kissed her knuckles with courtly
grace. Judith's hands tightened on the bowl she still
held while she imagined his lips touching her own skin.
She had never seen her mother looking so young and
flustered.

Conscious charm, she told herself. He was quite
capable of using it to get anything he wanted. From
women at least. Her mother, Marie, Penna, Genette —
he had them all eating out of his hand.

Silently, she turned and carried the bowl out through
the kitchen to the yard, where she emptied its contents
before dumping it back inside the door.

Then she picked up a hoe and made for the herb
garden. She did not want to sit in the kitchen watching
Oliver Burnett being charming to all the other women.
Since the time her gaze had made him uncomfortable
he had scarcely looked her way.

CHAPTER FOUR

SEVERAL days later, with no immediate task demanding her attention, Judith decided to walk down the valley to the bay in the hope of finding something worth salvaging among the rocks. High winds had prevailed over the last week and that should mean plenty of wreckage from disasters far beyond their ken.

Escape from the presence of Oliver Burnett had become imperative, for relations between them were strained. She knew why she had withdrawn into cool friendliness, but found it difficult to understand his manner. He laughed and joked with the rest of the household, teasing Genette into delightful confusion and making her mother blush with his blandishments. Even old Marie was not immune to his charm. Only for her did he reserve a polite formality. He no longer called her 'angel'.

She did not mind, of course she didn't, for it suited her own need to avoid deeper involvement. But she missed his bright, challenging gaze, his quirky smile, that sense of a special relationship which had at first seemed to spring up between them because of her part in his rescue.

Swine rooted among the remains of a crop of beans and she counted them in passing. All present and correct. Gulls swooped overhead and a rabbit scuttled back to its warren at her approach. She half turned to watch its tail disappear among the scrub and then stood quite still.

Master Burnett appeared to be following her. He

had seemed restless, impatient to recover quickly from the weakness left by privation and fever, insisting on taking exercise around the yard when no one had thought him fit enough. It seemed he felt able now to venture abroad. He waved and lengthened his stride in order to catch her up.

She waited, for without being rude she could do nothing else, watching his approach with mixed feelings.

The Sark men had been generous, the women industrious in making alterations to clothing, and also in washing, starching and ironing not only his shirt but the simple ruffs about his neck and wrists. The green velvet padded doublet suited him well, as did the feathered cap. But then, he would look dashing in whatever he wore. Or in nothing. She pushed that disturbing thought back where it belonged. She felt quite confused enough by the sudden changes in his attitude towards her. First teasing warmth and gratitude, then distant courtesy; now, apparently, a renewal of friendship.

He arrived, rather breathless, and greeted her with a sweeping bow.

'Mistress Judith! You are walking down to the shore?'

He had shaved his cheeks and trimmed his beard. The old blitheness of manner was back. As was the smile. She wished it were not, for her stomach gave an uncomfortable lurch and her knees began to shake.

'Aye, sir,' she admitted stiffly, dipping into a small curtsy in response to his salutation. ''Tis a fine day, and I had an hour to spare before the sun goes down.'

'You work too hard,' he observed lightly, though the sharpness of his half-hooded gaze belied the offhandedness of his tone. 'I should be honoured if you would allow me to accompany you. I have a fancy to renew acquaintance with the scene of my survival. I confess I retain but a dim memory of that momentous event.'

Judith's stomach turned another somersault at sight of the grin accompanying this remark. It had been so much easier to cope with her own feelings while he ignored her. Wanting to hide her expression, she began to walk on, leaving him to follow.

She kept her voice even by sheer determination. 'You were exhausted; small wonder your memory is dim. The effort to escape the tidal race proved almost too much for you. It was fortunate you did not get caught up in the undertow, for that is deadly.'

'The tides and currents around this island appear to be vastly treacherous and strong. How do your sailors and fishermen manage?'

'They are familiar with the waters and recognise the dangers. That is why they do not sail in strong winds or turbulent seas.'

The banter had left his voice and manner. A slight frown shadowed the clarity of his narrowed eyes. 'Like at the present moment?'

'Yes.'

'So we are cut off from the world?'

She gave him a quick glance and followed it up with a short, mirthless laugh. 'Most of us are always cut off, whatever the weather. Some are more fortunate and journey to Guernsey or Jersey for supplies. The Seigneur sometimes travels back to Jersey to oversee his fief of St Ouen.'

'Have you never left the island since you came here?' he enquired in surprise.

'No.'

'Poor angel.' His voice dropped, became deeper, more vibrant. 'The things I recall very clearly about my rescue are your face hovering over me and your quiet, confident voice asking for my hand. Had you gone wandering from the island, I would have drowned.'

The blood rose, colouring her cheeks, and would not be denied. 'I am glad I saw you and was able to pull you from the sea.' She laughed self-consciously. 'Mayhap 'twas fate that kept me here.'

'Destiny,' he mused, still serious. 'We can none of us escape our destiny. But — "kept you here"? Has there then been some thought of your leaving Sark?'

'Aye.' She wished she had chosen her words more carefully. She had no wish to remember the rejection she had seen in her suitor's eyes the moment they rested on her. Nor to discuss it. 'Marriage,' she said briefly. 'But the negotiations fell through.'

'To my good fortune!'

He halted in his tracks, that impossibly incorrigible smile making his green eyes dance. His fingers sought hers and carried them to his lips. He must surely feel them trembling! But he could not know of the strange, exquisite pain wrought by the feel of his firm lips on her roughened skin.

Judith recovered her hand as soon as possible without appearing ungracious. 'And now it seems I am destined to wed with the heir to La Sablonnerie, a tenement on Little Sark,' she informed him tonelessly.

'And you have no liking for the match?'

A gust of wind tore at his cap. He clapped a hand on top of his head to anchor it. A gull swooped, screaming, overhead.

Judith's hair, blowing freely in the wind, swirled about her face in a glorious disarray quite at odds with her contained expression. 'No. But I shall have little choice. Either that or grow into old age dependent upon my father while he lives and my brothers thereafter. At least if I marry I shall have the comfort of a family to raise.'

He remained silent for a moment, brooding on her composed features. This time it was he who made the first move to resume their walk.

When he spoke she was surprised at his abrupt change of subject. He swept an arm to indicate the fields through which they were passing.

'The land here looks fertile.'

Judith shook herself out of a dismal mental picture of life with Simon Perrier.

'It is. But it took a lot of clearing. When we arrived the land was overgrown with a mixture of blackthorn, bracken, brambles and furze. Sark was a barren wilderness, apart from the small patch the Seigneur de Carteret had cultivated as an experiment before committing himself to the venture.'

Oliver lifted his eyes to the towering bluffs on either side of the valley. 'Like that?' he asked.

'Exactly. I was up there,' she pointed to the end of Longue Pointe, 'when I saw something being swept through the passage between Sark and the Ile des Marchands. You will not see that until we reach the shore. I did not realise it was a man, but I ran down just the same. Down that path.'

Oliver looked where she indicated and saw the steep, narrow track winding through the thick growth and emerging on the small plateau they were rapidly approaching. To either side a bare, rugged, sheer rockface rose from the sea, merging with the bracken-covered slopes way above their heads. At the foot of these cliffs the retreating tide had revealed countless boulders littering the sea bed. Further out, a jagged outcrop promised doom to any unwary mariner.

Oliver stood, hands on hips, viewing the scene.

'Do you wish to climb down?' asked Judith. 'I intend to search the shore.'

'Indeed I do.'

'Then tread warily. The steps are difficult and probably slippery.'

'These are the ones you carried me up?'

'I only helped. Edward and Josué bore most of your weight.'

'Damnation!'

The oath seemed torn from him. A quick glance upwards revealed the frowning pain etched on his normally lively features.

'I am sorry,' she said sincerely. 'I did not wish to remind you, or to imply——'

'That my life was a poor exchange for that of your brother?' he said with uncharacteristic bitterness. 'And that Josué will probably be crippled for the remainder of his life?'

'No!' protested Judith, afraid of the passionate response she had roused in this man. She had thought him not only careless of danger, but also indifferent to the consequences of his actions. She had been wrong.

'No,' he agreed more gently. 'No, I know you did not. You are far too generous, angel. But nevertheless, it is true. I would gladly give my worthless life if I could restore Edward to you all.'

'But you cannot! And I am convinced your life is far from worthless! Are you not a merchant, buying and selling the cloth people need?'

This much he had told them, explaining his presence in Antwerp, where he had been arrested by the Spanish. He made no rejoinder as they gained the beach, but looked around, striding forward until he had the Ile des Marchands in view.

Waves lapped at their feet. Shingle, swept forward,

rumbled in protest as it was dragged back beneath the
sea again.

''Twas a miracle,' he muttered beneath his breath.
'Mistress Judith, I must return to England with all
speed. When will it be possible for me to sail?'

Judith's heart sank. He was so eager to be gone! But
she answered honestly.

'I do not know. Even when the wind moderates, the
sea will be rough. Two or three days. No sooner, I
think. But you should ask the Seigneur's captain.'

He turned to stare at her. 'The Seigneur has a ship?'

'Aye. 'Tis moored on the other side of the island, in
the Baie de la Motte, where he is having a harbour
constructed. The Eperquerie landing is not very convenient and lacks shelter from the north. He is building
a road down the valley and blasting a tunnel through
the bluff of rock separating it from the bay. With that
done, it will be easier to import all the things we need.
A man can get through now, but it will take years to
complete the work.'

'I'd like to see it.'

He spoke quite abruptly, his thoughts far from her
and the present. Judith smothered her disappointment
and answered with apparent indifference.

'Tomorrow, perhaps. I will show you.' She did not
look at him but changed the subject, pointing among
the rocks. 'See, there is plenty of driftwood to collect,
if nothing else. It helps with the fire. The furze burns
so quickly.'

She did not want to talk about his going away. His
advent and its consequences, though tragic, had been
the most exciting things to happen on Sark since she'd
been brought to live there. She ran ahead, lifting her
skirts and bounding from rock to rock to gather the
wreckage.

He shook off his sombre mood and joined her, laughing and teasing as he helped to collect and stack pieces of wet wood into a growing pile.

'How long since you came to the island?' he asked, as they made one last trip back among the rocks.

'Some six years. I had just passed my eleventh birthday at the time. I loved it then. It was exciting and new and yet I felt secure, since we all lived together in the ruins of St Magloire's monastery. To us children the island was one great playground!'

'There was a monastery here?'

'Ages ago. A thousand years, 'tis said. They had a water mill and a chapel. But the overcrowded conditions in the ruins did not suit the grown-ups. Maman was very unhappy. So Papa and the other men built shelters on their own tenements, primitive but private. You must have seen ours, Penna and Jasper live in it now we have a permanent house.'

He eyed her with some respect. 'You all work hard enough even today. It must have been even harder then.'

'We had help. But yes, it was. The trees and furze and rocks we cleared from the land went into building the shelter. Collecting this,' she grinned, flourishing a dripping baulk of timber, 'is easy work by comparison! Everything else we needed had to be shipped from Jersey or Guernsey. The animals — even the seed for our crops.'

'You have a merchant here?'

'Not one who imports; 'twould scarcely be worth anyone's while. Our needs are small by most standards. William Smith is our butcher and brewer, he trades in a few things besides.'

He stopped work for a moment, to stand gazing out across the sea. 'And that is Guernsey.'

'Aye. We should be up on the point. 'Twould be clearer from there. And you'd see Jethou and Herm, too.'

'It looks so near,' he mused.

'Seven miles, direct. An impossible journey if the wind is adverse. Jersey is easier.'

'What about France?'

'Brittany, yes. It is almost impossible to reach the Cotentin, because of the tide. We can sail to Jersey and St Malo, but not to Cherbourg.'

'I see. Interesting.'

'You have much experience of the sea, Master Burnett?'

'As a passenger, yes. I have been to the New World with John Hawkins. Three times.'

Her grey eyes lit up. 'You have seen the Spanish Main?'

'And many other parts of the world. But nothing,' he told her softly, 'can equal the magnificence of this island's coast.'

She met his teasing gaze steadily, feeling strangely let down that he did not appear to understand her ambivalent feelings about her home. 'I am not unaware of its beauties,' she protested stiffly. 'It is just that I feel trapped. Can you not understand that?'

'Aye. For at this moment I feel trapped myself.' He laughed suddenly, his momentary seriousness dispelled by that disturbing smile. 'But marry! There are far worse places in the world in which to be trapped! Let us enjoy the freedom we have to roam this shore!'

His irrepressible spirits bubbled over and carried Judith's with them. Sark seemed an altogether more attractive place with Oliver Burnett gracing it with his presence.

*   *   *

The following day she watched him eye the small ship owned by Helier de Carteret as it rocked at anchor off the new landing. They had walked across the island from west to east. The coastline of France appeared dimly upon the horizon.

'The weather is not auspicious,' Oliver remarked with a grimace. 'That brig would founder in these heavy seas.'

'And a larger vessel would be driven on the rocks. You must be patient, Master Burnett. In another day or two you will be stronger——'

'I am strong enough, angel. Shall we go down to the landing?'

'An it would please you, sir, and if you feel equal to the stiff climb back. We can use this path. Men are still working on the road.'

'It would please me, and I have no doubt that I shall survive the exertion.'

She had annoyed him, she thought, by dwelling upon his incapacity. He would deny it, laugh at it and stretch himself to the limit to prove that it did not exist. Just as she would.

The thought amused her, for they had so little else in common that a stubborn streak over admitting to physical weakness struck her as absurd.

She set off at a good pace with Oliver following rather like a goat. She had to admire his agility. Like the new road, the narrow path followed the line of the cleft and finished on a flat-topped escarpment between two small bays which were hidden from view behind rocks towering on either side. Judith led the way to what looked like the entrance to a cave.

'The bay is not ideal,' she explained as they ducked their heads to pass through what soon revealed itself as a rough-hewn tunnel. 'We have no pier or breakwater as yet, though the Seigneur plans to have both built, in time. The tunnel needs enlarging, too. But this landing is central, and the road up to the island's centre is shorter and less difficult than that from the Eperquerie.'

'You will not get a horse through here,' commented Oliver as they emerged on the other side and stood on the shingle beside several small fishing boats, hauled up to safety from the storm.

'Not until the tunnel is enlarged, but men will be able to drag their catches or cargoes to carts on the other side. At Eperquerie the only means of transporting the goods up the steep cliff is by sledge, and then there is a long trek across rough common ground before the going gets easier.'

Oliver nodded as though in understanding while he examined Helier's ship with a knowing eye. 'A sturdy little vessel,' he commented, 'about fifteen tons, at a guess. But will she not be grounded when the tide retreats?'

'Aye, and if the wind turns to the south she might well be driven on the rocks. But the Seigneur made the best practicable choice, Master Burnett. Although Sark has many bays it is also surrounded by rocks and by currents and racing tides. The most dangerous rocks are those which are never seen. Few of the inlets are approachable in safety and all are vulnerable to some direction of the wind. Our bay is used as a harbour sometimes, but is open to the westerlies and is only safely approachable at slack tide. The choice was not made lightly, Master Burnett.'

'I was not suggesting that it was. Yet smugglers used to haunt the island not long ago.' His voice took on a musing tone. 'They must have navigated the difficult waters in safety.'

'No doubt they did, but our people are honest traders and take no unnecessary risks. And the pirates could store their booty in caves, they did not have to cart it inland.' Judith's voice had taken on an edge. Her companion appeared unnecessarily critical of those who had succoured him and welcomed him into their midst. 'Shall we return, Master Burnett?'

He regarded her quizzically, making no move to fall in with her suggestion. 'Do not take offence, angel. I meant none, for I admire your colonists enormously. I would that such as you could cross the ocean to the New World. There, vast stretches of land lie ready for the taking——'

'You wish to settle over there, Master Burnett?'

'No, angel, not personally. My pioneering thirst has been slaked by those expeditions with John Hawkins. Drake brought me safely home from St Juan de Ulloa three years ago and I have no intention of crossing the ocean again. I am content to operate within the English Channel, and I have no desire to settle anywhere but in England. But I would like to see others do so.'

Judith frowned. 'You mentioned Hawkins before. But Drake? St Juan de Ulloa? Until you came I had heard none of these names.'

'Your ignorance astounds me, angel! John Hawkins is a fellow merchant from Plymouth. He gained the Queen's unofficial consent to trade in the Spanish Main. I joined him on two successful expeditions, but the third time I ventured forth. . .' He hesitated, unwilling to harrow her with tales of Spanish duplicity and cruelty. 'Suffice it to say that the expedition fell into a Spanish trap at St Juan de Ulloa, near Vera Cruz in Cartogena.'

'Ah!' she interrupted, eager to refute his accusation of ignorance. 'I did hear something of that betrayal!

The Seigneur expressed his anger and indignation to the Spaniards who came here searching for you!'

'I imagine any true subject of the Queen would have been disgusted by that incident. Few escaped death and most of those who did ended up in the dungeons of the Inquisition. Hawkins limped home on the damaged *Minion*, manned in the end by a dozen or so starving sailors. His brother had to send out a crew to bring the ship into Plymouth.'

'Were you. . .?'

Judith's anxious voice cut across his memories.

His firm lips curved into their habitual upward tilt. 'No, angel, I was more fortunate. I was aboard a ship captained by a clever, daring young seaman called Francis Drake, who had been given command of the *Judith* on the death of its original captain. He comes from Plymouth, too. Amid all the mayhem he slipped out of St Juan de Ulloa with his ship unscathed. We hung about for a full day waiting for others to join us, but none appeared and we thought them all lost. He did not know that Hawkins had leapt from his sinking ship to the *Minion* and escaped with other survivors. We did not see it. So Drake set sail for home.' A smile, grim for him, tightened the corners of his lips at the look on her face. 'Aye, angel. The *Judith*. Now perhaps you will understand why I was so surprised to discover your name. My guardian angel's name must be Judith.'

'I'm glad, Master Burnett,' was all Judith could find to say.

'Not nearly so glad as I am. And, angel — could you find it possible to address me as Oliver? There can surely be no need for formality between us — after all,' he added wickedly, his mood changing with its usual mercurial speed, 'there is little you do not know of me. . .'

Judith coloured hotly. 'On the contrary, sir! I know very little of you——'

'Everything that matters,' he interrupted softly. 'Your eyes give you away, angel. You do not regard me as a stranger. Will you not indulge me and call me Oliver?'

Her colour fled, leaving her pale and trembling. He reached out for her shoulders and drew her close. 'Judith, Judith, I owe you so much. Do not shut me from your understanding, from your affections.'

Judith did not possess the strength of will to resist the pull of his hands, the magnetism of his eyes, the seduction of his tone and words. She watched, fascinated, as his mouth came down to hers.

At its first touch her lids dropped as weakness invaded her limbs. Softly, caressingly, his lips teased hers, light as thistledown, searing as fire. His hands still gripped her shoulders and as his kiss deepened Judith felt the need to hold on to him, her only safety in a drowning sea of sensation. Her arms lifted to clasp him, her hands clutched at his back.

His sharp intake of breath, the tensing of the muscles under her fingers, warned Judith even before he lifted his head.

'Move your hands, angel,' he instructed on a gasp of strangled laughter. 'I fear my wounds are still too painful to bear even your delightful touch.'

But the interruption had brought Judith back to reality. After all the warnings, despite her own resolution, she had almost fallen under his spell! Her hands dropped and she pulled away.

'I think one kiss was enough, Master Burnett,' she said coolly. Although her heart cried out to capture this man for her own, she knew it for an impractical proposition. An adventurous man of such quicksilver responses could not possibly wish to do more than enjoy a diverting dalliance with her. He was recovering his strength fast, impatient to be off — and she was available to test his abilities, to relieve his boredom. And if she trapped him, as Mistress Quesle suggested, he would never forgive her.

He released her shoulders, but his fingers lingered on her flushed cheek while his thumb traced the sweet curve of her lips.

'Oliver,' he insisted. 'Did you not enjoy the kiss, Judith? I confess I found it quite enchanting. Was it your first?' Since Judith just stared at him he laughed and went on. 'I shall kiss you again, you know. It is my right, for how else should I show my gratitude?'

'You have no need to show gratitude!' cried Judith, backing away. 'Please, let us return to Beauregard! It is a fair walk, and you may need to rest ——'

'Afraid, angel?' he demanded softly. Then he grinned, quite certain of his charm. 'Anything to please you, angel. We will retrace our steps immediately.'

He turned and led the way back through the tunnel, leaving a startled and rather disgruntled Judith to follow. He had no need to be rude! However, at the other end she found him standing, a quizzical, teasing expression bringing laughter to his eyes. The dark rings outlining the green iris seemed unusually distinct. Perhaps because his lids had lifted with his eyebrows and his full gaze rested upon her, instead of the rather lazy, half-concealed scrutiny he more usually offered.

He guessed she had been annoyed by his suddenly taking her at her word, but she refused to let him see evidence in her demeanour.

'We may as well see how the road is progressing,' she told him tartly, and brushed past.

His hand snaked out and captured hers.

'Good,' he said complacently. 'We can walk side by
side, holding hands, like lovers. Narrow paths are so
restricting.'

Judith tried to tug her hand away, but his grip merely
tightened.

'We are not lovers,' she protested, and for all her
determination she could not control her breathing.
'Please, Master — Oliver, you are stretching my friendship beyond its limits!'

'Ah, but mere friendship is so tame,' he protested.
'Can we not pretend, and behave as lovers do? Allow
me to hold your hand. As you once held mine,' he
reminded her slyly.

'That was — that was an emergency!' she got out
eventually. But the protest was slight. His tone had
been too persuasive. Her hand felt too comfortable in
his, the contact gave her such a warm feeling of
closeness, of excitement, of promise. . .

Promise of what? she asked herself bitterly. But did
not have the resolution to attempt again to withdraw
her fingers.

She made one final effort to be sensible, saying
stiffly, 'I am not good at pretence.'

He began to ascend the hill, drawing her along with
him, swinging their clasped hands in time with their
steps.

'You think not? I would have said you were an
excellent performer,' he returned cheerfully.

The following day she took it for granted that Oliver
would wish to accompany her when her mother sent
her on an errand to Little Sark. Not to one of the other
tenements there, but to La Sablonnerie. Well, he
would no doubt see her suitor and it would do no harm
to remind him that she was almost betrothed. The way

he kept looking at her he needed something to cool his
ardour.

If only it were honest, a true attachment which could
blossom into something more lasting. . . .

But she had his measure. Dreams and reality did not
mix. A visit to La Sablonnerie would remind her, as
much as Oliver Burnett, where her future lay. She
suspected her mother of sending her on purpose. True,
she had a surplus of eggs from the ducks on the pond,
but there were other, nearer tenements where they
would be equally welcome.

'It is still blustery,' Ester warned as they set out. 'So
be careful.'

She had not looked pleased to find Master Burnett
determined to accompany her daughter but, after
expressing some doubts as to the wisdom of the proposal, had not forbidden the joint expedition.

'I still have so much of Sark to discover, Mistress Le
Grand,' Oliver had pointed out in his winning way.
'This is an excellent opportunity for me to explore your
beautiful island. And what better guide could I have?'

Judith had been half excited, half apprehensive at
the prospect of such an excursion. Once she had
managed to relax, the walk back yesterday had turned
into a light-hearted jaunt. Oliver had shown a lively
curiosity about everything they passed. He had paused
outside the long, low building of Le Manoir, eyeing it
with particular interest.

'I should like to meet your Seigneur,' he remarked.
'I am sure he would receive us. Shall we go in?'

'Not today.' He had squeezed her fingers. 'I do not
wish to interrupt our walk. But I must speak with him
before I leave the island.'

That remark had dampened her spirits slightly, but
not for long. Oliver's were high enough to be infec-

tious. At the brewery they stopped for a refreshing tankard of Will Smith's small ale. She had shown Oliver the bakehouse, where everyone without an oven took their risen dough, and the new mill, where all their grain must now be ground.

Oliver shook his head in wonder. 'You are obliged to use the Seigneur's mill? Such a practice died out long ago in England.'

'Helier de Carteret was granted feudal rights here, as his reward for organising the island's defences. The system works well enough. We are a happy community.'

'Because you are free and fortunate in your lord,' observed Oliver shrewdly. 'He does not abuse his power, as some of our barons did in the past. Still do, I suppose, though they have less opportunity to do so now that there are no longer villeins tied to their land.'

'Tell me about England!'

But he had merely laughed. ''Twould take an age, and we are nearly at your home! Wait until you see it, angel.'

She looked at him quickly. 'I doubt I ever shall.'

'Have faith, angel. I do not believe you are destined to spend your entire life here on Sark.'

He'd said no more, and they'd completed their journey in silence. But it had been a companionable silence. What he was thinking she had no idea. But her own imaginings had been galvanised by his words.

Perhaps, one day, he would bring his brigantine and let her sail with him back to England for a visit. She dared not hope for more.

CHAPTER FIVE

TODAY the expedition would take them south, into the sun, and with luck she would be able to show Oliver the coast of Jersey.

He carried the basket of eggs, but that still left him with a free hand which quickly claimed hers. Judith offered not even a token resistance, finding the touch of his fingers too delightful to refuse. When he looked at her and smiled she felt a tingle of expectancy which led to a clutch of fear. She did not trust him. Worse still, she did not trust herself.

He swung her along, up hill and down dale, for the treeless, cultivated plateau crowning Sark was far from flat; and, as they walked, the light-hearted mood of yesterday returned, and with it her confidence.

He must be older than her by at least ten years. He had travelled the world, seen things, experienced dangers she could only begin to imagine. His every word and action screamed 'gentleman'; the elegant way he wore even borrowed clothes proclaimed the same. His social standing must be high, higher than a mere merchant, and against all the present odds he exuded an air of wealth. Yet, despite her sturdy working clothes he regarded her as an equal — which of course she was, she hastily reminded herself, now her father owned land — and, incredibly, seemed to find her attractive. Determined to enjoy the day while she could, she thrust the memory of their destination aside.

As they approached La Coupée Oliver came to an abrupt halt.

'God's life!' He gazed in awe at the narrow neck of rock connecting the two parts of Sark. On either side almost sheer cliffs swept down to the sea far below. Along the ridge ran a narrow track. 'You did not tell me we were to go mountaineering!'

Judith chuckled as she began to lead him down. 'Scarcely mountaineering, Oliver! We merely have to negotiate a few yards of path with a drop on either side. Surely you are not afraid!'

Her tone teased. She knew by now that little scared Oliver Burnett. Rather, he sought danger. Otherwise he would never have set out on an expedition to Spanish territory on the other side of the Atlantic. Or gone to Antwerp when he knew Alva had initiated a wave of cruel persecution against all Protestants.

His eyes gleamed, his fingers tightened their hold. 'I am so scared, angel, that my knees are knocking together. Were it not for these eggs I would throw my arms around you and beg for your support!'

He almost sounded serious, but she knew he was joking. 'You will do no such thing, Master Burnett!' she scolded lightly. 'Stride the ridge like a true man!'

Saying which, she gave another teasing chuckle, freed her fingers and ran across the divide.

At the far side she turned, expecting to find him close behind her, laughing with exhilaration as she was laughing. But he was only halfway across, walking slowly and carefully, his gaze focused on the ground, his face grim.

'Oliver!' she called anxiously. 'Oliver, what is amiss?' She began to retrace her steps.

'Leave me!' he called roughly, concentrating on his feet.

Judith waited apprehensively, wondering what had happened to change him so.

He arrived at her side white and shaking, drew a deep breath, put down the basket and wiped his damp brow. As he relaxed, the colour began to seep back into his face.

'Marry!' he exclaimed, giving her a wry smile. 'My apologies, angel, for that sorry exhibition. But heights——' He shut his eyes as though to wipe out the memory. 'I could never usefully climb the ratlines. Hence my life at sea was spent on the deck. Though I filled in time by learning to navigate.' The irrepressible laughter bubbled up again but sounded rueful, lacking its usual humour. 'What must you think of me, angel? To be scared of falling off. . .'

Judith wanted to put her arms around him and assure him that she thought no less of him for something he could not help. She knew some people got dizzy on the edge of a shallow hole. She did not understand it, but could sympathise. She herself found small, dark enclosed places, places no one else seemed to mind, suffocatingly disagreeable.

She offered him her hand and he took it. 'I admire courage,' she said softly, 'and it took courage for you to make that crossing. I am only sorry that you will have to suffer again on the way back.'

'Oh, generous wench! Would that I could as easily forgive myself my weakness! But come!' He picked up the basket. 'Let us be on our way.'

At the top of the rise leading away from La Coupée Judith tugged him to a halt and turned round. 'Look,' she instructed breathlessly. 'You can see most of Great Sark from here. And the Ile des Marchands, with Herm and Jethou behind.'

Oliver looked back to the familiar small islands and then let his eyes roam to the breathtaking view to the east.

'Those bays,' he muttered. 'They look like safe anchorages.'

'They are, when they're sheltered from the wind. But getting inland from either Dixcart or Derrible is difficult.'

'I expect the pirates found a way.'

'No doubt. It is not impossible. Just impracticable for general use, like most other parts of the coast. Only goats can climb the Hog's Back, that spit of land separating the bays.'

He leapt on the name with an amused exclamation. 'An English name at last! 'Tis the first I've heard!'

'The holder of Le Grand Dixcart is an Englishman, Sieur William Smith, who was garrisoned on Guernsey. He named it. We practise our English on him and his children sometimes.'

'The brewer, eh? I must speak with him again,' murmured Oliver thoughtfully. 'He should be able to advise on navigation into his bay.'

'You seem extremely interested in anchorages,' Judith remarked impatiently. 'Do you not appreciate the beauty?'

'Oh, yes, angel, I appreciate beauty.' He wasn't looking at the view, but at her, and his eyes had regained all their lively teasing. 'I was merely planning for the future.'

His gaze made her blush. 'The future?' she asked rather breathlessly.

'Aye. For when I come back to Sark aboard my own vessel.'

She looked down, imagining a ship — his ship — riding at anchor in Dixcart bay. He did intend to come back to see her! Mayhap to take her away. . .

'Why not our bay?' she asked, despite her better judgement.

'You said yourself the tides were difficult there ——'

'But not impossible! And access would be better ——'

'I should need to use all the bays from time to time. Mostly the one we visited yesterday, no doubt.'

'You intend to come back often? Why?'

'I am a merchant,' he responded airily. 'I can supply many of your needs here. There is so much you lack.'

'Oh.' Her intense disappointment made her voice flat. 'I would hardly think it worth your while,' she muttered.

'There would, of course, be other attractions.'

Her heart lurched. His inference was plain from the tone of his voice. He *would* be coming back to see her! But in all probability she would by then be married — unless she stood out firmly enough. . .

'How could I not keep in touch with my guardian angel?' he went on lightly. 'To neglect to do so might blight my good fortune.'

They walked on in silence, Judith trying desperately to overcome her disillusion. For a moment she had dared to hope. . .he had been so attentive over the last few days, they had become so easy together. . .

But she had known in her heart the hope was false. It was as her mother and Penna had warned. He was grateful, bored now he was recovering his strength and spirits, and what better way for a man like him to amuse himself than by indulging in a meaningless dalliance with a willing maid? To her shame she had scarcely rebuffed him at all, and he had found it necessary to make the limitation of his intentions clear.

The sun still shone between bustling mountains of cloud, but to Judith a visit to Little Sark was always depressing. With Oliver's words ringing in her ears the day seemed positively gloomy. She quickened her pace, wanting nothing so much as to get her errand done and return home, where she could find solitude in which to indulge her misery.

Mistress Perrier greeted her effusively, accepted the eggs with embarrassing expressions of gratitude, welcomed Oliver with evident curiosity but doubtful enthusiasm and immediately ordered Simon to be fetched from the fields.

'No,' protested Judith quickly, 'do not bother your son! We cannot stay——'

'Nonsense! You will take a jug of ale and a spiced cake with us before you leave! Simon would be most upset to miss you, Judith, my dear. Run along, boy.' With an imperious wave of her plump hand she sped her chosen messenger on his way.

Judith had no choice but to await the arrival of her suitor. To her discomfort Oliver chose to seat himself on the bench by her side. Mistress Perrier deluged him with faintly hostile curiosity, firing a barrage of questions which he fielded deftly without giving away more than he intended.

Judith admired his skill. He knew he was the object of considerable speculation to the islanders, but never volunteered other than basic information about himself. She probably knew more about him than anyone else, she reflected, he had been more open with her over the last couple of days, yet her knowledge amounted to very little. He had his own vessel, but was he as rich as she imagined? He was well travelled, but did he still live in Plymouth? Was he wed? Was that why. . .? She faced the possibility squarely. He was old enough to have a family.

Having elicited all the information Oliver was willing to impart, Mistress Perrier went on talking. She was a great gossip. Judith sat in dismal silence imagining having to listen to that sharp, chattering voice every day of her life.

And then Simon arrived.

'Mistress Judith!' He entered heavily, bringing in the odour of the byre. 'What a pleasant surprise!'

'Good morrow, Master Perrier.' Judith kept her voice coolly polite. 'I came on an errand for my mother. I had no wish to call you in from your work——'

'You know I would not allow work to keep me from seeing you.' This was intended as a flirtatious compliment. His blobby face looked as animated as it ever would. His unformed lips, which somehow disappeared into his mouth without being seen, stretched into an admiring smile.

Judith shifted uncomfortably. The very idea of marrying this uncouth youth made her blood run cold. Yet he was heir to a profitable farm and a reasonable fortune. A good match by purely worldly standards.

His hands were dirty and he went over to a bucket of murky water and began to rinse them.

Revulsion sent a trickle of chilly fear down her spine. She sent up a fleeting prayer to the lord to spare her from the ordeal such a match must be.

'Master Burnett kindly offered to escort me here.' In the midst of her distress her mother's training came to her rescue. She found she could, quite steadily, make the right sociable noises. 'I do not believe you have yet met.'

Simon made a cursory gesture in Oliver's direction but his eyes never left Judith. Oliver rose to exchange courtesies and then, apparently unaffected by the other man's rudeness, gracefully draped himself back on the bench, starkly pointing up the contrast between the two men. Judith wanted to run from their presence and hide somewhere where she could weep.

'Have you agreed to our match yet?' Simon wiped his hands on a piece of cloth and came to stand over her. The stench of stale sweat and dung made her dizzy. 'Your father said it depended on you, though I don't see why it should. He should lay down the law, and my father told him so. Mother needs your help, and there will be plenty to keep you occupied about the farm until the babies start arriving——'

This speech was the longest Judith had ever heard him make and desperation enabled her to interrupt it. She stood up. Stretched to her full height, she headed him by half an inch.

As firmly as she could, she said, 'I am sorry, Master Perrier, but I cannot marry you.'

'*Cannot!*' shrilled his mother. '*Will* not more likely! What is wrong with my son, may I ask? If I were your mother I'd beat some sense into you, my girl!'

'But fortunately, you are not.' Judith's voice shook despite herself.

'Not good enough for you now, I suppose!' went on Mistress Perrier as though Judith had not spoken. 'Got yourself some fancy ideas now *he's* arrived on the scene!'

For the first time the threat posed by the stranger's presence dawned upon Simon Perrier. He stared at Oliver Burnett, and did not appear to like what he saw. His unprepossessing face drew into a scowl.

'Foreign devil!' he snarled.

Oliver lifted his brows, eyeing the young man up and down while continuing to lounge at his ease.

'To me, sir, you are a foreign oaf. The young lady is wise to refuse your generous offer of marriage.' The word 'generous' was spoken in a tone that made it an

insult in itself. Oliver rose languidly to his feet and
turned to Judith. Despite her shame at being subjected
to such a demeaning proposal in front of him, her gaze
seemed drawn upwards to meet his. 'Shall we leave?'
he enquired amiably.

His eyes held only amusement. He was laughing at
her. But then, he laughed at almost everything, and he
was offering her a means of dignified escape. She
nodded, unwilling to trust herself to speak.

'Then we will bid you both good day.'

He made an elegant, derisive bow before ushering
her out into the sunshine.

Dame Perrier's voice followed them. 'Well! Simon,
are you going to allow —— ?'

'It doesn't matter. I wasn't all that taken with the
wench anyway. But you and Father were keen for an
alliance with Le Grand and she is strong and would
have done ——'

Thankfully Oliver had led her out of earshot before
any further hurtful words could reach their ears.

She felt his touch on her shoulder but shrugged it
off. She stumbled on, blind to everything but her pain.
As though in sympathy the sun hid behind a huge black
cloud and the blustery wind rose. She was aware of
Oliver striding silently at her shoulder but not until
they reached La Coupée did the sound of a deeply
indrawn breath behind her pierce through her self-pity.
Then she remembered. She stopped.

'The path is wide enough for two,' she said. 'Hold
my arm.'

'Your hand will do, angel.'

His voice sounded breathless. She looked at him for
the first time since leaving La Sablonnerie. His eyes
held no hint of laughter. His amusement had foundered
in a sea of panic.

He grasped her offered hand, clasping it firmly and running his thumb caressingly over the back. His lips curved into a self-deprecating smile which failed to reach his eyes. 'Saved again, angel,' he murmured, and even now his voice was not completely devoid of humour. But this time he was attempting to laugh at himself.

''Tis not far,' she told him reassuringly as they set off. 'But I wish the wind had not risen. The gusts——'

As she spoke they were almost swept off their feet. Even Judith felt dizzy for a moment as she staggered in its force, her eyes drawn down to the sight of waves spuming over rocks hundreds of feet below. She felt Oliver's arms close around her, holding her safe, his body braced against the blast.

'We'd better crawl,' she managed to gasp.

'I, my angel, am not crawling anywhere. We'll be all right,' he came back immediately. The emergency seemed to have rid him of his vertigo. 'Come along, while there's a lull!'

They struggled the rest of the way clasped together and the moment they reached a sheltered dell on the other side collapsed in a heap, he half laughing, both panting for breath.

'Marry,' gasped Oliver, 'but I vow never to cross that ridge again! I like neither the place, the people nor the way!'

'The people are not really so bad,' Judith felt she should protest, 'you only met two of them, and under different circumstances even they are pleasant enough.'

'That I refuse to believe! Angel——'

He stopped suddenly, noticing the tears she could no longer hold back. He reached out gentle fingers and wiped them from her cheeks.

'Don't cry, my dear. Their spite is quite immaterial——'

'No, it is not!' Judith found herself sobbing and could not stop herself. 'He wanted me because I'm big and strong, I'd be a good worker, not for myself! You heard him! No one will ever want me for myself!'

For a moment Oliver was silent. Then she was gathered gently into his arms. And in the midst of her misery she felt the tender touch of his lips on her drowned eyes.

His voice came as a breath against her ear, warm and intimate. 'You cannot believe that, my dearest angel. To me you are generously and perfectly formed and most exquisitely fair.'

'Please don't tease me!' she whispered.

'I am not. You cannot see yourself so you cannot judge, but your height gives you dignity, presence, you move with grace and pride. . .and your features——' She felt his lips moving over her face, touching her forehead, her eyes again, her wet cheeks, her jaw and finally her mouth. 'Do you not know that you are quite lovely? As for your wonderful hair, so clean, so sweet-smelling. . .'

Judith did not need to look to realise that some emotion other than amusement had caused the unsteadiness in his voice. She wanted to believe him! Oh, how she wanted to believe him! If he were sincere. . .

He shifted. He was lying on top of her, his fingers threading through her tangled waves, holding her head still. His mouth descended, slowly, as his eyes searched her face. Then it claimed hers, gentle at first but soon seeking, demanding. His body pressed urgently down and Judith could not doubt the strength of his desire. Her own suppressed urges rose to meet his. Her hands gripped his head, pushing off the cap, already loosened by the wind, so that she could feel the crispness of his hair under her fingers. And she abandoned herself to his kiss with all the natural, inexperienced ardour at her command.

At last his mouth released hers. 'Marry, angel!' He was laughing again but it was breathless, incredulous laughter.

Judith was trembling from head to toe. Amazing sensations assailed her body in places she had not known could be stirred into such exquisite life. She shifted her arms to clutch him tighter and saw him wince.

'I'm sorry!' She let her arms fall away. They felt pretty weak anyway. 'Oh, Oliver, Oliver!'

Her voice quivered and she was crying again. Tears of some emotion akin to joy yet laced with sadness. She could capture him, she knew Mistress Quesle had told the truth, but her mother's warnings rang in her ears, together with the voice of her own common sense. He might already have a wife, and where would she be then? And she could not forget Oliver's own words. He would soon be gone, to return to the island only for business purposes.

'Don't cry, angel,' he pleaded. 'There's nothing to cry for.'

'I'm not,' she gulped.

'No?' he murmured, lapping the tears from her cheeks with a delicacy which seared. And he kissed her again.

She felt wonderful beneath him. Soft and eager. He had wanted her ever since he'd recovered enough to be capable of desire. Known that it would be wiser to ignore his impulses and tried to keep a distance between them. But the more he saw her, the more he

needed to conquer her cool beauty, her defensive
reserve, and his good intentions foundered in the storm
roused by her nearness. Besides, after his disgusting
exhibition over that cursedly narrow ridge the need to
demonstrate his manhood, to prove he was not some
puny weakling who disintegrated at the first sign of
danger, had become urgent.

His hands explored her body, fumbling over the
layers of her clothing. He needed to remove them, to
see and touch her satin skin. . .to conquer as he had
conquered women so often in the past. . .

But he could not. Not this virtuous maid, his angel
and his host's daughter.

He could not do it.

Instead, he controlled his raging desire, transforming
it into a tender, caring expression of reassuring adoration which made her tears flow even faster. But he
knew them to be tears of joy.

He could have taken her then. He knew she was
ready, willing, would not have protested. But in all
honour he could not deflower Judith Le Grand.

So lost in each other were they that neither heard
the sound of approaching footsteps, the sharp intake of
scandalised breath, the hurried retreat back into
Greater Sark of someone righteously bent on causing
trouble.

Judith arrived home flushed and apparently happy but
beneath the bright façade lay a heart aching for what
might have been. Not that the ache was too obtrusive
at that moment, nothing much could have disturbed
her present joy in the knowledge that Oliver found her
desirable. He had not taken her, but she knew he had
wanted to, and honoured him the more for his
restraint. She would have been powerless to resist had

he pressed himself upon her. And although at the time she had wanted him to, she was relieved that he had not. For her conscience was clear, she could meet her parents' eyes without shame.

Still immersed in the afterglow of their shared delight, neither was in the slightest prepared for the scene they walked into. Sieur Perrier was there, broad, red-faced and angry. He spoke first, giving no one else a chance.

'There they are! Just look at them! Guilt written all over their faces! How the pair of you can come back to a decent, God-fearing house after what I saw ——' Words failed him.

'Who is this man?' asked Oliver mildly. He still held Judith's hand, though unobtrusively, and gave it a reassuring squeeze before dropping it.

Pierre had returned for dinner. The entire adult family was present, even Marie, assiduously tending her pots and pretending not to listen.

'Sieur Nicolas Perrier,' said Pierre tiredly. 'Nicolas, I do not believe you have previously met Master Oliver Burnett.'

'But I have seen him! And what I saw — well! And to think I was ready to allow my son to marry this. . . this wanton!'

'Mind your language, sir.' Oliver's voice was still mild, but very firm. 'I will not have Mistress Judith spoken of in such terms. And as for what you saw. . . what exactly *did* you think you saw?'

'Fornication! Blatant fornication in full view of anyone who passed! Right beside the track! She should be ducked in the pond as a loose woman!'

'You were mistaken, sir. Neither Mistress Judith nor I have indulged in fornication by any track today. Please apologise to the lady.'

'Apologise!' Perrier was almost apoplectic. 'I will not! You were tumbling her! And she shall not wed with my son!'

Judith spoke for the first time since entering the house. 'I have already told your son that I will not marry him. I would rather remain unwed.'

Shocked, taken aback for an instant, Perrier quickly recovered himself. 'And what respectable man would want to wed you now, wench? When people discover——'

'You will not spread your lies.' Oliver's voice had taken on a dangerous edge. His hand hovered, as though seeking the hilt of an absent sword, then dropped back to his side. 'Nothing untoward happened between Mistress Judith and myself today. Nothing of which either of us has reason to be ashamed.'

'That is not what it looked like to me!'

'Nevertheless, that is the truth.' Judith tried to imagine what the man *had* seen. Two people clasped together. Rumpled skirts, for Oliver had been caressing her skin, and the memory brought its own tremor of delight. But there had been nothing else for anyone to see. She met Perrier's eyes fearlessly. 'A few kisses — what are they?'

'Enough to compromise——'

Oliver still appeared languid but as he took a step towards Perrier an unmistakable cloak of authority descended upon him.

'I asked you to apologise to the lady. An you do not, sir, I must ask you to step outside with me.'

Perrier hesitated, awed by the sudden transformation in Oliver's manner. No longer could he or anyone else imagine him bullying a guilty philanderer into shame. He faced a determined man of action, a man used to giving orders and having them obeyed. While Perrier continued to contemplate the phenomenon, Pierre's voice rasped into the fray.

'No! I'll have no more violence here. Nicolas, I would be obliged if you would keep your own counsel and leave this matter to me. I think we agree that the marriage we had planned between our children will not now take place. Neither party any longer desires it. If you value the friendship between us, you will say no more on this matter, here or anywhere else.'

Perrier looked as though he still might argue, but in the end prudence won and he shrugged. 'As you like, Pierre. But if I were you I'd take a strap to that daughter of yours. Teach her a lesson she won't forget.'

'I think you can leave me to deal with my own daughter, Nicolas. And now we will bid you good day. No doubt your dinner is waiting.'

As Nicolas Perrier departed Oliver made a move towards the door. Pierre Le Grand called him sharply.

'Master Burnett! You will do me the courtesy of remaining here. I wish to speak with you.'

Oliver halted, eyed the man who dared to stand between him and his own brand of justice with respectful amusement, shrugged his shoulders and gave one of his quirky smiles. He bowed. 'I am at your command, sir.'

'We will retire to the solar, where we can be private.'

'Father——'

'Not now, daughter. Remain here with your mother. I will speak with you later. Come, Master Burnett.'

Oliver turned to Judith and lifted her hand to his lips. His eyes smiled reassuringly into hers. 'Do not worry, angel.' He breathed the words, pitched for her ears alone. 'All will be well, you will see.'

* * *

But all was not well. Not altogether reassured by Judith's protestations, her mother had been hurt, anxious, angry that a daughter of hers could behave in such an apparently wanton manner, whatever had truly transpired.

'I knew no good would come of allowing you to nurse him! You have betrayed my trust!'

'Maman, I have not!' Judith faced her mother squarely. She could not control the high colour in her cheeks, but her eyes remained clear and unafraid. 'Simon Perrier had made it quite clear that he was marrying me for my usefulness, not my looks or my character. Oliver——' her voice shook and she swallowed '—Master Burnett was merely attempting to demonstrate that I am not unattractive——'

'Whoever said you were?' demanded Ester impatiently.

'Marie, for one!'

'Humph!' grunted Marie. 'I didn't say that! But you could've made more of yourself. The way you behaved, I thought you didn't care! Haven't I kept on telling you——?'

Genette's smug voice cut across her words. 'I've told her, too! I care what *I* look like!'

'Enough, Marie. And you, too, Genette. I sometimes think you care too much for *your* appearance, my girl. I suggest you go and find something useful to do outside.'

'Come and help me to shift the animals' tethers,' said Josué quickly, rising to his feet. He went across and kissed Judith on the cheek. 'I believe you,' he told her simply. 'Oliver would not take advantage of you. And I never liked that Simon much.' He eyed her speculatively. 'You've always looked fine to me.

You've no need to worry.' He gave her another kiss. 'Come along, Genette.'

Judith gave her brother a grateful smile as he shepherded Genette from the house.

'You let that unfortunate incident when you were scarcely fifteen upset you too much,' said Ester once they had gone. 'I have done my best to reassure you.'

'I know, Maman. But—well, you are prejudiced.' So was Josué. 'You would tell me I looked all right even if I didn't.'

'And Simon Perrier——'

'Wanted me for my usefulness, as I've just told you. He was not "smitten" as you call it with me, but with how hard I could work! So I told him I would not marry him. I do not like him or his mother. I would have been miserable at La Sablonnerie. Surely you would not wish me to be unhappy?'

Her voice took on an unconscious note of pleading. When Ester replied her tone had softened.

'Foolish child. No one would have forced you. But you must be sensible!'

'Yes, Maman.'

But she did not feel sensible. Her heart was in the grip of wild longings, her body charged with restless energy.

And then her father returned, much mollified, to announce that Master Burnett was willing to make restitution for placing her in a compromising situation by marrying her.

And Oliver had the effrontery to walk across to her, put an arm about her waist, take her chin in his fingers and kiss her on the lips in front of them all.

Judith flushed scarlet. 'No!' she cried. She tried to free herself, but Oliver would not let her go. 'Master

Burnett can have no wish to wed me! I will not have
him forced into marriage!'

'You should have thought of that before behaving in
such a wanton manner!' rasped Pierre. 'Before the
night the Spaniards came——' Words failed him. 'I
would not have believed any daughter of mine capable
of such disgraceful conduct!'

'It was the only way I could think of to save Master
Burnett!' cried Judith. 'He was not fit enough to defend
himself! Would you have had me hand him over to the
Inquisition? And today——' The tears began to brim
over as she realised the debasement those wonderful,
reassuring moments in Oliver's arms had suffered,
thanks to Nicolas Perrier. She would never forgive
him.

'Angel.' Oliver's soft voice and the gentle pressure
of his fingers under her chin compelled her to lift
shamed eyes to meet his. 'Angel,' he repeated, 'have
you an aversion to marrying me?'

He was quite serious, his green gaze clear and
steady, although some deep emotion smouldered in its
depths.

She was forced into an honest—well, almost
honest—answer.

'I d-don't think so. In fact I—I would be honoured
to be your wife, Master Burnett. But you would feel
yourself trapped, and that would never do. We do not
love one another.' He did not love her. But she was
beginning to wonder about that statement as far as her
own feelings were concerned. She tried to make her
voice sound final. 'We would stand little chance of
happiness and therefore I do not think we should
marry.'

'Love!' snorted her father. 'When did love matter in
arranging a marriage? You appear to like each other,

and by all accounts there is no physical problem.' Scorn dripped from his voice. He took a steadying breath and went on more reasonably. 'A better basis than most for happiness, I would have said! Provided there is not actual antipathy, respect and affection grow. Ask your mother.'

The last was said on a growl. Her father did not like exposing his feelings, especially with Marie listening.

Ester walked across to link her arm with her husband's. 'But I loved you from the moment we met, Pierre. Did you not know?' she asked calmly. 'And afterwards I had the joy of watching your regard for me grow.'

Judith suspected this was not the answer her father had expected. Her mother was telling her that love on one side was enough. To begin with.

But not if the other person felt trapped. Resentment, not love, would grow. And yet. . . The prospect of marriage with Oliver Burnett was tempting, and not only because of her feelings for him. It offered escape from Sark. . . It was, she recognised, exactly what she wanted. And he was offering it again.

'Marry me anyway, angel,' Oliver went on as though there had been no interruption. His gaze had rested steadily on her face throughout, intent, yet revealing nothing of his inner thoughts. 'I was not forced. I volunteered.'

'But you would not have done ——'

'Mayhap not. But I do not regret my decision.'

He leaned forward to kiss her again. The touch of his lips, firm yet gentle, sent fire streaking along Judith's nerves. Her legs trembled. She put out a hand to support herself, grasping the arm he had put about her waist.

She met his gaze again. This time he could not hide

the tiny devilish glints in the depths of his eyes. He knew the effect his kiss had had on her. 'Why not?' he whispered, adding outrageously, 'We shall both enjoy the bridal bed.'

Prudence told her she should continue to refuse. But why should she not believe him when he said his offer had been freely made? And how could she listen to prudence when his arms beckoned?

'Very well,' she whispered, and lowered her eyes in confusion as his blazed with the sudden, undisguised joy of possession.

He masked his feelings quickly. When he released her to turn to her parents he was smiling with all his normal gay inconsequence.

'Marry, sir,' he drawled, 'but your daughter is difficult to persuade!'

'Stubborn as a mule!' snorted old Marie from her stool. No one took exception to her intervention. Marie's special privileges had been established long ago. 'All I hope is, you'll condescend to wear a decent gown for your wedding, my lass. You'll have to mend your ways now, or you'll shame your husband before his family and all his fine friends!'

Oliver burst into loud chuckles. 'What makes you think I have fine friends, Marie? Mistress Judith looks beautiful to me just as she is! My family will love her and as for my friends — she will more than hold her own.'

Although glad of his defence, Judith wished he had been a little more positive. She had taken little pride in her appearance before his advent, and then another kind of pride had prevented her from changing her ways. Besides, she only had one decent dress and she could not wear that for every day. If he had said that a few new gowns and a body servant to tend her needs

would soon put that little matter right she would have
understood. But he had seemed to imply that she
would do just as she was. Dressed in country working
clothes and heavy leather shoes, with a hooded woollen
cloak to keep her warm and dry. That was not how the
Seigneur's wife, Margaret de Carteret, dressed. Even
her own mother wore more becoming clothes, for she
had been a woman of some consequence in St Helier.

Judith began to wonder how Oliver Burnett lived
when at home in England. She had not stopped to
question what kind of life he would take her to.

But it did not matter. She would be with him. Even
La Sablonnerie would seem like heaven with him.

Her father had taken up the conversation, brushing
aside old Marie's opinion.

'Master Burnett, we must go immediately to see the
Seigneur and then Pastor Brevint.' He addressed
Judith. 'We are agreed that the sooner you are wed,
the better. We can thrash out a legal settlement later.
Master Burnett has promised to put his lawyers in
touch. If possible I will arrange the ceremony for the
morrow, before dinner. Have either of you any
objection?'

'It is a little soon ——'

'None.'

Judith broke off her objection as Oliver's firm voice
cut across it. It seemed she had little choice but to rush
headlong into a marriage for which she was desperately
ill-prepared.

CHAPTER SIX

'You should consider yourself extremely fortunate!'

Judith knew it, but did not appreciate having the fact rubbed in. Dinner had been eaten in a strained atmosphere made tolerable only by Oliver's behaving as though he hadn't a care in the world. Yet even his manner had seemed forced to Judith. Now he had gone with her father to see the Seigneur — he would have his wish to meet Helier de Carteret fulfilled, she thought wryly — before seeking out Cosmé Brevint to arrange the ceremony.

She answered her mother's remark with an undignified snort. 'Whatever he says now, Maman, he was forced into proposing marriage. If Papa had not listened to Sieur Perrier, if he had not been so scandalised over nothing——'

'Sieur Perrier reported nought but what he saw! You have admitted——'

'I have admitted nothing wrong! Maman, did you never kiss and cuddle when you were young? Is it so terrible to enjoy a man's admiration?'

'His admiration, no! But admiration does not necessarily extend to "kissing and cuddling", as you so vulgarly put it. And no, I did not. My virginity and reputation were carefully guarded until an advantageous match had been arranged and I was safely wed. Whatever else you may or may not have done, you have endangered your reputation. You, my girl, have enjoyed far too much freedom on this island. But things are so different here. . . I have been unable to chaperon you as I should. . . I have allowed you to run wild. . .'

Her mother, unused to playing the stern parent, looked for a moment so forlorn and guilty that Judith swiftly went over to give her a hug. 'No harm has come of it, Maman. Nor would it have done.' She stood back and sighed. 'Although I feel I have cheated Master Burnett into marriage. He was simply being kind and. . .and reassuring. But now——' she sniffed back foolish tears '—now, thanks to Sieur Perrier, everything has been made to seem wrong, dirty. . .'

Despite her attempt at control the tears began to roll down Judith's cheeks and her mother stared at her in consternation. Judith so seldom wept! Even when hurt as a child she had tightened her lips and refused to cry. But Judith was no longer a child, and new, deep emotions had brought the tears to the surface.

'There, there, my love!' Now it was Ester's turn to offer consolation. She drew Judith down to sit beside her and patted her hand. 'Don't cry! One can do nothing on this island without some busybody seeing and talking and thinking the worst.' Her tone sounded surprisingly bitter. 'Threatening to have you treated as a loose woman indeed! It would please his mean soul to see you humiliated, no doubt, ducked or driven around the island in a cart, exposed to public ridicule and contempt.'

Judith gave a little choked moan and Ester drew her closer. 'But do cheer up! Sieur Perrier's threats were empty! We would never have allowed it! Neither, I believe, would Master Burnett.'

'No!' Judith swiped at her cheeks with the backs of her hands. '*He*,' her voice shook, 'is a true gentleman! And grateful to me for rescuing him. He feels he owes me a duty!'

'Nonsense, child! If I am any judge, he is not at all averse to the match! Come now, I did not mean to make you cry! You'll make your eyes red and puffy and what will Master Burnett think of his bride then?'

Judith sniffed again and smoothed her still-wet cheeks with stiff fingers, running a knuckle along her lower lids to remove the moisture gathered there. He would think she regretted the interlude and did not wish to marry him, neither of which was true. She was crying for besmirched memories, for fear of forfeiting his regard. . .

'That's better!' Ester smiled and stood up briskly. 'You must wash you hair and have a bath. Your best dress will need ironing and the ruffs must be goffered——'

She cut off as a shadow darkened the open doorway. Penna came in, smiling and holding out her arms to Judith.

'Judith, my dear! Genette tells me you are to be wed!'

'Aye, Penna.' Judith gave a cracked laugh as she accepted Penna's embrace. 'Did she enlighten you as to the circumstances?'

'I received a full account of the scene with Sieur Perrier. That man is a menace, and so is his wife. I never liked the idea of your marrying Simon Perrier, my love. But who was I to argue with your father?' she asked with a wry shake of her head. 'He saw only the prospect of you as mistress of La Sablonnerie.'

'I was as much to blame.' Ester's choked voice filled the little silence which had fallen. 'Neither of us realised that the Perriers viewed the marriage chiefly as the acquisition of another labourer on the farm. You must forgive our blindness, Judith.'

'At least,' said Judith, attempting another laugh,

'you did not threaten to beat me into submission, as many parents would. But let us forget all that! There is so much to do if I am to look my best! And I do want to look my best,' she admitted with an unconsciously wistful smile. 'Penna, could you see to my dress? You are so clever with the iron.'

'Of course, my lovely! And I shall tend you myself! I have been longing for the day you wed a man you could admire and love — and I am certain Master Burnett is that — and by tomorrow you will look a picture! Master Burnett will not be able to take his eyes from you, just you wait and see!'

Judith accepted the flattery with a hesitant laugh. Despite his assurances and those of others, she still doubted her appearance. For some reason he appeared to like it, but she did not look at all like any of the women in the portraits she had seen.

She shrugged. 'If I were Genette I might believe you. Her features are the admiration of everyone! And I have only the one decent dress,' she added wistfully.

'You will have more,' Ester hastened to inform her daughter. 'Master Burnett assured your father that he had a tidy fortune. You will have no need to fear penury.'

Obtaining personal information from Oliver Burnett was as difficult as squeezing juice from apples, thought Judith, remembering William Smith screwing down his cider press. But this drop of hard-won news did please her. She would gladly have borne a life of penury with Oliver Burnett, but penury threatened other problems she could do without. She had enough already.

Later, choosing a moment when they were alone, Penna added to them. 'Genette is jealous of you, Judith.'

'Jealous? You jest, Penna! Why should Genette be jealous of *me*?'

'Because you are to marry such an attractive and wealthy young man. She cannot understand why Master Burnett did not choose her!'

Judith reviewed Genette's recent attitude and sighed. 'She probably is jealous, a little, but she'll get over it. Master Burnett thinks of her as a charming child.'

This she believed and hoped was true. He certainly treated her young sister with the indulgence normally reserved for infants. And once they had left the island she could put Genette's jealousy behind her with the Perriers and everything else that irked her about it.

'It's understandable, I suppose, she's growing up fast and wants to be wed. And she knows quite well she's attractive, I've seen her testing her wiles on any young man who will look her way.'

Judith eyed Penna with amusement. 'God knows there are few enough on this island!'

'Nevertheless, she is the one your parents should watch, and your father should arrange a marriage for her as soon as possible. However, Master Burnett has never had eyes for anyone but you, my dear, so you have no need for concern. Treat her kindly.'

Hoping Penna was right about Oliver Burnett's regard, Judith promised, and turned the subject to her wardrobe. Her clothes were spread out on the bed and kettles of water steamed over the fire when Pierre returned, alone.

'Helier gave his approval,' he told the women. 'He offered Master Burnett the hospitality of Le Manoir; he is to sleep there overnight.' He paused, frowning as though puzzled, then went on with a shrug. 'He seemed much taken by your future husband, daughter. It seems he looks forward to entertaining him. You are to be wed there, too, and he has offered Master Burnett the continued use of his guest chamber for your bridal night. Pastor Brevint will perform the ceremony at eleven o'clock on the morrow.' He looked directly at Judith, his eyes less hostile than earlier. 'I trust these arrangements meet with your approval, daughter?'

'Thank you, Papa. I will be ready.'

Judith spoke submissively, not wishing to further antagonise her father. In fact she desperately desired his understanding and forgiveness, feeling guilty over causing the family so much embarrassment. Although she did not consider what had occurred wrong, she did realise that it had given rise to gossip and cast a slur upon the good name of Le Grand. She should not have allowed Oliver so much liberty; she should have been stronger. . . .

She struggled not to allow her disappointment to show, but her heart sank and the nerves she had been suppressing attacked her stomach as she realised she would not see her bridegroom again before the ceremony. Supposing he had begun to regret. . . She needed the reassurance of his presence, of his smile.

Quelling a sudden desire to be sick, to curl into a corner and hide, she tried on the dress which had been made to impress the suitor from Guernsey.

It had failed dismally on that occasion, but it was all she had. It showed some regard for fashion and the material was of the best her father could afford within the limits imposed by law. Unlike men, women did not face imprisonment or fines for breaking the Sumptuary Laws, but they did invite ridicule if they dressed above their station. She tied the bell-shaped farthingale at her waist, slipped the stiff, cream-patterned brown brocade of the petticoat over it, tied its strings and smoothed it down over the hoops. She donned the matching bodice and then Penna hooked her into the rich, coppery velvet of the overdress.

Penna and her mother regarded her critically. They said nothing and Judith began to feel uncomfortable under their scrutiny.

'Hum,' said Penna at last. 'You've grown, Judith. 'I'll have to let it down. Otherwise it looks very nice.'

Judith stuck her foot out and regarded her ankle dubiously. 'Is there enough hem? And what about the embroidery?'

Penna bent down and examined the garment closely, giving special attention to the elaborately worked border. 'There's enough, and the stitching does not go through. The decoration will be a little high, that is all.'

'The top is a bit loose,' Judith observed, not entirely displeased by the discovery.

'You've grown taller and thinner,' remarked her mother.

'There's enough padding to disguise the bad fit.' Penna cocked her head on one side, considering. 'By the time I've ironed the loops at the top of the sleeves and you've got the ruff on at collar and cuffs you'll look splendid.'

'But I am even taller and the fact that I'm thinner than I was won't show,' objected Judith gloomily.

A complacent grin spread over Penna's plump face. 'Most men like the feel of soft flesh,' she observed, ignoring Ester's scandalised expression. 'The lacing down the seam at the back is as tight as it will go, but I can probably manage to take the waist in a bit.' She pinched the material between her fingers. 'Yes, I can do that.'

Bathed and finally certain that her dress would do

her reasonable credit, Judith retired to join Genette in
their bed.

'For all your pious talk you're nothing but a strumpet,' sniffed Genette accusingly.

Judith stiffened, outraged. 'How dare you?' she
demanded fiercely. ''Tis not so long ago you were
calling me a prude! Besides, you know nothing about
such things! You cannot possibly understand——'

'I understand you've tricked Master Burnett into
marriage. That's what you wanted, wasn't it?'

Genette's petulant tones floated out of the darkness
to rasp an already raw nerve. Judith clenched her fists,
longing to hit her silly young sister.

'Genette, if you don't watch your tongue you'll grow
up into shrew!' Her voice shook. 'I had no
intention——' She broke off. 'But why should I explain
myself to you? Penna thinks you're jealous. I hope that
accounts for your stupidity and bad temper. You
should pray the lord for forgiveness——'

'Don't you preach at me!'

'I'm not!' Judith drew in a steadying breath and went
on in a more conciliatory tone. 'You are far too young
for Master Burnett——'

'Two years too young, I suppose! Don't be ridiculous, Judith. He cannot yet be thirty and girls of my
age wed men far older than that! But no, you had to
trap him before I had a chance!'

'I did not trap him!' It hadn't been like that at all,
but she would never convince Genette. Or plenty of
other people, she thought glumly. Judith hated the
childish quarrel, wanted to keep her promise to Penna,
but could not ignore her sister's spite. 'After he
recovered you had as much chance as I did to impress
him with your maturity! Is it my fault if he treats you
as a child?'

'He doesn't!'

'Yes, he does, and it's because you are!'

With this final, damning statement Judith flung over on her side, turning her back on her sister. Genette retaliated by doing the same. Deep, resentful silence reigned.

Before long Genette's steady breathing told Judith her sister had fallen asleep. Genette's emotions were all on the surface. Nothing disturbed her enough to interfere with her rest. But Judith's mind seethed, images flashed at random across her inner vision. She tried to imagine what life with Oliver Burnett would be like, but somehow her mind refused to look forward, only back, reviewing every word, every look, they had ever exchanged. And every touch.

She woke late, heavy-eyed and nervous. Genette had gone. Judith yawned, stretched and got up.

The hens still needed feeding and there were other chores she must perform before she began to dress for her wedding.

But when she joined the others she found that nothing was expected of her except to prepare for her departure half an hour before the ceremony. She would walk to Le Manoir, her light shoes protected by heavy wooden pattens strapped on beneath the soles, her body swathed in her best cloak. Luckily the ground had dried and the wind moderated.

Genette could not display hostility in front of the family and in fact seemed to be regretting her outburst of the previous night. Perhaps, thought Judith cynically, she did not want their parents to notice they'd quarrelled. Genette would not wish to incur their wrath; she liked to be favourite. And Judith herself, absurdly happy despite her nervousness and doubts, had not the heart to nurture resentment.

Her party arrived at Le Manoir to find the de Carterets and others waiting to greet them. The Seigneur's wife had always been friendly and reached up to kiss the bride as a servant relieved Judith of her cloak. Mistress Brevint kissed her, too. Behind their parents stood the three de Carteret sons, Philippe, Amais and William. And beyond them, Oliver Burnett.

Her gaze returned briefly to Philippe. She could understand her infatuation with him. His honest good looks and strong, shapely figure had made him stand out from the other young men of Sark, even his brothers, for they were still boys. Yet now she saw only his immaturity. And although the widening of his eyes in admiration fed her vanity, it did not make her pulses race as it would have done only weeks since.

Irresistibly, her eyes sought those of her bridegroom.

No admiration there. Just the twin sparks of devilment flashing out to ignite their usual fire in her breast. His quirky, irrepressible smile drew her to his side like a magnet.

He made an elaborate bow and took her hand.

'Marry,' he whispered, 'but this is a better end than I had feared when I leapt into the sea!'

He could not treat even marriage seriously! This was but another adventure to him, a trip into the unknown similar to his voyages across the Atlantic. Assailed with sudden doubts, Judith felt her lovely, slow smile of greeting die and she tugged to retrieve her hand.

He refused to release it. Instead he carried it to his lips. His firm grip and warm, caressing mouth renewed her confidence. She had no need to worry. It was just his way. He would meet this challenge with the same lively sense of humour, the same courage as he met everything else in his life.

'You do not mind?' she whispered.

'Mind, angel? Nay, but I look forward to our bedding!'

His deeply murmured words teased, but she could discern no trace of reluctance, of resentment, in his attitude. Rather, he seemed to be revelling in the situation, impatient to begin the ceremony, to bring forward the moment he anticipated with such apparent fervour, for he immediately led her across to Pastor Brevint, who stood waiting in austere solemnity to join them in matrimony.

He conducted the ceremony in High French, which everyone understood. When a beautifully wrought gold ring was placed upon her finger Judith wondered fleetingly where Oliver had obtained it. There had been no rings on his fingers and nowhere for him to conceal one. . .

At this point her musings brought uncomfortable colour to her cheeks and she abandoned them. The ring fitted surprisingly well and she could wear it proudly. It must have been provided by someone on the island, like the change of garments he wore. Were she not mistaken, the new outfit had been acquired by Philippe de Carteret on his last visit to Jersey. She recognised the padded, slashed trunk hose, black with a saffron lining, and the matching, richly embroidered doublet, the small ruff and falling band. He had been very proud of it. It looked better on her bridegroom, who had more shapely legs to fill the long white nether-stocks and whose broad shoulders stretched the doublet impressively. A sword hung at his hip.

The dubious background to the marriage did not inhibit the revelry which followed. The Seigneur acted

as host and provided the feast. If her father resented
the matter being taken from his hands he showed no
sign, expressing gratitude to his old friend for setting
such a sumptuous banquet.

To Judith it all seemed unnecessary. She touched the
ring on her finger for reassurance. It scarcely seemed
possible, but she was wed, satisfying the moral scruples
of this strictly Presbyterian community. They had no
need to make such a fuss of the occasion. The goose
was much too rich for her queasy stomach. She nibbled
a leg of capon instead.

'You are not enjoying yourself, angel?'

Oliver, observant as usual, had seen her comparative
gloom and lack of appetite. Everyone else was too
occupied in eating and drinking to notice. He reached
out to refill her wine goblet.

'There was no need for a banquet,' she muttered.

'Which only serves to keep us from our bed,' he
murmured provokingly. 'Cheer up, angel. 'Twill not be
long now.'

'That was not ——'

His chuckle broke across her protest. 'Was it not,
angel? But then, you know nothing of the joy of bed-
sport.'

'And how should I?' she hissed indignantly. 'I am
merely an ignorant virgin, unversed ——'

'Unversed, but not unresponsive, wife.'

She coloured at his words. 'Do not embarrass me,
sir,' she pleaded.

'No one can hear ——'

'That is not the point! 'Twas because I responded
that we are in this coil!'

'Coil?' he enquired softly. 'Do you find it a coil,
wife?'

'It must be, for you,' she muttered defensively. 'For

myself, I have little to lose and much to gain. . .my
reputation. . .'

'I had hoped you would not dislike the union, angel.'

His quiet voice brought home to Judith that she was
being ungracious. He had put her welfare and honour
before his own wishes and freedom. But how could she
tell him that marriage to him represented her idea of
heaven on earth when he had never pretended to love
her?

'I do not dislike it,' she muttered.

'Excellent! And I'll warrant you will like it all the
better by morning!'

The uncontrollable colour rose again in her cheeks.
She could not meet his eyes. But coupling was as
natural as living. Why should she feel embarrassed?
Because everyone made such an issue of protecting a
maid's virginity, she supposed. Fornication and adul-
tery were both sins, true, but within the bonds of
wedlock. . .

Common sense reasserted itself. She had nothing of
which to be ashamed. *She* had not initiated the incident
or precipitated the scene afterwards. Neither did
Master Burnett give the impression of a man forced
into wedlock against his will. She doubted whether
even her formidable father could have coerced such a
man had he set his mind against the match. So he was
not averse to the marriage, though he would not have
proposed it himself. She was quite certain of that. He
had never even hinted. . . Why he had acceded so
readily she had yet to discover. He did nothing without
good reason.

She lifted her head and met his gaze squarely.

'I do not know why you agreed to wed me, Master
Burnett. I do not believe it was out of either guilt or

gratitude. But I shall endeavour to be a good wife — in every way.'

'Then I can ask for nothing more,' he said. But despite a suspicion of his normal smile playing about his lips he seemed somewhat disappointed.

CHAPTER SEVEN

WHEN the time came for them to retire the gathering accompanied them to the door of their chamber but, to Judith's immense relief, did not insist on observing the custom of bedding the bridal pair. Oliver it was who, laughing but audaciously firm, shut the heavy door in their faces. Thus, with the jovial blessings of the company ringing in her ears, Judith found herself alone with her husband.

'Thank you,' she murmured and, in answer to his quizzical look, explained. 'For not letting them in.'

He chuckled. 'An intrusive custom, which I sincerely hope is fast dying out.' With careless ease he discarded belt and sword, threw off his doublet and stepped across to lay caressing hands upon her shoulders. Wine lay heavy on his breath, but he was not drunk. Compared to most of the others at the feast he had partaken sparingly of both food and drink. 'An you need assistance with your gown, I will play the serving-woman,' he offered softly, drawing her closer, 'and you shall take the place of my lackey – who, I earnestly hope, is back in England,' he added with a wry grimace.

He had never mentioned the man before, just as he seldom spoke of his family except in passing. But now was not the time to probe into his private life. Nothing mattered but being here, with him. The ring on her finger gave her the right.

Judith trembled as he folded her into his embrace. Not with fear, not with embarrassment, but with sheer, joyous anticipation. She had already experienced the exquisite pleasure of his touch. All shyness had left her now the moment had come, for as his wife she could accept his caresses without fear of censure.

His long, firm body, pressed against hers, made her feel feminine, secure. Her arms rose confidently to encircle his neck and as his mouth met hers her lips parted in expectation.

He drew a sudden, harsh breath before accepting the invitation to explore the innermost recesses of her mouth. His tongue penetrated, tasted, and hers sought to stroke, to savour, to discover.

While her fingers tangled in the springiness of his hair, his hands shifted over her body, impatient to remove the inhibiting layers of thick cloth separating them. He drew back, his breathing deep and uneven.

'Turn round, angel.'

His hands urged, his fingers unerringly found the hooks at her side. Tossing the overdress to the floor, he paused only to lift her heavy hair and kiss the nape of her neck, sending thrilling tremors down her spine, before undoing the fastenings at the back of the bodice. With that gone it was the work of moments to untie the strings holding up petticoat and farthingale. Judith stood, trembling, clad only in her shift, ruffs and hose. Genette's voice echoed faintly in her head. 'You're such a prude, Judith.' A tiny smile touched her lips.

Oliver gathered her close. 'You are not afraid, my angel?'

'No.' She smiled again, a wide, confident smile. 'No,' she repeated, and lifted clinging lips to his even as her hands sought the belt of his trunk-hose. 'Help me,' she whispered.

With a soft laugh he complied, guiding her fingers to the fastenings, to the points supporting his nether-stocks. Breathlessly, she reached up to remove the ruff and falling band, then lifted the tail of his shirt to urge it over his head.

'I don't want to hurt your back,' she whispered.

He chuckled in delight, brushing off her concern. 'Nay, you will not, for it has almost healed over the last couple of days. But what happened to the shy, ignorant, unversed virgin?' he teased as he stood before her, as magnificently naked as the day he'd arrived on the shore.

Judith laughed breathlessly. 'I do not believe she ever existed!'

'I never believed she did! But you have the advantage, wife!'

Judith trembled anew as he reached out to remove her ruffs, stroked the hose from her legs with sensuous attention to knee and ankle, and finally deprived her of her shift.

With nowhere to hide, she stood proudly, allowing him to gaze his fill, knowing the flickering candle-flame flattered her skin and brought out the coppery lights in her hair.

'Lovely,' he murmured. 'My lovely, beautiful angel-wife.'

For the first time, Judith allowed herself to believe him. Basking in his admiration, she drew a deep breath and her full breasts stirred.

The effect on Oliver was instantaneous. She caught the flare of passion, the tensing of his muscles and then there was no time to notice anything else, for she had been gathered into his arms and laid on the huge bed. He followed her down, drew the curtains close and pulled the covers over them, proving undeniably that his back could take the friction. For a while it was all warm, moist, seeking lips, sensitive, knowing hands, quick breathing and murmured words of endearment.

Excitement rose in Judith until she could scarcely contain it. In desperation she began to kiss and nip at his neck and this seemed to have the desired effect.

'God!' he murmured. 'Woman, are you trying to drive me mad?' And he rose above her.

He held still for a moment. Judith thought in revenge. But then, his breathing under control, he spoke again.

'Now, my angel,' he whispered. 'Now. I'll be gentle.'

He was, although she could feel him shaking with suppressed passion as he leashed his body in. Despite her own urgency, gratitude overwhelmed her at this restraint, the gentleness with which he explored before, with one decisive thrust, he broke through the slender barrier protecting her virginity.

She could not help the scream which rose to her throat, for the pain seared. But as he lay quietly inside her, soothing and waiting, she knew the short, sharp agony had been nothing, since it had brought the exquisite pleasure of being joined with her husband.

Soon he began to move again, and sensations quite unlike anything she had known before enraptured her body. And then, in a sudden panting flurry, it was over. She lay, clasping his heaving body close, unwilling to abandon the intimacy holding them locked together.

They lay quietly entwined for a long time after Oliver regained his steady breathing. He seemed content to rest on her, supporting his main weight with his elbows.

Eventually he stirred, lifting his head from the pillow beside hers, pushing up to lift his torso a little so that he could look down into her face. He turned his hands inwards to touch it, tracing its tender lines with wondering fingers.

'You ravish me, wife,' he murmured. 'So warm, so

lovely, so exciting.' And she felt him stir again inside her. 'Next time it will be better for you.'

'It couldn't be,' protested Judith, exploring the tender scars on his back with careful, loving fingers. 'It hardly hurt at all, and then it was wonderful, exquisite. . .'

He gave his breathless little laugh. 'Dear, sweet angel, you know nothing! Wait until I have regained my strength! Then I shall teach you to come with me to a place such as you have never dreamed. . .'

'Oliver, husband.' The word came awkwardly to her tongue and she fingered her wedding-ring again, to make quite sure she was not dreaming. 'You have given me so much delight already! What more can there be?'

He laughed again. 'I have given you pain, and a certain pleasure while I slaked my own thirst. Believe me, the best is yet to come.'

'Don't go!'

Her cry was urgent, but he had already slipped from her to lie at her side so that he could woo her again. His lovemaking this time was different—languorous, unhurried. While he explored her face with his lips, his hands found the rich swell of her breasts. Oh, those clever, teasing fingers! Judith gasped under their ministrations. And then his mouth was where his hands had been and his fingers were exploring more secret places.

Judith melted under his touch. Wallowing in a sea of ecstatic sensation, content to go wherever the tide took her, she wondered idly whether she would ever reach solid ground again. But then she gasped as his beard scraped over her sensitised skin. She gasped, quite sure she would split in two if Oliver did not take her soon. . .

'Please!' she begged huskily. 'Please, husband!'

He moved over her immediately, his flesh warm and reassuring against hers. But there he rested, kissing her first, then smiling down into her passion-glazed eyes.

'You want me, sweetheart?'

Apart from a slight breathlessness and the rapid beating of his heart, he seemed entirely composed. Judith did not understand how he could delay.

'Yes!' she cried urgently. And repeated an agonised, 'Please!'

'How much?' he enquired, still amused, and stroked her eyebrow with his finger. The sensation reached right down to the place where she wanted him to be. And then, without waiting for the answer Judith found it impossible to formulate, he posed another question. 'Enough to guide me home?'

His words brought her reeling senses back for a moment as they sank in. She knew what he wanted, but did she have the courage? Shyness almost overcame her, but she had denied prudery thus far and she had no use for even its last feeble manifestation where her husband was concerned. She nodded.

He drew a deep breath and then gave a cry of undisguised pleasure as he felt her touch. 'My wife,' he murmured thickly as the tremors shook his body, and Judith could hear no trace of laughter in his ardent voice.

There was no pain this time, only slow, stroking pleasure, until everything exploded in a cataclysm of sensation which sent Judith spinning from reality into a wondrous place shaped and inhabited by Oliver. . . Oliver. . .Oliver. . .

She returned to earth knowing she was crying his name. It seemed to take him longer to recover, for he lay so still and silent she thought in panic that he might be dead. But then the shudders began.

'Oh, my dearest angel-wife,' he murmured when at last he could speak. 'I had no idea. . .'

He trailed off, drawing her closer to nestle comfortably in his arms. She fitted herself to his contours with an ease which might have come of long practice, but actually needed none. With her head on his shoulder, his lips on her forehead, she dropped contentedly to sleep.

Oliver had gone!

Judith sat up behind the bed-curtains, aware that someone was moving about in the room, tending the fire, bringing hot water. She could hear the rustle of the servant's dress, so it was not her husband. She fondled her wedding-ring again, reassuring herself that it had not all been a dream.

Yes, she was wed. Well and truly wed, if the aches and pains in her body were anything to go by! Yet the discomfort only added to her sense of wellbeing and she sank back into her pillow to luxuriate in the knowledge that Oliver found her desirable and had transported her to the gratifying, delightful status of womanhood. The bed beside her still felt faintly warm, and Oliver's particular odour remained caught in the linen. Oh, no, she had not been dreaming!

But now he had gone.

He must have woken and crept away without disturbing her. He might intend to come back and make love to her again. Mind, she would need to get up herself first.

She stretched and yawned, hoping he would not be long, knowing they would be lucky to have a chamber to themselves once they returned to Beauregard. She would prefer for them to share with Josué, rather than Genette. Josué was less impressionable, less inquisitive and unlikely to be jealous!

But Maman would take care of the new household arrangements. And whatever was decided would not be for long. Once the weather cleared Oliver would want to return to England.

Her excitement rose at the thought of taking ship across the channel to Plymouth. She did not like the sea. The crossing from Jersey had been distinctly unpleasant, she had not enjoyed the cramped and damp conditions, the sickening, frightening lurch and roll of the ship. But she would endure any hardship if it meant being with her husband. And she would see his home, be introduced to his parents, meet his brothers and sisters and their families. John, Henry, Audrey and Catherine. She recited his siblings' names, determined not to forget. Oliver was the youngest. He had told them that much.

The servant left the room. Judith decided to get up. With a final stretch, she pushed back the heavy curtain and slipped from the bed.

Grey light filtered in through the small window. Judith made her toilet and with new eagerness picked up the glass hand-mirror lying beside the ewer. At home a rather scratched steel one served the entire household, so this was a novelty and Judith wondered at the silvery surface which reflected her face so clearly, with only the slighest waviness here and there. It was rather like looking at herself in the still waters of a pond, but with her image so much brighter and clearer, especially now the light was stronger.

She turned her head this way and that, trying to see what others, particularly Oliver, saw, but succeeded only in viewing familiar, unremarkable features. She

tidied her hair, mirror in one hand, comb in the other,
letting the waves ripple through its teeth and crackle
and spring back into position. No sun shone through
the small window to bring out the highlights. It looked
quite dull and ordinarily brown. She was not sorry to
twist it up and cover it, now she was a matron. She
pinned a gauze cap loaned by her mother over a rather
untidy knot and smiled at herself in satisfaction.

But where could Oliver be? His old clothes had
gone, though those he'd worn for the wedding were
laid out over a chest. It was not until she went to touch
them that she saw the sheet of paper resting on top.

It was addressed to her. 'Mine own sweet angel-
wife.' She did not need the signature to tell her who it
was from.

Her heart began to pound in her ears. She sank
down, almost too agitated to make sense of the words
he had written. But the gist was all too clear.

Overnight, the wind had dropped to a fresh breeze,
the sea had moderated and the *St Ouen* was sailing on
the early tide. The Seigneur had most kindly instructed
his sea-captain to transport Oliver to Plymouth, the
moment conditions allowed. He went on to remind her
that from the first he had made it clear that he had
urgent business in England. Unfortunately the notice
had been far too short for him to ask her to leave with
him. He had not wished to cast a gloom over their
bridal night and so had said nothing, although he had
been informed of the change in the weather late the
previous day. He begged her forgiveness for departing
in such a scurrilous manner, but he had thought it best
not to prolong a painful parting and promised to return
at the first opportunity to fetch her. And he had signed
himself, 'Your most devoted servant and husband,
Oliver Burnett.'

Judith sat, stunned. He had known last night that the ship would sail at dawn. He had made love to her and he hadn't told her.

How could he? Tears blurred her eyes so that she could no longer see the painful words. She crumpled the paper in her hand.

What would everyone think? He had been forced into marrying her, had bedded her and left. He had wanted to bed her from the first. Well, he had had his way.

She caught her breath. Mayhap he did not consider the ceremony on Sark as legally binding in England! He inclined towards English Catholicism rather than the more extreme Presbyterianism Helier de Carteret and Cosmé Brevint saw practised among the island community. But neither he nor she were Papist. The difference in emphasis could not affect the legality of the ceremony. But he might see things differently.

Had he engaged in a, to him, meaningless rite in order to deceive her and so gain his own end?

She shivered as cold sweat broke out on her palms. Surely she had not misjudged him so badly? Her laughing companion of the last days could not be so devious. Until yesterday she had not completely trusted him not to tumble her were she to drop her guard — yet when he had his chance he had not taken it. She did not understand him at all.

And then, suddenly, she was on her feet, fastening on her pattens, snatching up her cloak. The *St Ouen* might still be lying at anchor, waiting for the tide!

Servants gawped in astonishment at the sight of the new bride racing from the house, cloak flying and cap askew.

The way to the Baie de la Motte seemed never-ending, though she knew it to be less than half a

league. Fit as she had thought herself, she entered the
tunnel gasping for breath, holding the stitch in her side,
aware of a distressing wheeze in her windpipe. Eyes
fixed on the circle of light at the far end, she forced
herself on, knowing her headlong rush to be almost at
an end.

One or two fishermen preparing to put to sea greeted
her briefly. Apart from them the beach was deserted.
Fifty yards off-shore the *St Ouen* was weighing anchor.
Even the seamen's chanting of 'Yo-heave-ho!' could
not obliterate the squeak of the capstan as the men
bent to the spokes to wind in the cable.

Because the captain had caught the last of the rising
tide the brig had been riding stern to shore, though
slightly askew because of wind and currents. As the
anchor cable shortened the ship rode forward and as
she moved the breeze lifted and filled the lower sails.
By the time the cry went up, 'Anchor aweigh!' she had
caught enough wind to drive her. An order echoed and
the men and boys scrambling about on the ratlines and
yards began to unfurl the topsails.

It was a pretty sight, but Judith had eyes only for the
tiny figure which appeared on the poop deck beneath
the billowing spanker.

He doffed his hat and waved it widely through the
air. Judith tore off her cap and returned the salute,
helpless tears streaking her cheeks.

He must have been watching the shore through the
great cabin window or he would not have seen her.
The thought sent a tiny glow of comfort to her heart.
He had been looking back, not forward. As though he
regretted leaving.

She was glad she had come, but cross with herself
for wasting so much time before setting out. Had she
arrived earlier she would have gone aboard willy-nilly.

He could not have refused to say goodbye, even had he stubbornly declined to take her with him. He knew she had few possessions, must guess she would have gone with nothing but the clothes she stood up in. The shortness of the notice had been an excuse, not a reason for leaving her behind.

But he had said he would come back. Because she loved him, she must believe it. Meanwhile, she must survive the pitying looks, the snide remarks and the jeers of everyone she knew.

How could he do this to her? she asked herself in anguish. And as the ship taking him away from her passed out of sight anger began to bubble up inside her, a fury which overcame her self-pity and obscured her love. She wiped the tears from her cheeks and sniffed, straightening her shoulders. She would show him! She would show *them*! No one would see her mope and moan. She would take up her life again as though yesterday — last night — had never been. If he came back she would greet him coolly, show him that he could not take her complaisance for granted.

Though, as his wife, she would be at his command, unable to deny him anything he asked.

Once the first unpleasantness of astonishment, censure, indignation and, in some quarters, unconcealed glee, had been weathered, Judith carried on much as before, except that she continued to assume the dignity of a cap, reminding everyone that she was no longer an innocent child, but a woman wed, despite the absence of her husband.

Christmas came, and the New Year of 1572. But Oliver Burnett did not.

During the winter the roads were improved, tools mended and the fields ploughed ready for planting in

the spring. Judith devoted much of her time to planning
and digging a small garden for the enjoyment of the
family, based on the one they had left behind on
Jersey. The project gave her a purpose, and hard work
made her so tired at night that she dropped off into
exhausted slumber instead of lying hour after hour
longing for her husband's touch, wondering why Oliver
had not returned, or even written to her.

Perhaps it was the weather. Sea travel in winter was
not recommended, yet plenty of ships did sail. Every
time a vessel put into harbour, she hoped Oliver was
on it, but he never was. He had mentioned his own
ship once, the *Mermaid*, but she looked for it in vain.

Then, with planting well under way, Helier de
Carteret announced his intention of travelling to
England to report in person to the Queen. He was
pleased with the progress of his little colony after six
years of unremitting effort and wanted Elizabeth's
approval. He proposed taking Peirre Le Grand with
him, to deal with any legal questions which might arise.

It was Margaret de Carteret who suggested Judith
accompany them. She herself was travelling with her
husband, and since Ester had been laid low with a
fever and remained too weak to travel, Margaret
thought it would be nice if Judith could keep her
company. Judith would be on hand to see to her
father's comfort, too.

'Oh, but I could not leave Maman,' said Judith
regretfully.

'Yes, you could, my dear. She will have Marie and
Penna to look after her, as well as Genette. She will do
well enough, you will see. And would you not like to
see England? Who knows, you might manage a visit to
your husband's home.'

Judith coloured painfully. That had been her first thought. Mistress de Carteret must have read her mind!

They were strolling in Judith's new garden, which consisted of a great deal of brown earth broken up by numerous pinpricks of green, with the bare branches of small trees and bushes rising above to promise fruit in the future. Rustic trellis had been erected along the north side, which one day would support the climbing roses and vines planted at its feet.

Margaret stopped by a budding apple tree, reaching out to stroke a slender branch.

'This was an excellent idea of yours, Judith. Your mother will enjoy this garden when it matures. Another few years and this tree will provide welcome shade in the summer. I must order something similar for Le Manoir.'

'You do not seem to pine for Jersey as she does,' murmured Judith, and then hoped she had not been disloyal. 'You set such a wonderful example to all the other wives here, and it cannot have been easy for you.'

'Like all other women, I go where my husband leads. I suppose his enthusiasm for this venture rubbed off on me, for I found the experiment a stimulating challenge.' She chuckled. 'I must be a pioneer at heart. But Mistress Le Grand is not, I think,' she went on, sobering. 'It is a pity she cannot travel to London; she would have appreciated the English Court far more than I shall!'

'Do you not wish to go, mistress?' asked Judith, quite unable to understand anyone's reluctance to experience the reputed glitter and luxury of Elizabeth's Court.

Margaret de Carteret laughed. 'Of course I do! In any case, if my lord commands, I obey! Would you not follow your husband to the ends of the earth if he asked?'

'He did not ask,' said Judith, the shake in her voice betraying her hurt.

'I know, my dear.' Margaret sought to ease the pain her unconsidered words had given. 'But he will come back, of that I am convinced. He is not a man to break his bond, or to forget his debts.'

Judith glanced down at her wedding-ring, a constant source not only of reassurance, but also of speculation. 'He must owe someone for this.'

'Aye! I parted with one of my precious jewels reluctantly, but I could not see you wed without a ring!'

'It is beautiful and I love it. I guessed it must have come from Le Manoir. I do thank you, Mistress de Carteret.'

'No need, my dear. But you must have faith in your husband. He was most anxious to please you and, I know, desolate to have to leave so soon after the wedding. He did not explain fully, but he gave us to understand his business was of the utmost urgency, and of importance to England. Otherwise, the Seigneur would not have offered him the use of the St Ouen.'

Judith sighed. 'No. But to hear nothing. . .'

She let her voice trail off. Margaret captured and patted her hand.

'You will find him in England. Or at the very least discover where he is. He may have ventured across the Atlantic again.'

'Yes.' Judith made no further comment. After what he had said she did not think that explanation likely. But he might have returned to Antwerp and been recaptured by the Spanish. She shivered. Not knowing was the worse part.

As the days had turned into weeks and the weeks to months she had tried to cut Oliver from her thoughts. But try as she might, his image kept appearing in her mind; she heard his laugh, imagined his touch, even caught the scent of him at the oddest moments.

She had found it impossible to forget him. Not to worry about him. She prayed that, wherever he was, he had not forgotten her. If he were still alive.

Oliver paced restlessly, cursing the capricious woman who kept him prisoner in London.

His companion, Sir Charles Mead, sat sprawled on a wooden chair, one richly brocaded arm resting on a small table while he idly tossed dice. He waved a languid hand.

'Do sit down, my dear fellow, or you will wear the boards through! Besides, I find your energy quite exhausting.'

Oliver swung round to face the friend with whom he shared the lodging and planted his hands on his hips.

'Why won't she let me go, Charles?' he demanded angrily.

The older man laughed. 'You should have known better than to catch her eye in the first place, and to do her a service in the second.'

'I wish to God I'd never accompanied Hawkins to Court in '65!'

'That was when she took a fancy to you, was it? Young, personable — not surprising, when you know her. Our Virgin Sovereign thrives on the adoration of a court of young men like you, my dear Oliver.'

Oliver grimaced wryly. 'I wish she would confine her attentions to Dudley. He appears to welcome them.'

'You should be hoping for a knighthood, or some lucrative sinecure. Settle down, Oliver. Enjoy the pleasures of the Court. Come, toss some dice with me! Or we could play a hand or two of cent, if you prefer.'

Oliver shook an impatient hand. All trace of amiable merriment was absent from his face, replaced by what could almost be called a scowl.

'Idling my days away does not suit me. I want to be pursuing the enemy in the brigantine, not directing its operations from here. I can give only the broadest of orders, I am forced to leave my sea-captain to find his own targets.'

'I thought Blackler was one of the best sea-dogs to come out of Plymouth, not counting Hawkins and Drake. You've said so often enough!'

'He is, but as I've told you before, we work as a team. Blackler runs the ship, takes on the crew, I rely on his seamanship to engage the enemy and corner our prey. But I have always sought out the destinations and cargoes of the Spanish vessels we attack.'

'And of course, when you're aboard you are the master, fighting hand-to-hand if necessary and parleying with the other party. I know you thrive on that kind of thing, Oliver, though I must confess, I could never understand why.'

A small smile twitched Oliver's lips as he regarded the stout figure of the indolent Charles Mead. Charles would never understand the intoxication of danger faced and overcome, the thrill of dicing with death. Wagering for money was but a poor substitute which he despised; although, like all other men, he indulged in it from time to time.

He had worn a mask when his ship became a privateer, of course, just as the brig changed its name from *Mermaid* to *Sea Hawk* and ran up a different flag. A plain black one, with the bird in flight outlined in white. He reckoned that in the years since the betrayal

at San Juan de Ulloa he had done as much damage to
Spain's fleet and taken as much treasure as Drake and
others had in more distant waters.

'Besides,' he said slowly, speaking his thought aloud,
'I promised to return to Sark.'

'Ah!' exclaimed Charles with a chuckle. 'Now we
come to the nub of it! You are pining for the fair
Judith!'

A faint tinge of colour crept into Oliver's cheeks.
Luckily the room was gloomy enough to hide his
discomfort. He had not realised he had voiced his
musings. The frequency with which his thoughts
returned to his bride surprised him. His angel! The
smile Judith would instantly have recognised flickered
across his features. He had immediately fallen under
her elusive spell. Yet marriage had not entered his
mind until circumstances had made it inevitable. He
had not realised how deeply enmeshed he had become
by her quiet, restful charm. He was still amazed at
himself, for young virgins did not usually appeal to
him; he preferred his women more mature, experienced, able to indulge in a satisfying flirtation which
committed neither party.

'Mind your tongue, Charles,' he admonished his
friend. 'You are bound to the utmost secrecy. I have
not even been able to keep my promise to consult my
lawyers over a marriage settlement. If Elizabeth found
out —' He gave an exaggerated shudder.

'I shall not betray you, my friend, but I cannot
conceive how you came to marry the wench. Was it at
swordpoint?'

'Nay, you know it was not. I was not entirely averse
to the match, for Judith will make me an eminently
suitable and agreeable wife when I wish to settle down.'

Suitable, agreeable — and desirable! His pulses

stirred at the memory of their bridal night. He had
expected pleasure, but known better than to hope for
rapture. Yet he had found it.

He sighed and stirred, attempting to subdue his
wayward libido, glad again of the poor light.

Judith had been completely innocent. Yet so mature.
He had thought his enslavement a temporary thing, a
reaction to escape from peril, a momentary need for
solace and the natural desire for a woman who, however ingenuous, unconsciously exuded an air of sensuality. And it had been unconscious. She had been so
convinced of her lack of attraction!

But he must have fallen deeper in the mire of
enslavement than he had imagined, and it irked him.
A man who had always relished the chase and enjoyed
the inevitable conquest, he resented his present condition. Other women had lost their allure.

'I think,' said Charles judiciously, 'she's got you
under some kind of spell. Why else are you shunning
the pleasures so many ladies are willing to offer? It's
not like you, my friend!'

The other man had so nearly mirrored his own
thoughts that Oliver snorted. If he could only see her
again, mayhap he would be cured. Memory was a
peculiar thing, gilding every lily, rendering the most
prosaic event momentous. Under the strange circumstances of his stay on Sark she had appeared to him as
an unusual, desirable young girl he could not, in
honour, bed. But that unfortunate encounter with the
self-righteous Perrier had led to complications of a
most intractable kind. He had wed her, since it meant
he could bed her, and he had met no other woman he
wished to make his wife. But then circumstances had
forced him to leave. The sight of her lonely figure
standing on the shore as he sailed out of sight haunted

him. He had not had time to sate himself with her; she remained on his blood, spoiling him for the pleasures offered by the ladies of the Court.

'If I could but see her again, bed her again!' he muttered.

'You would soon realise that she was just an ordinary woman, like any other,' grinned Charles. 'You'd be free of her spell and ready to indulge in your usual amorous diversions!'

'Maybe.' Oliver continued to pace restlessly. 'But I cannot return to Sark or send for her to join me here. I am completely bound, and I do not relish the feeling!'

'Have you written to your wife?'

'No.'

An uneasy conscience told him he should have done so. He had tried. But when he picked up a pen the words refused to come. He respected her too much to lie. How could he explain to his strong-minded, practical, unworldly angel that her carefree, venturesome husband was tied to Court by invisible strings from which he could not free himself? Or that he had been quite unable to tell the old witch that he was wed? Admitting to a fear of heights paled by comparison.

'If you please, master.'

Oliver turned as his lackey entered, slanting the man a glance of enquiry. A solid fellow of about his own age, cautious where his master was rash but courageous as a lion, Lambert was the best of men to have behind one in adversity. He had accompanied Oliver on his adventurous journey to Paris and almost been caught, with him, in Antwerp. That the man had escaped and made his way back to London with the information Oliver had been detailed to deliver had given Oliver immense relief and pleasure on his own return. He

suspected that Lambert had been equally pleased to
see him.

'What is it?'

'A message from Cap'n Blackler, master. He's at the
tavern and awaits your orders for the cargo he's got
aboard the brig, which he's got moored down by the
Tower.'

'Ah!' A brilliant smile lit Oliver's face, all thoughts
of Judith wiped immediately from his mind. 'So he's
back! A successful voyage, too, by the sound of it. I'll
go at once. Come along, man! There'll be plenty of
merchandise to shift, I imagine. The Prince of Orange
will rejoice! The Queen will be pleased, too, for she
must have her cut!'

'Mayhap she will reward you with your freedom,'
grunted Charles, rising to his feet. 'I assume you have
no objection to my coming with you? I could do with a
little merry company!'

Oliver laughed as he buckled on his sword and flung
a short fur-trimmed cloak around his widely padded
shoulders. All his usual careless good-humour had
returned with the prospect of action. 'By all means!' he
cried, clapping his friend on the back as the small party
ventured out into the crowded, filthy streets, malodorous even in the chilliness of a dreary February
afternoon.

CHAPTER EIGHT

SOON after Easter, with the weather settled fair, Judith embarked on the *St Ouen*, bound for Plymouth. Small cubicles, no more than box beds, had been partitioned off the sides of the great cabin, and she was allocated one of these. It afforded some degree of privacy, although the servants and several men in the party would lay their bed-rolls in the cabin itself at night.

She could hear the sea-captain pacing overhead and the shouts and movement on deck as the crew scuttled about their tasks. Everything seemed to creak and groan as the sails filled with wind and the vessel plunged its way over the waves.

At least she had a kind of shelf on which to sleep, with a mattress on top and space beneath for her travelling chest, and a night stand with a basin and ewer set into holes so that they shouldn't topple off. The water in the ewer was slopping alarmingly.

It seemed quite rough and Judith began to feel queasy. A frightening, dizzying view of heaving sea surmounted by steep, spiralling cliffs could be seen through the tall windows at the stern, but the air was stuffy and the movement seemed to get worse. She gulped and swallowed, holding her stomach to ease the sickness. Fixing her eye on the cabin door, she began a stubborn, lurching progress towards the open deck.

'Where are you going?'

Her father's sharp voice failed to slow her steps. If she stopped she would disgrace herself.

'On deck. I feel sick,' she gulped.

'You cannot go out there alone!'

'Then someone come with me! Please!'

Margaret de Carteret's maid spoke up. 'I will, with my mistress's permission. I feel a little unwell myself.'

'By all means.'

Margaret's compliance came instantly. Thomasse was to serve both ladies, for Judith would need help with her toilet in London, but had no servant of her own, though her father had engaged his own lackey for this trip, a man called Hiou. Helier had brought him over from Jersey.

The thought drifted over the edges of her mind as she concentrated on reaching the side of the ship before her breakfast came up. As they left the cabin a blast of cold air almost took her breath. But then she gulped it in, deep into her lungs, revelling in its salty freshness. How she wished she were a good sailor! It was so depressing to feel ill when she should be enjoying the adventure. This might be the only time she left Sark's shores, and the experience was being ruined!

Annoyed with herself, she stumbled to the side. It was no use leaning over the rail in front of the cabin, she would only be sick over the helmsman working the tipstaff on the half-deck below.

Thomasse joined her and the two women gripped the rail, shutting their eyes against the heaving, swirling waves, the swinging, swooping cliffs and the dancing outcrops of rock, known as moies, through which the ship was threading its way.

'I am told 'twill be better once we round the Bec du Nez,' groaned Thomasse.

Judith opened her eyes for a moment. A moie loomed too close, leaning at an improbable angle. She shut them again quickly. 'I hope the sea-captain knows what he is doing!'

It was so stupid to feel sick! But she couldn't help it. And suddenly the nausea overcame her. She emptied her stomach but felt little better.

Suddenly she remembered Oliver crossing La Coupée. The ghost of a smile crossed her wan face. What a fine pair they would make at sea! He must have felt then just as bad as she did now. But he had not allowed it to stop him, and under pressure had behaved with conspicuous bravery despite the way he felt. She glanced up at the swaying masts, at the seamen in their baggy venetians and fur hats still clambering about high in the rigging, hanging on like monkeys. Faced with imminent disaster, Oliver would climb those frightening ratlines and do whatever had to be done.

She straightened her shoulders and took another deep, deep breath. Oliver! Would she see him in England? She was determined not to seek him out, a supplicant for his attention. Without invitation she could scarcely present herself at his home, even could she find it. But she could attempt to discover his whereabouts. And she desperately wanted to know why he had ignored her existence for the past six months.

Not that it took much imagination to find an answer to that question. He had been forced into marriage, but his life held no place for a wife.

The wind whipped at her cap and sent tendrils of hair flying about her face. Having rounded the northernmost point of Sark, the captain took advantage of the north-easterly flow of the flood tide to clear Guernsey. Soon he would have to set a north-westerly course for Plymouth. Everyone hoped the favourable wind would hold.

Now the sea was calmer, Judith's sickness receded. Looking at Thomasse, she could see the colour returned to the woman's face, and knew her own had probably lost its ghastly tinge.

'This is better,' she observed brightly.

'Aye, mistress.' Thomasse smiled, though somewhat thinly. 'I have always feared the sea, it has claimed too many lives. But it is especially perilous around our island. I am thankful to be clear of it!'

'So am I.'

Judith's heartfelt agreement included delight at escaping the confines of a place which had become something of a prison for her, especially over the last few months. Whatever the journey held in the way of danger from pirates or storms, she would never be sorry to have left Sark's shores.

England beckoned, an England governed by a Protestant Queen who was yet merciful to Roman Catholics, so long as they did not plot against her. With Spain's Duke of Alva presiding over the destruction of Protestants in the Netherlands, many had fled to England, and the money-market of Antwerp had been badly disrupted. This was bad enough, but Mary Queen of Scots, a refugee from her own people enjoying the English Queen's hospitality, had managed to stir up a couple of uprisings by Catholics in the north, which had mercifully been defeated because the vast majority of her English subjects, both Catholic and Protestant, had stood four-square behind their Queen. But Elizabeth could never feel entirely secure. Word had reached Sark of the assassination plot dreamt up by a Florentine banker called Roberto Ridolfi. In some mysterious way it had been discovered and defeated and the Duke of Norfolk had been arrested and sentenced to death for his part in it. Ridolfi had escaped.

Judith could scarcely imagine what this Queen, who

stood up to the power of Pope and Church and to the might of Spain, could be like. She considered herself incredibly lucky to be on her way to the English Court.

After the Channel Islands, England seemed to go on forever. The Seigneur had been anxious to reach London as soon as possible and so they had spent the night anchored in the Cattewater among a flotilla of other ships, and been rowed ashore early the following morning. Solid hacks, ordered in advance, awaited them. They mounted up immediately and began the overland journey to England's capital city.

Judith had never learned to ride properly. Of course, she had climbed up on the back of their cart-horse from time to time while it was being led, and the amiable creature had borne her weight stoically, barely noticing she was there. But that did not mean she was capable of controlling a horse of her own, so she found herself riding pillion behind her father's lackey. Thomasse was thrown up behind the Seigneur's servant, Coysh.

Judith found the saddle uncomfortable and disliked being dependent on Hiou's indifferent horsemanship. But they rode beside Mistress de Carteret, who, surprisingly, proved to be an excellent horsewoman, and soon Judith forgot such minor inconveniences in the excitement of seeing and exclaiming over so many new sights. Plymouth, soon left behind, looked extensive and crowded, the buildings tumbling down from a high green promontory to the water's edge. Devonshire was hilly, the lumpy countryside divided up into small fields not unlike those in Sark.

The King's Highway — a great road linking Plymouth with Exeter and beyond that with London itself — carried many travellers, mostly on foot, but quite a

few, like themselves, rode horses while others made do
with mules or donkeys.

After only a couple of hours in the saddle she was
glad to dismount at Ivybridge for refreshment and a
change of horses. As they travelled on the road became
ever more crowded.

'Curse these cattle!' muttered her father as they
came up behind a herd of cows. 'Make way for us, my
man!' he shouted imperiously.

Judith had never seen such a busy road. Since they
had all been forced to rein in until the herdsman had
cleared the way, she amused herself by studying the
cart beside her. The driver, wearing a coarse linen shirt
under a sleeveless doublet made of brown kersey, his
woollen jerkin bundled on the seat beside him, sat
hunched patiently on his seat, the reins drooping
through grimy, horny fingers to rest on the backs of a
pair of bony horses. The nearside grey had lowered its
head to graze the verge while the black curled its
tongue round an isolated tuft of grass at its feet. She
wondered idly what was underneath the tilt, but it was
impossible to see. Vegetables, maybe, or cloth.

Looking ahead, she could see a train of mules,
loaded panniers swaying on their backs, and beyond
them a flock of sheep. Having been warned it was
market day in Ashburton they had feared their progress
might be slow.

A horn sounded behind them and people turned to
look, Judith with them. Everyone moved over as fast
as they could as a steaming horse galloped up, scattering people right and left, its rider sounding imperiously
to clear the way. Even her father shifted instinctively
aside and Hiou dug his heels into their mount and
edged ahead of the cart. Galvanised, the herdsman

soon cleared a passage and the rider sped on, leaving confusion and a barrage of good English oaths behind.

'Who was he?' wondered Judith as they took advantage of the passage he had cleared to spur forward and pass the herd themselves.

'A government messenger. He'll be in London by the evening of the morrow.'

Her father had been to England before, she remembered, and was therefore knowledgeable.

'When shall we be there?' she asked.

'We shall stop overnight tonight at Exeter, hope to be in Yeovil by tomorrow, then spend the next nights in Salisbury, Andover and Basingstoke. It will take us six days, more if we are held up, despite our use of post-horses.'

Six days, thought Judith ruefully, and I am already longing for the next rest!

Seven hours and three new horses later, she dismounted for the last time that day in the courtyard of an inn near the towering Norman cathedral in Exeter, aching, sore and weary to the bone, wondering whether she could endure five more such days. Though they would presumably rest on Sunday.

The ladies shared one room, the gentlemen another, with their respective servants, not one of whom could speak English, which was inconvenient, for they could not be sent on an errand in an inn where nobody spoke anything else.

'I think I am too tired to eat,' Judith sighed wearily, gingerly stretching her back and massaging her behind.

'Nonsense, child! You ate very little on board the *St Ouen*, and if you do not eat now you will never reach London at all, and that would never do!'

Margaret de Carteret's rallying tone made Judith smile ruefully.

'I still feel as though I'm heaving about at sea, though I no longer feel sick. I wish I weren't such a bad sailor! How long before I recover my land legs, I wonder?'

'You'll be all right after a good night's sleep, believe me,' said Margaret, laughing.

When a tray of food was brought up by a serving wench — so that the ladies would be saved the necessity of presenting themselves in the rowdy taproom — Judith suddenly realised how hungry she was and fell ravenously on the hot vegetable stew, and then the Friday fish, digging into the yellow butter and spreading it on the wheaten bread with relish.

'I'm glad to see you have recovered your appetite,' remarked Margaret drily.

Judith pulled a face, but her mouth was too full to answer.

As the journey continued the countryside changed, became flatter and more rolling, with huge fields, some looking big enough to swallow Sark whole. They stretched as far as the eye could see in every direction hour after hour and day after day. A small hamlet, sometimes attached to a larger house, often nestled in some dell. Clumps of woodland, some quite extensive, topped hills or clad the slopes. On the far side of the vast plain of Salisbury they came at last to Andover.

Despite the interest of the journey, she was glad when they entered the outskirts of London. They had crossed the river at Staines and, having passed through the village of Chelsea, entered Westminster late on a sunny May evening.

The Queen was in residence in Whitehall Palace, for her standard bearing the lilies of France and the leopards of England fluttered from a flagpole above as they travelled the road passing through its midst. Helier de Carteret had taken lodgings as near as possible, in the region of Charing Cross. Judith, tired as she was, could not help but be interested in the imposing buildings lining the riverbank, the houses crowding the narrow side-streets, the thronging people. She had become used to the stink of the towns they had passed through. London was worse rather than better, and she raised a perfumed handkerchief to her nose.

'It will be at least a week before we can be presented to the Queen,' Margaret told Judith. 'The Seigneur has asked to be allowed the privilege of delivering his report personally, and we shall accompany him to Court. Meanwhile, we may take a rest after the journey and try to find our way about the Cities of Westminster and London. There must be merchants here with goods to sell, and we must find someone to sew suitable dresses. The men will need a tailor, too.'

Judith was reminded of Oliver. Not that it took much to bring her husband to mind. Did he trade in London? she wondered. He had never said so. She tried to imagine him in the long gown of a merchant, and failed. He had looked so right in the gentleman's outfit loaned for their wedding. The short cloak had added an air of dash which suited him. Not that his being dressed as custom demanded would have made any difference to her feelings. Whatever his garb, she would have been proud to become his wife. As a lawyer her father had worn a long gown until they moved to Sark, and she had always considered it gave him a distinguished appearance.

Most mornings dawned hazily bright but chilly. Smoke rose thickly from the chimneys as the inhabitants of London uncovered their fires and stirred them into new life. Even candles and other forms of lighting

had to be extinguished when the bell sounded for
couvrefeu, for fire spread rapidly through the crowded,
timber-framed houses. People still talked of the time,
ten years since, when the wooden steeple of St Paul's
had been struck by lightning and burned down. That
disaster had been caused by a storm, but fire started in
so many ways and Londoners feared it as much as the
plague.

The days sped past, busy and full of interest, as they
explored the narrow, confined streets darkened by
overhanging upper storeys. Judith came to expect the
constant cries of "Ware!' as pails were emptied from
above into the drainage kennel running down the
middle of the street, but thought she would never get
used to the all-pervading stench. Sark had at least
supplied plentiful fresh air and, surprisingly, a sense of
space lacking in the town. Both ladies purchased sweet-
smelling pomanders to hang from their girdles and
gingerly walked the streets with the herbs held to their
noses. The perfume helped a little, but not much. After
an hour or two Judith was glad to escape the crowded
streets for the open fields which lay to the north. But
there was little time for such pleasures. Many hours
were spent with the dressmaker, for several fittings had
to be endured before everyone was satisfied. But at
last the gorgeous dresses were ready.

Thomasse helped both ladies into their farthingales
and then into the new gowns. Judith thought Mistress
de Carteret looked splendid in a decorative, tight-
fitting gown of midnight blue spangled with mother-of-
pearl and silver thread. The silk petticoat, of a similar
colour, was so richly embroidered with flowers and
leaves as to appear multi-coloured. A high collar
supported a white ruff edged in blue, which matched

those at her wrists. A small jewelled cap sat flat on top of her head.

'You look beautiful, mistress,' she whispered.

Margaret smiled affectionately. A real fondness had grown up between the two women despite the difference in their station and age. 'You too, Judith! Here, let me hold the mirror for you!' She slowly lifted the hand-mirror up and down so that Judith could see herself from top to toe. 'There! Did I not tell you that cream sarcenet would suit you? Isn't the quilting fine? And the tiny seed-pearls reflect the sheen and set it off beautifully. The saffron-shot brocade of the petticoat looks splendid beneath it.'

Judith fingered her ruff, attached to the high collar above the close-fitting bodice. 'I can scarce move my head,' she complained with a wry grin. 'Papa has been more than generous. But — are you certain the colour is right?'

'Quite sure, my dear. I would not allow you to appear in anything which was not suitable. See now, let me fasten this delightful necklace your mother gave you about your throat.' She stood back and held the mirror up again. 'The silk makes a perfect background for those loops of tiny pearls, and the little gold pendant. And your lovely hair shows to advantage beneath that cap.'

Judith laughed slightly, her face flushed with pleasure. The cap, wired into a becoming shape and decorated with yet more pearls waving in stiff little droplets, did suit her. She wished Oliver could see her now. Where was he?

'I suppose a lot of Englishmen, as well as Flemish refugees, will have gone on that expedition to the Netherlands we've heard so much about since we arrived,' she mused, hoping Oliver was not among them.

'Probably, though 'twas only four or five thousand men in all. No doubt the Prince of Orange would have welcomed more. And to think it all came about because the Queen expelled Count de la Marck and his Sea Beggars from Dover, for fear of Spanish reprisals!'

'Well, I did hear that our merchants pleaded for it, too, for the Sea Beggars were falling on our ships as well as Spanish ones. You'd have thought they'd have had more sense!' she added disgustedly. 'Fancy robbing the hand that fed them!'

The Sea Beggars had caused the new flare-up of rebellion in Zeeland and if Oliver had gone. . . She dared not think of it.

'Whatever the reason for Elizabeth's decision, it made de la Marck desperate for a base nearer home than La Rochelle and so he fell on Brielle — and took it from the Spanish!'

'And managed to raise the whole island of — what is it called. . .something beginning with V?'

'W, actually, though it is pronounced as a V. Walcheren.'

'Walcheren, yes. It declared for the Prince of Orange.'

'And when de la Marck asked her to send back some of the Flemish refugees to help him, Elizabeth reluctantly agreed. I wish we had been here on May Day, when she went to review the volunteers before they set off from Greenwich. My husband says she is noted for changing her mind, and that was certainly a volte-face! But her best courtiers will still be here in England, you may be sure, Leicester and the rest.'

'I long to see what they are like! I am so grateful to you for suggesting I come!' Judith drew a breath.

Despite her excitement over going to Court, she could not long forget her overriding concern. 'Mistress de Carteret, when do you think we may be returning to Plymouth? Will there be time to seek out information on my husband's whereabouts before we embark for home?'

'I shall not allow Helier to set sail before he has traced Master Burnett, never fear. Sark is in good hands; Philippe has a sound head on his shoulders and plenty of older de Carteret relatives to guide him. Julien at La Fripperie and Hiou at La Moinerie, not to mention Jean out at La Duvallerie. Sark will go on very well without its Seigneur for a few extra days!'

With that Judith had to be content. Helier de Carteret had been granted an audience on the following day, when he would present his report and all his party to the Queen.

The distance to Whitehall Palace being short, the ladies were carried in hired litters while the men walked, traversing once again the road which cut through the centre of the palace. Another right-of-way led up through the courtyards from the public landing-stage on the Thames. The ordinary, common people, going about their business, could easily catch sight of their Queen as she went about hers, and often did, raising a spontaneous cheer as she passed. That day, though, her business lay inside the palace.

The party turned in through an archway. The Seigneur dismissed the litter-bearers and stated his business to an official. They were promptly ushered across courtyards, along corridors and through vast rooms until they came to the ante-room to the Presence Chamber where the Queen was holding Court.

At last it was their turn to enter. Although enor-

mous, the magnificent room seemed crowded. Courtiers stood or knelt in loose ranks about the Queen,
their sumptuous costumes providing a confusing kal-
eidoscope, mainly in black and white, the sombre
colours made brilliant by the jewellery adorning both
men and women alike.

Elizabeth's splendid figure immediately drew
Judith's awed gaze. Everyone else paled into insignificance beside the regal form of the Sovereign, clad in
gleaming cloth of gold and displaying jewels more
magnificent than those of anyone else. Hair the colour
of carrots had been piled high beneath a cap which
consisted entirely of strung jewels as far as Judith could
see, and a huge ruff of delicate, stiffened lace stood up
to frame her startlingly white face. Flanked by her
maids of honour, all clad in white, her wide skirts
spread about her, she sat on a dais in an elaborately
carved and gilded chair: not quite a throne, for this was
not a State occasion.

The walk to the dais seemed endless. As the party
trod solemnly towards the Queen, led by a black-
gowned official, Judith felt the prickle of awareness
that came when someone stared at you. She looked
distractedly at the ranks flanking their path on the left,
knowing instinctively where that disturbing scrutiny
was coming from — and almost stopped in her tracks.

The room spun. She closed her eyes momentarily
while she regained her equilibrium then, still moving
forward but on decidedly unsteady legs, she lifted her
lids to meet the bright, inscrutable gaze of her husband,
who stood in a group of other courtiers. Gorgeously
apparelled in a slashed doublet of black velvet
embroidered with silver and lined with palest grey, his
expression guarded, he appeared almost as a stranger

until that merry, rakish smile suddenly lit his face and he bowed his head in acknowledgement.

Judith dredged up an uncertain smile in return and walked on in a daze. The occasion had strung her nerves quite taut enough, without the added shock of encountering Oliver in a place where she had least expected to find him. Questions teemed through her mind, unformed, irrational, as though it were not her brain doing the thinking. And then they had stopped and dropped to their knees as the Seigneur paid homage to his overlord and offered her the parchment, painstakingly written by his clerk, containing an account of his progress to date in colonising Sark.

The Queen bade them rise and graciously accepted the scroll. Encouraged, Helier de Carteret then begged leave to present his wife, his friend and lawyer Sieur Pierre Le Grand, and Sieur Le Grand's daughter, Mistress Judith Burnett.

Elizabeth's eyes narrowed in that extraordinary white, painted face. As Judith rose from her deep curtsy she saw small creases had been drawn on the smooth forehead.

'Mistress Burnett.' The Queen's brows arched. 'Your name is not uncommon, yet I wonder — are you by chance related to Master Oliver Burnett?' She looked beyond Judith. 'Master Burnett, here is someone bearing your name. Are you acquainted?'

Judith shivered as warm fingers momentarily brushed hers. Oliver slid gracefully to one knee as he faced his Sovereign.

'Your Grace, Mistress Judith is my wife.'

A buzz of hushed excitement ran through the chamber. This was drama indeed!

Elizabeth was abruptly more erect in her chair, her face coldly furious.

'You are wed, sir? Without my permission? Why was it not sought, pray?'

Judith heard Oliver's sharp intake of breath, but his calm, faintly amused expression did not waver. 'Madam, the circumstances were. . .unusual.'

'They would need to be! And for how long has this deception been practised on us?'

'Since my return in October, Your Grace.'

The Queen snorted into the expectant silence. 'Afraid to admit to your disobedience, eh, sirrah?'

'Indeed, Madam. I must beg Your Grace's indulgence and forgiveness.' Oliver placed his hand on his breast in a theatrical gesture. 'Since the one who possesses my heart and devotion is beyond my reach, I wed where I could.'

Judith's pulse beat like a drum in her ears. His words seemed to thrust a sword into her heart. He loved another.

But the Queen had drawn herself up and Judith could feel the force of her anger like a wave washing over her. Whatever was the problem? Surely Oliver was entitled to marry whom and when he chose, even if he did not love the woman. But it seemed not.

'You know full well the consequences of disobedience, sir.' Elizabeth used one beautiful hand to make an imperative gesture to one of her officers. 'Have him taken to the Tower.'

Judith gasped, as did her companions, and a rustle of anticipation ran around the assembly. Oliver merely bowed his head in acquiescence.

William Cecil, recently created Lord Burghley, stepped forward. 'Your command must be obeyed, of course, ma'am,' acknowledged her principal secretary, 'but may I beg leave to suggest that the Fleet would be a more appropriate place of confinement? Master

Burnett has offended against Your Grace, but is not guilty of treason against the State. On the contary he has rendered it worthy service.'

For an instant the Queen looked as though she might argue, but in the end she shrugged. 'Do as you see fit, as long as our displeasure is made manifest by the punishment and we do not have to behold his wretched face again!'

'Oliver,' muttered Judith as her husband rose to his feet at the approach of a couple of guards. 'What have you done to deserve this?'

'Wed without the Royal Blessing,' he murmured, his smile rueful. 'But do not concern yourself, angel. She always relents. A few weeks of discomfort and all will be forgiven.'

There was no time for more. 'Oh, husband!' whispered Judith fearfully as the guards lined up on either side of him and, having deprived Oliver of his sword, began to lead him away. With an anguished kind of pride she noted that his casual air remained steadfast as he walked from the chamber.

The Queen waved her hand again and they were dismissed. How she managed to get out of the chamber without disgracing herself Judith never afterwards knew.

'That dreadful woman!' muttered Margaret de Carteret as they gained the comparative space and freedom of the ante-room.

'Hush, wife!' Helier hissed harshly. 'Do you want us all to end up in the Tower?' His worried frown deepened. 'I trust this catastrophe will not affect her judgement of my report. . . .'

Margaret subsided, keeping her indignation to herself until such time as they were alone. The party made its way back to the lodging in subdued silence.

'My poor love!' cried Margaret the moment they
were inside, and took Judith into a motherly embrace.

Judith accepted the comfort gratefully, but did not
cry. Tears would be of no practical help. The knowledge that Oliver loved some other woman had killed
something inside her. Yet it did not alter the fact that
she bled for him, sent to prison for marrying her under
pressure.

She had not known what risk he ran, or she would
have refused to go ahead with the ceremony. But
perhaps that was exactly why he had not confided his
dilemma. The hazard involved had made her the more
desirable in his eyes.

She had scarcely removed her cloak and given it to
Thomasse to take to her bedchamber when a loud
knock on the door sent a servant hurrying to open it.
Coysh presented himself, a doubtful expression on his
severe face.

'Who is it?' demanded Helier irritably.

'A gentleman, sir. By what I could make out, for his
French is very strange, he says his name is Charles
Mead, he is a friend of Master Oliver Burnett, and
wishes to speak with Mistress Burnett——'

'Oh,' cried Judith, 'I must see him—he may come
up, may he not, Seigneur?'

Helier assented and Coysh departed to fetch the
visitor.

'Sit down, my dear,' advised Margaret. 'Come, sit
by me on this settle.'

Judith wanted to pace the floor, but obediently sat
on the edge of the padded seat. Her father had not so
far said a word, but stood in brooding silence in the
darkest corner of the room. Suddenly, he spoke.

'You are not pregnant. Was the marriage
consummated?'

Judith gasped, flushed, and nodded mutely. No one had questioned that fact before.

'Pity,' was all Pierre Le Grand said.

Charles Mead — Sir Charles Mead, it soon transpired — was shown in and bowed to the company. Judith realised at once that she had seen him standing with Oliver, a shorter, rotund but elegant figure in midnight blue brocade.

'Mistress Burnett, your husband sent me after you to add my reassurances to his. He has been awaiting a suitable opportunity to inform Her Majesty of his marriage, but it did not arise. He regrets the unfortunate scene to which you were exposed this morning.'

'Will he be all right?'

Her anxious tone brought a brief smile of sympathy to Charles's face. 'I believe so, mistress. Her Majesty is wont to punish her favourites for disobedience, but her displeasure seldom lasts for long, and your husband has the means to make his stay in the Fleet tolerable.'

'Money, you mean?'

'Indeed, mistress. Gold will buy a decent lodging, food, heat and light. He will also be allowed to receive visitors ——'

Judith was on her feet. 'I must go to him at once ——'

Charles lifted a restraining hand. 'Nay, mistress. Not today. Allow him to settle in. I will come to escort you — an you will allow me the privilege — as soon as possible.'

Judith subsided disconsolately. 'How soon will that be?'

'Tomorrow, perhaps. I will wait upon you again at noon on the morrow.'

'Think you the Queen's displeasure will extend to us?' demanded Helier.

Charles shook his head. 'Nay, Seigneur. 'Tis unlikely
to extend beyond Oliver's person. Otherwise I should
be in the Fleet with him, since I am known to be his
friend and we share a lodging in Whitehall Palace! Her
Majesty passed your document to the Secretary of
State to peruse. He will give it a full and fair reading,
and guide her response.'

'Good.' Helier's relief was evident. 'This is a shock-
ing business for Mistress Burnett. She had been expecting her husband to return to Sark for her.'

'I know, Seigneur. It distressed Oliver that he could
not, for the Queen demanded his attendance here at
Court.'

'He could have written.'

Charles bowed in the direction of the voice coming
from the shadows. 'Indeed, Sieur Le Grand. I offer no
excuse on his behalf for that neglect. He must explain
it himself.'

'If he can!'

'Papa, please!' Judith wanted no further berating of
her absent spouse. 'I am sure Oliver will be able to
explain everything when I see him tomorrow.'

Her smile touched something deep inside Charles.
He cursed his friend for a fool to toy with his wife's
affections. But he looked likely to pay dearly for his
careless conduct.

'Mistress,' he murmured, 'I will do my best to make
your visit possible.'

He left then, his business done. Judith wished she
could have spoken longer with him, asked him all the
questions tumbling through her mind, but with her
father and the de Carterets present that had been
impossible. Perhaps tomorrow.

But tomorrow she would see Oliver. Her pulse
quickened. What would his chamber be like? Dark and

dank? She shivered in fear. Men died in prison, mostly
from one of the fevers endemic in such places. But Sir
Charles had promised that gold could buy comfort.
And Oliver had gold.

So perhaps they would meet in reasonable conditions. Sir Charles would be present, of course. Unless
he courteously absented himself to leave them
alone. ...

Oliver. It mattered not one whit that he did not love
her. She longed for his touch, his kiss. How she had
missed his lively humour, his reckless courage, his
merry smile. Seeing him again, however briefly, had
brought all the old feelings flooding back.

But she must not forget that he had abandoned her,
suddenly and without real explanation. She could not
just fall into his arms as though nothing were amiss.

'Don't let the fellow bamboozle you, daughter.'

Pierre's harsh words brought Judith back to the
room, to the friends gathered about her in concern.

She straightened her shoulders and tilted her determined chin. 'I won't, Papa,' she promised.

CHAPTER NINE

CHARLES MEAD arrived as promised, and only a little late. Her father had declared his intention of accompanying them but Judith managed to dissuade him, though she did bow to demands that she take Thomasse with her. Charles's lackey was waiting below and joined them as they set out to walk the comparatively short distance to Fleet Bridge.

Judith had been this way before, previously continuing on to pass through Lud Gate into the City of London and St Paul's in order to visit various tradesmen in the area. That day she scarcely saw the impressive residences of the rich which lined the Thames to her right. Nor did she respond in anything other than monosyllables to Sir Charles's efforts at polite conversation. Sensing her abstraction, he soon relapsed into companionable silence.

The river curled away as they passed through Temple Bar and traversed Fleet Street. Judith felt the tension building in her. Before long she would see Oliver again. Touch him. Make certain he was real, that his presence yesterday had not been a figment of her imagination.

She knew it was not, yet reality seemed difficult to grasp. The Fleet, filthy and stinking, was real enough, yet she scarcely noticed its turgid, refuse-laden waters as they passed over the bridge and approached the forbidding edifice. Not far now.

She gagged as they passed inside its portals and she caught a whiff of the well-nigh insupportable stench.

Her face paled at the thought of the fastidious Oliver confined within these walls! No wonder prisoners died like flies of the putrid fever! Surely incarceration in the Tower would have been preferable? Except, she remembered grimly, that few people left the Tower unless it was to walk to the scaffold.

Jerked abruptly back to unpalatable reality, she heard Sir Charles exchange a few words with the turnkey and saw silver pass hands. They were escorted along putrid corridors, the cries of desperate prisoners assailing their ears from behind the grilled gates, until they came to a quieter wing of the establishment. The warder led them up a dank staircase to clearer air and a floor where individual cells were guarded by heavy oak doors. The turnkey opened one, called out some supposedly witty remark to the prisoner, stood aside for them all to file in, then went out and slammed the door on them. To Judith, the clunk of the engaging lock held all the horror of disaster.

She blinked in the brightness streaming in through a high, narrow window. Momentarily dazzled, she did not at first see Oliver, standing in shadow beyond the beam of sunlight.

'Well, angel!' His voice held its characteristic laugh and as her eyes adjusted she could see the familiar curve of his lips. 'Marry, but it seems you are destined to discover me in desperate situations! Would that you could fish me out of these troubled waters!'

'Don't joke, Oliver! This is no laughing matter!'

In her distress, Judith's voice came out more sharply than she intended. Charles quickly intervened.

'Oliver is known for his ability to laugh in the face of adversity, Mistress Judith! How are you, my friend? Comfortable?'

'Comfortable enough, I thank you, Charles. See, I

have Lambert in attendance, I have a bed, we possess mattresses and blankets, a table and chair, a candle or two, a quill and ink and paper on which to write! Though exactly what I shall write I have yet to decide. Oh, and I have books to read. A Geneva Bible and Foxe's *Book of Martyrs*.'

Charles chuckled. 'That one should stiffen your resolve in certain enterprises!'

'Undoubtedly. But now, think you you could take yourself and the others off, so that I may have a few moments alone with my wife? We have need to discuss certain matters in private. I am most grateful to you for bringing her, Charles, but your continued presence would render the favour rather less worthy of my thanks!'

A heavy sigh belied the grin on Charles's good-natured, rather dissolute face. 'I know when I am not welcome!'

He turned and rapped on the door. Eventually a response came in the shape of the individual whose duty it was to look after the more important prisoners. More silver changed hands and, having promised to return in an hour, Charles departed with all the servants, Thomasse expressing doubts over leaving her mistress, which Judith dismissed, and Lambert scowling at being parted from his master.

The warder leered. 'An hour, then, master. Enjoy yourselves.'

Oliver gave the man the most repressive look Judith had ever seen on his face, but his gaoler merely winked and chuckled, forcing the phlegm to rattle in his throat. Judith suppressed a shiver as the lock turned again.

'Well, wife.'

Oliver's quiet voice still held the lilt of laughter. Judith jerked back her wandering thoughts and gave a

nervous laugh. It was strange being alone with him
again, especially here, in this awful place, with that
lewd warder imagining. . .

'The stench is not so bad up here,' she offered as the
first reasonable remark to come into her head.

He stepped forward into the light, which caught the
silver embroidery and grey silken lining behind the
slashing of his doublet and trunk hose. He still wore
yesterday's fashionable garments, quite out of place in
those surroundings. He looked his usual elegant self
apart from his ruffs, which were drooping rather sadly.

And from the tiny lines of strain struggling to break
through the careless mask he wore.

Her heart felt squeezed. 'I'm sorry,' she whispered.

'*You* are sorry, angel!' He came closer and took her
gloved hands into a strong clasp. ''Tis I who should be
apologising.'

Pushing back her ruffs and cuffs, he kissed the inside
of each wrist in turn. The touch of his dry, warm mouth
sent shivers of longing trickling down Judith's spine.

'Why did you let them force you into marrying me?'
she asked, and the quiver in her voice she could not
suppress only deepened her distress. 'You knew you
should not, and you. . .you love someone else.'

'Do I?' He sounded genuinely surprised.

'You told the Queen so.'

'Ah!' His mischievous smile flashed out. 'Come,
sweet angel, let us sit here, together.' He drew her
towards the narrow bed set in the dimness behind the
shaft of light and they sat, his shoulder brushing hers
in an intimacy which set her nerves on fire. He held on
to one of her hands, clasping it in both of his.

He spoke low, as though afraid he could be overheard. 'You must understand, wife, that although

Elizabeth glories in being known as the Virgin Queen, she is in fact a rather embittered old maid.'

'But I've heard——'

'Oh, she talks of marriage to the Duke of Alençon but it is largely a diplomatic stratagem, meant to strengthen the recent treaty with France. She enjoys the flattery of being wooed, but 'tis my belief she will never commit herself to marry him. For a start, he must be twenty years her junior, and short where she is tall.'

Judith spoke with feeling. 'It is a great disadvantage for a woman to be tall.'

He chuckled, and his arm crept round to squeeze her shoulders. 'Nonsense! I for one like a woman of stature!' There was a moment's silence while he turned her face to his and lightly kissed her lips. Judith shivered, helpless to withstand her immediate response to his touch. But he quickly dismissed the distraction and returned to his theme. 'In fairness, Alençon's envoy is most reassuring in the reports he brings of the young man, and I think she finds the proposition attractive politically despite his youth, his alleged pockmarks and lack of height. And *he* would not be averse to the match. He would become King of England!'

Judith offered no comment except to frown. Oliver therefore continued. 'She may be tempted to wed with him, but I do not believe she will ever finally bring herself to allow a foreigner, let alone one who is not truly Protestant, to rule over England. Her sister Mary made that mistake and the Spanish are hated more than ever by the average Englishman.'

'Because they persecute Protestants!'

'Not only for that. Foreign rule goes against their grain. If she could have married Leicester — but despite her love for him she could not bring herself to do it after all the suspicion over his wife Amy Robsart's death, and now he is consoling himself with Lady Douglas Sheffield. The Queen is jealous, but although Christopher Hatton is a favourite and she's recently promoted him to an important post, she refuses to consider him as a husband. She should, for I believe he is, perhaps, the one man who truly loves her.'

'How could any man ——?' began Judith disgustedly, but Oliver cut her off.

'She is a woman who invokes deep emotions in courtiers in general, though it does not normally go further than paying her a special homage because she is a woman. Hatton's feelings have gone beyond that, but who can say what makes a man love a woman?'

'Or a woman a man,' murmured Judith.

He slanted her a smile. 'Quite so. But I digress. You must understand that she feeds on the admiration and flattery of her gentlemen courtiers—those she chooses as favourites must pretend to be in love with her ——'

'Was that what you were doing?' demanded Judith breathlessly. If only she could believe that!

'Of course. And they must beg her permission to marry elsewhere, must solicit her forgiveness for seeking the fruits of matrimony with some other woman.'

'Which you failed to do. Why did you not tell my father all this?' demanded Judith. 'He would not have forced you to disobey the Queen and earn her displeasure!'

'I knew the risk I ran, angel, but—I had my reasons for not imparting the information then. Besides,' he lifted his head arrogantly and waved a dismissive hand, 'I could not allow the whim of an ageing virgin to dictate my actions in such an important matter! I have no liking for the role of courtier. Were it not for—

certain circumstances—I would have disregarded her wishes and left Court long before this.'

Judith did not like to ask what the circumstances were. 'She is not that old,' she protested instead, though why she should defend that vicious woman she did not know.

'She is approaching forty, and will soon be too old to bear children. She enjoys having young men about her paying court, and we oblige in order to keep her favour and earn preferment—besides, as I said, she inspires homage and loyalty, if not love. Her company is stimulating. She is a great Queen. Men go out and conquer new worlds for her sake.'

'Were you doing what you were doing when you were caught by the Spaniards for her sake?' asked Judith curiously, and surprised in herself a touch of jealousy.

'Perhaps, my sweet. But that is another story and this is not the time to tell it,' he retorted lightly. 'Right now I should be on my knees to you begging forgiveness for my neglect over the past months.'

He made a move as though to put his words into action. 'Don't do that!' cried Judith anxiously, regarding the rather grimy boards with disfavour. 'You will ruin your nether-stocks!'

'Oh, practical Judith!' Now he really was laughing. 'Do not worry, I will look to my costume, at least until Lambert brings me a change of apparel.' He quickly sobered, as far as he was able given his normal blithe approach to life. 'Elizabeth would not grant me permission to leave Court and I could not find a convenient opportunity to inform her of my matrimonial state,' he explained. 'So I could not return to Sark.'

'I waited for a letter,' said Judith quietly.

Her heart had stopped pounding. His arm still lay about her shoulders but otherwise they were sitting like old friends discussing matters of little concern to themselves. She was not sure whether to be glad or sorry. He was almost like a stranger now. She had never really known him.

He took his arm away and put both elbows on his knees, threading his fingers through his disordered hair. 'You did not know my circumstances. What could I have said?' he asked, and the hint of desperation in his voice gave Judith pause.

'I understand, husband,' she said wearily. 'I would agree to an annulment, but that is scarcely possible.' Her voice caught as her fingers twisted together in agitation. 'I will retire to Sark and leave you to court the Queen.'

'No!' The violence of his denial astounded her. And then, quite disregarding the inconvenient farthingale, in a whirlwind of movement he caught her to him, swung her bodily on the bed and stretched out beside her, pulling her so painfully close that she could scarcely breathe.

'No,' he repeated more quietly, kissing her forehead. Her stylish hat had come off despite the skewer-like pins and she wondered dazedly where it was. 'I have missed you, wife,' he went on huskily. 'When I saw you yesterday I could scarce believe my eyes! So gorgeous, so stately. . .'

His voice trailed off rather breathlessly. He kissed her lips fiercely, demanding the full surrender of her mouth.

Judith's response was tempered by a justifiably stubborn determination not to let him off too easily. He had behaved badly and although she forgave him, he must not imagine she had not been hurt. She kept her lips firmly clamped together. Feeling her resistance, Oliver soon released her mouth.

'Then imagine *my* astonishment!' she demanded as
soon as she was able. Her lips felt swollen and painful
and she ran her tongue over them to ease the discomfort. 'I do not know how I completed that walk to the
dais.'

'My poor angel!' Oliver sounded pleasingly repen-
tant. He kissed her lips lightly, as though aware that he
had made them tender. 'But when I am free again we
shall be together, I promise.'

His hands began to roam. Judith, pliantly absorbed
in the pleasure of his nearness, forgot her determination to resist his advances and took a while to realise
the urgency possessing him. Her own desire was rising
fast, she was his, his wife, but. . .but she could not. . .
She struggled to free her lips.

'Oliver! Please, not here.'

'Marry, why not, angel? It has been too long——'

'And whose fault was that, pray?'

He made a sound of exasperation. 'I have
explained——'

'Oh, that's not the reason! It's that warder. He will
know and I could not bear it!'

He chuckled, trying to set her reluctance aside as a
joke. 'Why so modest?' Then, since she did not
respond, he tightened his hold, demanding compliance.
'You are my wife, and I want you!'

'Then you should have found a way to come to
Sark—or to bring me here!' Judith sobbed in her
agitation. 'I cannot, will not be so debased as to. . .
to. . .' she couldn't say it '. . .under these conditions!'

He released her abruptly and sat up. 'Marry, then I
shall have to send out for a strumpet.'

He did not mean it, for he would not be able to
touch such a woman if she came. But Judith's refusal
stung him. He could not understand her scruples.

Judith felt the chill of his frosty displeasure, knew the devastation of jealousy and loss. Her prudery would force him into other arms. Probably familiar arms. But she was as she was. Hurt made her voice sharp.

'Do you always use the same woman? Or do you spread your favours?'

'I spread them, of course,' he averred suavely. 'There is safety in numbers.'

'I might have guessed you were a libertine,' she choked. 'A man like you——'

'What do you mean,' he demanded dangerously, '"a man like me"?'

Judith gulped but could not reply. A full-blooded, persuasive, magnetic man no woman could resist, she might have said. But her voice had deserted her. And, to cap her humiliation, she began to weep in earnest. She, who never normally cried! She turned her head into the lumpy pillow and let the tears flow.

Oliver regarded his wife in sudden contrition. His fevered libido had abated, leaving him vaguely aching. It had been so long and he wanted her so much! Caught in the sudden grip of a desire to lose himself in the paradise of possession, he had forgotten he was supposed to be a gentleman.

But she was right. This was no place to pursue a fragile, budding relationship which needed nursing and could only be besmirched by the obscene surroundings.

'I did not mean it,' he confessed softly. 'About the strumpet. I've been no monk in the past, but since I met you. . . Angel, no other woman has had the power to stir me.'

His voice held such rueful sincerity that Judith was inclined to believe him. A surge of happiness flooded

her. Perhaps, after all, he was hers, as she had thought
on their bridal night.

She sniffed loudly, mopped at her eyes and tried to
sit up. She did not spurn Oliver's helping hand as he
moved away to let her slide her feet to the floor.
Batting down a farthingale threatening her modesty,
she resumed her seat on the edge of the bed. Oliver
continued to stand.

She looked up at him in his elegant clothes, a
tentative smile hovering on her lips. But then renewed
sight of his costume roused an unwelcome memory,
ruining the effect of his flattering words.

'Not even the woman leaning on your arm at Court
yesterday?' she blurted.

She had scarcely registered her at the time, and yet
now, suddenly, her image was imprinted on her mind.
Bejewelled, dainty, fair-haired, her face whitened and
painted like all the other Court ladies, she had been
laughing up at Oliver until she realised his distraction
and discovered its source. Then she had darted Judith
such a look. . .

'An old friend, no more,' Oliver assured her quickly.

But he had known instantly who she meant, and
assumed a trifle too much unconcern. Judith suspected
the pair of being more than friends.

Yet he had sounded so sincere. Perhaps any liaison
was in the past.

'An old lover, perhaps?' she probed, unable to help
herself.

He turned away irritably. 'Yes, if you must have it!'
He swung back to crouch down beside her, taking
possession of one of her hands. The smile spreading
over his face seemed more self-mocking than humorous. 'But believe me, wife,' he said gruffly, 'what I said
before is the absolute truth. You are the only woman I

desire now. The past is past. It is you I want and no
other.'

She forced down the irrational surge of jealousy
threatening to swamp her immediate happiness. The
past *was* past and did not matter. The future did.

'How long will the Queen keep you here?' she
wondered anxiously.

He squeezed her hand in wordless accord. 'Until her
pique lessens and she thinks I have been punished
enough. Although favoured by her, I am not her
favourite — Leicester will always be that, though
Hatton is running him close these days. But I do have
access to her Privy Chamber and we have spent some
profitable and enjoyable hours together. She sometimes calls me her Brain.'

Judith frowned, puzzled. 'Why?'

'Because when we talk she is able to sort her ideas, I
believe. Burghley is her Spirit, Leicester her Eyes,
Hatton her Lids, Alençon her Frog! 'Tis her way of
nicknaming people.'

'Huh,' muttered Judith. It all sounded rather childish
to her. 'Could you not apply to her for leniency?'

'Prostrate myself, you mean?' Scorn made him sound
insufferably arrogant and he sprang up, drawing himself to his full height. 'I may try to avoid giving offence
and attempt to flatter my way out of trouble, but
plead? You do not yet know me, wife!'

'I realise that, husband!' Judith wrapped the hand he
had dropped in her other, missing the lost warmth of
his touch. 'I become more aware of it with every
moment that passes! I am ignorant of your past and am
discovering things about your nature I would perhaps
prefer not to know! You are proud, arrogant, and
stupid!'

Anger at his sudden change of mood, his dismissal

of her idea out of hand and with it the precious unity they had just achieved, brought tears to sting her lids again, but this time she managed to blink them back.

'Stupid?' That had pricked him. The arrogance had intensified. 'When the Queen deigns to call me her Brain?'

'Not that sort of stupid! Just silly stupid! Silly to let pride stop you from asking her to relent. She does not know the circumstances under which we wed. She condemned you unheard, which is intolerable!'

'But not unusual in a sovereign. I know Elizabeth, wife. You do not. Your presence precipitated this crisis, so please allow me to extricate myself from the result in the way I know to be best.'

Judith's anger abruptly dissipated in a cloud of misery.

'I would not have attended Court with the Seigneur had I known you were there,' she said. Her voice shook. His inference had hurt. 'You cannot blame me for what happened!'

Suddenly the smile she loved illuminated his face. Oliver could not be repressed for long. He dropped back on his haunches to take both her hands in his. 'Oh, angel! Why are we quarrelling? Marry, but we must have better things to do than try to apportion blame when 'twas no one's fault!' He pulled her hands against his chest. 'Tell me, how have you been coping? Did you have a pleasant journey from Sark? I am avid for news!'

'As am I! You are right, husband.' Judith smiled her rare, slow smile. 'The origin of this mess was not of our making, although both of us must perhaps bear some blame. We should not be accusing or condemning — we can leave that to others!'

Oliver lifted the hands he held to his lips. She could

feel the warmth of his kisses through the thin silk of her gloves. He stood, drawing her up into a gentle hold. His lingering kiss melted her bones until she was forced to cling to him for support.

'Oh, Oliver.' She buried her face in his padded doublet. 'I am so worried for you. Hold me.'

His arms tightened, but only in reassurance. He spoke into the nest of her hair. 'I am a survivor, angel. Do not worry over me.'

'I will try not to.' She lifted shadowed eyes to ask anxiously, 'How do you eat? Have you victuals enough?'

The lilt in his voice betrayed his restored high spirits. 'Lambert sees to that. He purchases meals at the local tavern and brings them in. I have food and wine in plenty, angel, but I relish most your wifely concern.'

Standing there in the security of his embrace it did seem that her worries were groundless. Being in amity with him again brought deep contentment. She relaxed and nestled her head on his shoulder. 'The hour must almost be up,' she sighed regretfully.

Oliver glanced across her head to the hour-glass the warder had turned as he left. The sand had almost run through.

'A few moments only, angel. And I would prefer you not to come again. It is not right for you to be exposed to the sights and sounds of this place. You run the risk of fever just by entering its portals.'

'And what of you?' she whispered. 'Who will tend you if you fall victim to some illness —— ?'

'Lambert,' said Oliver swiftly. 'He has seen me through many a tight spot in the past and will do so again. But I shall not catch a putrid fever. I had a slight attack as a child and it seems now to pass me by. I shall be all right, but you, living on small islands all your life, you may not be so immune.'

'But I must come, husband! I owe you a duty! Besides, I could not bear for us to be parted again so soon!'

'My sweet, it would be better so. I do not think I shall be here for long, but if you have returned to Sark before my release I swear I will come straight to you. Nothing shall stop me. I have flirted with the Queen's favour for long enough. I do not like Court life, and shall not try to return. I have my own life to lead.'

'I did not like Court,' Judith averred. 'All those painted women! Why do they whiten their faces so?'

'Fashion,' said Oliver succinctly. 'They ruin their complexions.' He ran a tender finger down Judith's cheek, then followed it with his lips. 'Your skin feels like silk, not pumice stone.'

She ignored the implication of that comparison. 'Does it?' She rubbed her cheek against his. 'So does yours.'

He laughed softly. 'Lambert shaved me shortly before you were due!'

'Aha! You wished to impress me, sir?'

'I did, and apologise most humbly for the sad state of my ruffs. Talking of sad states, may I suggest you replace your hat before the sand runs out?'

'My hair!'

Judith released herself and patted frantically at her unruly tresses, pushing in falling pins and tucking stray strands into place beneath her small cap, all askew, trying to restore the style Thomasse had achieved for her. Oliver retrieved her hat from the floor, brushed it off and handed it to her gravely.

'No mirror, I fear.'

Judith put it on and skewered it in place more firmly than before.

'Is that all right?'

'Beautiful.' He leaned forward and touched her ready lips with his. 'God be with you, my wife. Until we meet again.'

They were just in time. Before Judith had time to do more than return his kiss, they heard the door opening. When the gaoler entered Judith was seated demurely on the chair while Oliver stood by the window.

'Time's up,' announced the man unnecessarily.

'Where is my friend?' asked Oliver sharply.

'Waitin' in the street. They wouldn't let 'im in agin. I'll see the lady reaches 'im safe and sound.'

Judith did not like his tone. Neither, apparently, did Oliver.

'Where is my lackey?' he demanded abruptly.

''Ow should I know, yer honour? He i'n't outside.'

'Gone for supplies, I suppose,' muttered Oliver. He drew a breath and assumed his most arrogant, commanding air. 'If anything should happen to my wife, gaoler, the Queen shall hear of it. Take very good care of her.'

'Yer wife, be she? Very tasty, if I might say so! But I thought as how you was out of favour wiv 'er Majesty?'

'You may not say so! And mind your business, fellow, and your manners. Mistress Burnett has many influential friends at Court.' Oliver strolled over and took Judith's trembling fingers in a strong, reassuring clasp. 'I shall watch from the window,' he murmured. 'Charles will see that you are safe.'

'I shall be all right, Oliver.' Judith knew that to show her fear of the man and her distress at leaving would only make matters worse for him. She controlled her

emotions with a supreme effort. 'God be with you, my
dear husband. We shall meet again soon.'

'So I promise.' He kissed the hand he held. 'Farewell, wife.'

For a moment their fingers clung. Then Judith gathered her pride about her and walked from the room
without a backward glance.

Judith waited while the man locked the door. Even
his doubtful escort would be welcome in that awful
place.

''Is wife, is yer?' He gave a gappy, blackened grin as
he led the way, but there was a new if grudging respect
in his voice. Judith felt reassured, though his stench
was powerful and she had a job not to shrink away.

'That's right.'

'Thought you was more of a lady-friend, like. They
be what usually visits the gentlemen in 'ere.'

Judith had very few coins with her. She felt desperate
to do something to help Oliver so she took what she
had from her pouch as she descended the stairs ahead
of the man. The fetid air at the foot forced her to make
hurried tracks for the entrance, where she stopped to
offer him the money.

'Look to Master Burnett's comfort, if you please.
There will be more for you if he comes safely out of
here.'

The man's greasy, greedy hand quickly swallowed
the silver. ''Ow much?'

Judith hesitated. She had no idea of the amount to
offer. 'Master Burnett is not a poor man,' she tempor-
ised. 'He will wish to reward any kindness you may
show him. In any case, I will reward you.'

''Ow much?' he repeated.

Judith looked round wildly for inspiration and relief

swamped her when she saw the sturdy figure of Sir Charles striding towards her.

'Wait!' she instructed the warder and sped forward to meet Oliver's friend. 'Sir Charles!' He greeted her with a smile and bow. 'How much should I promise this man if Oliver emerges safe and sound from this iniquitous place?' she asked urgently.

He considered. 'A couple of angels should suffice.'

'You are certain that is enough? Oliver can surely afford more.'

'Unnecessary. That will be a fortune to the fellow.'

'Then please come and add your promise to mine. I may not be here to keep my end of the bargain,' she admitted in a low, tense voice.

He looked slightly surprised, but did as she asked. And like the gentleman he was asked no intrusive questions during their return to Charing Cross.

Judith looked back at the prison once. She searched the narrow windows of the upper floors for any sign of Oliver, but in vain. Nevertheless, she waved.

CHAPTER TEN

JUDITH fretted away the days. Conscience whispered that her husband was confined to that appalling place because of her; and there was nothing she could do about it.

She would have ignored Oliver's prohibition on visiting, but no one would escort her to the Fleet. She could not go on her own, even she realised that would be the height of folly. So she was forced to rely on Sir Charles for information and comfort.

He visited his friend faithfully and cheerfully accepted the role of go-between. He took such things as wine and candles and returned, to Judith's secret delight, with a romantic poem penned in Oliver's flowing hand.

She had not realised him to be so accomplished. Sir Charles merely laughed at her astonishment.

'Any courtier worthy of the name can pen a few lines of verse, Mistress Judith. Why, I myself am no mean hand at the task! And with little else to occupy his time, Oliver has found an outlet for his energies!'

Judith shook her head and sighed. 'I know so little about him!'

'Have you never seen your husband dance, dear Mistress Judith? Or heard him play the lyre? I can assure you, he is as accomplished in these things as he is in the gentle art of flirtation.'

'Flirtation? Is that an accomplishment?' Judith asked dourly, her pleasure dissipating fast.

'Indeed it is, at Court. A harmless exchange of looks

and sighs, a game indulged in by many to alleviate the
boredom of waiting upon Her Majesty. And, of course,
Oliver has developed it to perfection with the Queen.
She depends upon his every word — when Leicester or
Hatton are not on hand to amuse her.'

He had flirted with her. What were Sir Charles's
words? 'A harmless exchange of looks and sighs.' A
game. Was that all his pursuit of her had been? Well,
if so he had paid dearly for indulging his whim in a
place where such conduct was not understood.

When Charles had gone she read Oliver's verse
again, not certain how much sincerity it held.

   Angel of Sark, most beauteous and kind,
With courage so prodigious: your image fills my
   mind.
Your hair, so curling soft and lustrous in its shade,
   Your eyes, so clear and shining, with honesty their
   trade,
Your lips, so full, so tender, their touch igniting fire.
Keep faith, my angel-wife, th'art all of my desire.

He did not mention love, yet surely those words
could not be merely flirtatious? Even if they were, she
thought defiantly, she did not care. They were beautiful. She lifted the paper to her lips and kissed it.

On Sunday they all attended church in the Abbey.
Failure to do so would have rendered them liable to a
fine. Recusants often paid this rather than attend a
service read from the Third Book of Common Prayer,
ordained by law for use in English churches, which
they considered heretical.

Repressive legislation had been introduced against
Roman Catholics after the Northern Rising last
November twelvemonth, when Pope Pius V had issued

a papal bull deposing Elizabeth. He had declared that
Roman Catholics were absolved from their allegiance
to her. It followed that an attempt to assassinate or
overthrow her would not be treasonable, a sin, since in
his eyes she was no longer Queen. All the Romanists
wanted was to place Catholic Mary of Scots on the
throne and return England to the papal fold. Of course,
no one else took any notice of the papal bull.

But there had been a rare old turmoil last year when
Ridolfi had conspired to assassinate Elizabeth so that
Mary could succeed her. The ripples were still running
through the country. Since their arrival in London
Judith had discovered that King Philip of Spain and the
Duke of Alva, who was supposed to bring an army to
invade from the Netherlands, had been wary of the
rash plan. The plot had been discovered and the
conspirators arrested at about the same time as Oliver
had been washed up on Sark. The Duke of Norfolk
still languished in the Tower awaiting Elizabeth's signature on a warrant for his execution.

Sir Charles said all this had badly upset Elizabeth.
'She hardly knew who to trust,' he told Judith, 'and
Oliver's return to Court came at just the critical time.
He has proved himself loyal beyond doubt, which
meant she could talk to him freely.'

'How has he proved his loyalty?' Judith wanted to
know.

But Charles had shaken his head.

'Oliver will tell you when the time is right. It is not
my place to reveal secrets that belong to your husband.'

'The Queen does not appear to reward loyalty with
compassion,' Judith had muttered rebelliously.

Elizabeth attended the service with all her Court,
but the Seigneur and his party sat at the back with the
lesser worshippers. Judith caught a glimpse of Sir

Charles down the length of the nave but fixed her eyes on the regal head, willing the Queen to relent, unable to concentrate on anything else.

She found the ceremonial rather popish after the austere Presbyterianism of Sark, yet in her abstracted state oddly comforting. Whereas spoken words went over her head, the ceremonial and singing lifted her spirit in a way she had never imagined possible. She knew she could grow to like the Anglican form of service, falling as it did between the two extremes of Christian doctrine.

Calmer and more cheerful, she returned to the lodgings to find Sir Charles waiting for her.

'I have had an idea,' he told her once their greetings were exchanged. 'Should you wish it, I could approach the Queen to ask her to grant you a privy audience. If she agrees, you could explain the circumstances which compelled Oliver to enter into matrimony.'

'He was not all that reluctant!' protested Judith defensively.

'Of course not! Do not mistake me. No man would be reluctant to take a bride such as you, Mistress Judith,' Charles assured her gallantly. 'In fact, Oliver has confessed he could not resist the temptation to make you his! But nevertheless, to comply with your father's demand was an act of bravery on his part. He well knew the consequences were his marriage to be discovered.'

'I told him he should have explained,' muttered Judith miserably.

'But listen. Elizabeth dislikes extreme Protestantism as heartily as Roman Catholicism. Play on that, emphasise the bigoted nature of the man who exposed you. Assure her of Oliver's innocence of the charge of ravishment. Plead with her. She may listen to you.'

Judith's face lit up. 'Do you think so, Sir Charles?' It fell again. 'But wouldn't Oliver be angry? He absolutely refused to plead with her.'

Charles shrugged. 'His pride will be the death of him yet! Request the Queen to keep your secret. She may agree, if you catch her in a good mood, for she is of a devious nature and after all the conspiracies mounted against her it may amuse her to indulge in a harmless one of her own. It is my belief she already regrets her hasty action but lacks an excuse to retract her order. She misses Oliver.'

'He says he will not return to Court.'

'Brave man! But there is no need to inform Her Majesty! It is usual for her to impose a short period of banishment from Court. He need not emerge from his retirement to his estates.'

Judith allowed that puzzling statement to pass while she thought, her face serious. She would be risking Oliver's wrath, but what did that matter if she could secure his release?

'Very well. Thank you, Sir Charles. When may I hope to be admitted to her presence?'

'That I cannot say. A week perhaps, no more.'

The Seigneur haunted Whitehall waiting for a response to his report. A few days later he returned to the lodgings, jubilantly waving a parchment.

'Signed by Her Majesty herself!' he exclaimed. 'She is satisfied that I have abided by the Letters Patent she granted me seven years ago, and is impressed by my progress in colonising and defending Sark. In recognition of this, she has granted me the means to defend the island more effectively!'

'How?' demanded Margaret. 'Must you find more than forty men to carry muskets?'

'Nay, wife! She has ordered six fine pieces of artillery with all their appurtenances to be supplied from her munitions in the Tower!'

'Cannon to defend the landings?' asked Pierre eagerly.

'Aye. Two culverins, two sakers and two falcons, with fifty iron shots and two hundred pounds of powder for each.'

He waited for the exclamations of satisfaction to subside before imparting further news.

'And it says here that Her Majesty has graciously bestowed upon me a small brass cannon as a personal gift, to be so inscribed and dated this year of grace, 1572!'

'Helier! How wonderful!' exclaimed Margaret.

The Seigneur held up a restraining hand. 'But that is not all. She has also seen fit to grant me the island in Fief Haubert — I now owe homage directly to the Crown.'

Amid the congratulations which followed, Pierre's laugh rang out. 'So if called upon to do so, you must provide an armoured knight, fully armed and mounted, to fight for the Queen!'

De Carteret grinned. 'No doubt a payment in silver will suffice!'

In all the excitement only Judith remained silent, nursing her reservations.

'Then you will be returning home shortly?' she asked when the others had done.

'I must pay my homage and arrange for the shipment, but that should not take above a week. We may start for home within ten days. I had already sent for the St Ouen to be brought round into the Thames. We will sail from Gravesend.'

'I shall not be sailing with you,' she said quietly.

'Of course you will!' exclaimed her father. 'I shall not leave you alone here in London with no man to protect you. If your husband were free that would be another matter. But as he is not, you will return with me!'

'No, Papa. My duty is to my husband. I must wait here for his release. I shall be perfectly all right. I can stay on here. I shall engage servants and Sir Charles will no doubt offer his support if necessary.'

'What will you do for money?' asked her father coldly.

'My husband is rich. You have told me so yourself.' Since Oliver had expressly told her to return to Sark and wait for him there, she wondered whether he would, in fact, supply her with the means to defy him. But she would meet that obstacle when it arose. Mayhap her father would relent, or Sir Charles advance her a loan. Or she could use her husband's credit. But she was determined not to put the sea between them again, whatever Oliver said.

If only the Queen would agree to see her! So far Sir Charles had no progress to report. He had been unable to approach Elizabeth himself, let alone arrange a private audience for her. The uncertainty, the waiting, was beginning to fray her normally steady nerves.

It took two more days for Sir Charles to bring her news.

'It is arranged!' he told her happily. 'I will escort you to Whitehall on Monday to see the latest drama performed, and afterwards, when the Queen retires to her private quarters, I am to take you to her.'

Judith felt dizzy with relief. 'Thank God! Sir Charles, how may I thank you?'

'To see you happy is reward enough, my dear.

Oliver,' he added grimly, 'does not yet appreciate what a treasure he has found in you.'

Oliver, meanwhile, was finding it difficult to push his wife from his thoughts. He had almost forgotten how desirable she was, a steady, restful creature enveloped in an aura of deep sensuality. A bewitching combination which had caught him, all unwillingly, in her toils. God, how he wanted the witch! Whenever he attempted to write an essay on the situation in the Netherlands to pass the time, he found himself writing, instead, a poem about Judith. One he had sent to her by Charles, only to regret the gesture later. The rest he had torn to shreds. She would think him a foolish, love-sick boy!

He scratched busily again by the light of a guttering candle, for lacking exercise he found sleep elusive, then sat back and scrutinised what he had written.

Angel, siren, murderess of my peace,
I loathe, I hate, I pray for my release!
Oh! to loose the chains that bind me close,
Oh! to forget, to abandon, to dispose
Of a wife who makes me question, sees me, all deranged,
From heedless venturer to dutied husband changed.

He read the words he had written, a wry smile on his mobile lips. He did not know whether he meant them or not. Judith was his angel and his devil, haunting him in whichever guise she appeared. With an impatient sigh he tore this latest composition to shreds, discarding it with all the others.

Concentration on anything else seemed beyond him. He might just as well retire, even if he could not sleep. 'Come, Lambert,' he cried. 'To bed!'

'Aye, master, and about time, too,' grumbled Lambert, waking from an uneasy doze and scrambling hurriedly to his feet.

The play was just about to begin when Sir Charles escorted Judith into the chamber. She settled into a seat several rows behind the Queen, who was laughing and joking with some of her maids of honour. Both Leicester and Hatton were in close attendance. It wasn't fair, thought Judith. Leicester and Elizabeth were of an age, yet he looked to be in his prime, whereas she had begun to show her years. Yet there could be no doubt of the affection existing between them. They behaved quite like an old married couple, Robert Dudley claiming the privileges of a husband and Elizabeth allowing it. Sir Christopher Hatton, she thought, was jealous.

Her appearance with Sir Charles initiated a great deal of interest and speculation. Despite this and her nervousness over the coming interview, Judith soon became absorbed in the spectacle offered by the players, who were re-enacting the villainies of Richard III. She sternly quelled the slight feeling of disapproval, engendered by the preaching of Cosmé Brevint, as she listened to their sonorous voices rising above the rustle of movement and whispered conversation. Dressed in eye-catching costumes, they strutted about the stage making extravagant gestures which could not fail to catch her attention and feed her imagination.

She clapped with the rest when it was over. It had been wonderful and she could not see why Pastor Brevint was so set against the drama. Had it not been for her mission. . .

'Now?' she whispered to Sir Charles.

'Not yet. The Queen will want to dance before she

retires. Hear, the musicians are tuning up for a pavane.
Do you wish to take part?'

'Oh, no! I have never learned to dance.' Pastor
Brevint did not approve of dancing, either.

'Then we will watch together,' smiled Sir Charles
good-naturedly.

All could join in the stately pavane, even the lawyers, merchants and other men wearing long gowns.

'Oliver does not wear a merchant's gown,' Judith
remarked inconsequentially as the company began the
movements.

'He does on the Continent, for he goes there on
business, but here he is a gentleman first,' explained
her companion.

The dance ended. The musicians struck up another
tune and to Judith's surprise all the men began to
discard their rapiers, handing them to their lackeys.

'Why are they doing that?' Judith wanted to know.
Court was a strange place, full of surprising behaviour.

Charles chuckled. 'They are about to dance the
volta — very energetic and they might trip over a dan-
gling rapier! This, you must know, is considered a
daring dance, for the gentleman clasps the lady by the
waist and lifts her into the air.' Seeing Judith's surprised and rather disapproving look, he hastened to set
her mind at ease. 'The Queen not only allows it, but
joins in herself. See, she is taking the floor now.'

Judith watched in some surprise as the Queen and
her courtiers cavorted about, and gasped aloud the first
time Her Majesty was lifted high in the air by Leicester.
She thought they all looked rather more amusing than
graceful, leaping and whirling, the men unable to grasp
their partners properly for swaying farthingales and
stiff, padded stomachers. She tried to imagine Oliver
taking part in such a scene and decided he would cut a

better figure than many of the corpulent courtiers panting and sweating as a result of their exertions.

She longed intensely for him to be there. How she would love to be able to dance with him.

After expending so much energy the Queen seemed ready to retire. Everyone made obeisance as she swept from the room, followed by some of her maids of honour and other favourites.

'Now,' said Charles, 'follow me.'

He had to state his business and they were made to wait, but before long the equerry returned to lead Judith into the presence. Charles gave her arm an encouraging squeeze.

Elizabeth had been divested of her formal gown and farthingale and had on a comfortable night gown of a soft green colour. She waved Judith forward.

Judith made the deepest, most graceful curtsy of which she was capable. 'Your Grace.'

'Well, mistress, what is it you want?' demanded Elizabeth sharply.

Tongue-tied for a moment, Judith cleared her throat. All she knew was that she could not possibly be frank in the presence of so many people. Four white-faced ladies and several men, including Leicester and Hatton, lounged close about their Sovereign. It was an intimate, almost a family scene which must be familiar to Oliver, but Judith felt like an intruder.

'Your Grace,' she managed at last, 'what I have to say is — delicate. I do not feel able to speak freely in the presence of the gentlemen.'

'Then perhaps you should not waste our time!' snapped Elizabeth. Then, seeing something of Judith's inner agony reflected on the girl's face, she abruptly relented, waving the men gathered about her to a far corner of the room. Once they were out of earshot she beckoned Judith closer. 'Come, girl, speak up!'

Judith suddenly found herself on her knees, her hands clasped urgently in front of her. 'Madam, I come to plead for my husband, Master Oliver Burnett. You do not know the circumstances under which he disobeyed you.'

'We are listening,' snapped Elizabeth impatiently.

There was only one thing for it. Judith launched into a description of Oliver's remarkable arrival on Sark, his recovery, her distress over the marriage proposed for her, their being seen as he comforted her, the pressure brought to bear by her father due to the extreme prudery of Sieur Nicolas Perrier, which had led him to assume the worst.

'Believe me, Your Grace, Master Burnett did not ravish me,' she finished. 'Mayhap he behaved imprudently in his desire to comfort and reassure me, but it was no more. Prior to that moment he had no intention of asking me to be his wife.'

When she had done, 'He was flogged, you say?' demanded Elizabeth, her eyes narrowed in thought. 'He said little of his experiences beyond an implication of shipwreck which had delayed his return.'

'That, I think, is his way, Madam.'

'I know his way.' Haughtily. 'But mayhap I did judge too severely. How long has he been in the Fleet?'

'For almost two weeks, Madam.'

'Hmm. Very well, I will see to it. You may go.'

Judith bowed her head. 'Thank you, Madam. May I beg one further favour?'

'Well, what is it?' the autocratic voice snapped.

'Your Majesty must know that my husband is a proud man. He would not appreciate my intervention on his behalf. Let him believe that the matter rests entirely between Your Grace and himself, that he owes his early release entirely to Your Grace's own change of heart, to your great mercy and favour.'

'Won't plead for himself, eh?' grunted Elizabeth, but Judith caught a gleam of approval in the sharp eyes. 'Very well. I will not mention this audience, and neither will anyone else, on pain of my displeasure!' She raised her voice. 'D'you hear that, all of you? I have not spoken with this child! Mention this meeting to anyone outside this room at your peril!'

A murmur of assent went around the chamber. Elizabeth nodded imperiously. 'So be it!'

Judith rose stiffly to her feet, made another obeisance and backed to the door.

'Well?' demanded Charles, offering his arm for support as an unusually subdued Judith emerged from the Presence.

'She said she would see to it. I think she means to release him. And has promised not to mention this interview, and charged her attendants to do the same.' Her husky voice shook. 'Oh, Sir Charles, I do pray she keeps her word!'

'I know she has a reputation for vacillation, but mayhap that is a good thing, for others will think Oliver's speedy release typical of her sudden changes of mind. He will discover that you attended Court with me, no doubt; too many people saw us to be able to keep your visit quiet. But if Elizabeth's warning is heeded he need never know that you spoke to the Queen.'

'How long do you think it will be?' asked Judith anxiously. 'Before he is released, I mean?'

'Her Majesty alone knows,' said Charles ruefully. 'She is capricious. She may keep you waiting, or she may act immediately. Time will tell.'

* * *

Helier swore his allegiance to the Queen two days later, and the Sark party declared their readiness to return immediately.

'Change your mind, child,' pleaded Pierre that evening, having called her to his bedchamber. Their departure for Gravesend had been set for the next day, sailing for the one after. 'Oliver would not expect you to stay on here alone. He may be imprisoned for months——'

'Do not say so!' cried Judith fiercely. 'I believe Her Majesty will speedily relent! But even if she does not, I shall remain here. Mistress de Carteret understands! She has offered for Thomasse to remain with me, and Thomasse is agreeable, so I shall not be entirely alone and the servants hired with the lodgings will remain. Please, Papa! Please do not try to force me!'

'You are a wedded woman now, Judith. You are at your husband's command, not mine. Does he wish you to remain?'

'He has not forbidden it,' said Judith accurately.

'Then I suppose I must bow to your wishes, much as I disagree with your decision. Have you money?'

Judith clenched her fists, determined not to show embarrassment at the question. 'Oliver has funds, but they are not immediately available to me. I would appreciate a loan, Papa.'

'Very well,' agreed Pierre grudgingly. 'I will see to it before we leave.'

'Thank you, Papa.'

If Judith had thought to kiss her father in gratitude, his forbidding expression squashed the idea dead. He was not pleased with her.

She returned to the room they all used for sitting and eating and took up the embroidery she was working. She was not particularly good at it but it kept her hands occupied while she waited for news. Oliver might appreciate a falling collar decorated by his wife's hand. If not, it would not matter, she told herself stoutly. Someone else would.

A disturbance at the entrance caught her attention. She looked across at Margaret, the only other occupant of the room. They heard voices and leaping footsteps on the stairs. Judith sat, needle poised, as though turned to stone.

The door swung back and Oliver stood framed in the opening, the rakish, magical smile she remembered so well curving his lips.

'Marry, angel, but you do look the very picture of a dutiful wife!' he pronounced lightly.

'Master Burnett!' exclaimed Margaret de Carteret. But neither of them heard her.

Judith sat mesmerised. His green eyes sparkled with mischief, yet burned with something which set her heart thumping. She rose slowly to her feet, fighting to draw breath.

Her own eyes luminous with joy, she held out her hands. 'Oh, Oliver! She has released you at last!' she choked.

CHAPTER ELEVEN

HE HAD acquired the pallor of confinement. The darkness of his hair and beard emphasised the paleness of his face. A tide of tenderness welled up inside her, but she couldn't rush forward and fling herself in his arms as she wanted to do with Mistress de Carteret there and with the Seigneur, her father and Sir Charles pressing into the doorway behind him. So she waited for him to stride forward and take her offered hands.

He lifted each one to his lips in turn, and the lingering warmth of his mouth lit a fire in her heart. Then he was bending over Mistress de Carteret's hand and swinging round to greet the men entering behind him.

Charles, of course, had brought him. He gave Judith a broad wink when no one else was looking. 'Just come from the Presence,' he murmured as he made his bow. 'All is forgiven, though he is banished from Court for the nonce.'

'Which,' announced Oliver with a laugh, having overheard the last, 'is no disfavour! The Queen begins her progress soon, and her courtiers must trail about the country after her enduring unnecessary hardships, quarrelling over mean accommodation and generally wishing they were elsewhere. *She* takes her bed with her; *they* must make do with whatever is offered!'

'You should see the length of her baggage train!' interjected Charles with a laugh. 'I must say, I envy you, Oliver.'

'So you may, my friend! I shall be enjoying my own

189

acres! I am come to tell you, wife, that we shall be leaving for Kent on the morrow. I trust you can be ready?'

'Kent?' murmured Judith stupidly. She had anticipated a return to Plymouth.

'My lands at Harvel are but two leagues from Gravesend. I think you will like the manor house.'

'Gravesend?' Helier clapped him on the shoulder. 'We sail from Gravesend on the day following the morrow! We had intended leaving here tomorrow and spending the night on board the *St Ouen*. We were loath to leave Mistress Judith behind, but she refused to quit London without you.'

Oliver's eyes were bright on hers. He did not seem displeased. 'You thought to disobey my orders, wife?'

'I could not leave you, husband,' she said steadily. 'My duty lay here.'

'Oh, valiant heart!' he murmured. ''Tis no wonder you hold me captive with your charm.'

He had spoken low, so that the others would not hear. Judith wondered whether she had mistaken what he said, for she could scarcely believe her ears. She held him captive? 'Twas the other way about!

Yet perhaps she had heard aright, for a rueful smile now turned the corners of his mouth. A reluctant captive, then.

'Mayhap we may travel together,' suggested Helier heartily. 'Our animals are ordered, our baggage ready. 'Tis only Mistress Judith and Thomasse who have still to pack.'

'Thomasse is Mistress de Carteret's maid and was to remain with me,' Judith hurried to explain.

'She may still wish to,' said Margaret cheerfully. 'I think she prefers England to Sark. I can always find another woman to tend me upon my return.'

Judith's face lit up as she turned to the older woman. 'You are kindness itself,' she exclaimed. 'It would please me greatly to have Thomasse as my serving-woman. If you have no objection, husband?'

'I? No, none. I remember her well. There are servants in plenty at Harvel, of course, but it would be good for you to have someone you know.' He swept a brilliant smile around the company. 'So that is settled. I will present myself here one hour after sunrise.'

'I cannot manage a horse,' Judith felt bound to explain. Oliver had to know. Perhaps he guessed, for there had been few horses on Sark.

'Ah, yes, you mentioned animals, Seigneur — but are you not travelling by barge? 'Tis by far the speediest method of reaching Gravesend. Your baggage will be more easily carried so.'

'Barge?' repeated Helier. 'Ha! I had not bethought me of that!'

'Nor I,' admitted Pierre ruefully. ''Tis many years since I was last in London! I had quite forgot its ways.'

'Then I shall arrange it,' said Oliver briskly, 'and be here to escort you to Whitehall steps.'

A gleaming smile lit Judith's face. The thought of sharing a horse with Hiou again had not been comfort-able. And Lambert was yet a stranger. But Oliver had solved her problem at a stroke!

'You can cancel your horses?' he asked, and the Seigneur quickly assured him there would be no problem.

He made ready to depart. There were so many questions she wished to ask! They had not had a single moment alone together and now he was leaving.

'The sun will soon be going down and I have much to arrange before I leave Whitehall,' he excused himself to de Carteret. 'We meet again on the morrow, then. *Adieu*.'

Judith thought perhaps she was included in this general farewell, but no. Oliver came to her and, before the whole company, bent his head and kissed her lips. The heady feel of his mouth on hers almost undid Judith's calm. But the touch was gone in a moment and his brilliant smile encompassed her whole being as he stood back, his hands on her shoulders, and surveyed his prize.

She was as he remembered, his angel. Gentle and yielding, stubborn and independent, yet, he suspected, highly romantic. She saw him as entirely hers because she had rescued him from almost certain death. But he belonged to no one but himself, not even the Queen of England! Certainly not to William Cecil or Francis Walsingham, though being close to the seat of power had its attractions. No, his angel could not shackle him. The *Sea Hawk* called, and he would answer her cry ere long.

He lifted one hand to caress his wife's smooth cheek. 'Until the morrow, angel,' he murmured, and bent to kiss her again. He should have resisted the temptation, for the feel of her made him restless for more intimate commerce. But tomorrow night nothing should prevent him from tasting her honey, of drinking his fill at the fountain of all pleasure.

'God keep you, husband,' whispered Judith.

He swung about, his cape stirring the dust caught in a beam of rosy sunlight. One final, flourishing bow, and he had gone.

A late May heatwave had hit London and they were all glad to leave its fetid streets. Others seemed to have the same idea, for strings of baggage trains headed in

all directions from the Capital, high-born and newly
rich alike travelling on horseback, in litters or, like
them, in barges, to find the fresher air of the
countryside.

'The Queen will not delay her departure long,'
Oliver predicted. 'Whitehall will soon become
untenable.'

Leaning contentedly on the rail beside him, one
hand covered reassuringly by his, Judith knew a luxur-
ious sense of happiness. She rubbed her cheek against
his padded shoulder.

'I am glad we are not to accompany her. Where will
she go?'

She did not see it, for her eyes were fixed on the
river's ever-changing bank, but Oliver's smile held
amused indulgence as he gave reply. The accord
between them grew with every bend and twist of the
water's course. He'd been a monk for so long. The
delights ahead spread a glow of anticipation throughout
his body.

'She makes a regular round of her own palaces—
Richmond, Hampton Court, Greenwich, Eltham and
Windsor mostly but she sometimes visits Hatfield,
Hunsdon or Woodstock. In the summer, though, she
often chooses to go further afield into provincial
England, to stay with one of her richer subjects.'

He turned his head, hoping to glimpse her face. But
all he could see was the glow of a few curls peeping
from under the stylish hat on her head, whose curling
feathers threatened his eye. 'Twas a pity, for the sight
of her serene face brought him inexplicable contentment. But he would have plenty of opportunity later to
indulge in restful contemplation of her features. For
the moment he gave up and joined her in observing the

194   ESCAPE TO DESTINY

passing scene, the bustling wharves and deserted
stretches of marshy bank.

They had already passed the Tower, when Judith
had exclaimed over the threatening sight of the
Traitor's Gate and he had had to reassure her that he
was unlikely to enter there, and Greenwich Palace.
Her ingenuous enjoyment and wonder emphasised her
youth and lack of wordly experience. Rejoicing in
them, he appreciated the sights and sounds anew, as
though through her eyes, while most of his attention
was focused on the warmth of her body, pressed against
his, the small, capable hand clasped in his own, sending
a thrill through him whenever it tightened its grip. His
longing for the night to come intensified with every
moment that passed.

He kept his voice light, allowing no trace of the
emotions seething through him to show, when he took
up the conversation again. 'I know she would like to
visit Bristol and York, but she is a woman who changes
her mind on a whim, so no one can be sure where she
is going until she has actually set out. The people love
to see her, though, and she is always ready to stop to
receive their homage. Perhaps that is why she is so
well-loved.'

'She is, isn't she? Yet she is so. . .so. . .'

'Autocratic?' suggested Oliver on a laugh. 'But then,
she is the Queen and has, so far, managed to keep
both the Pope and the Spanish at bay!'

'Will it come to war?' wondered Judith anxiously.

'Mayhap. But not yet, I think. Meanwhile, perhaps
she will visit Kenilworth again. Leicester has been
building extensively there to make the castle more fit
to receive her. We shall see.'

Yes, they would see. Judith relapsed into contented
silence, enjoying the unexpected pleasure of the jour-

ney. The river held barely a ripple despite a cooling
breeze which blew the many vessels on their courses,
and no qualm of seasickness spoilt the day. Now and
again the Seigneur or her father came over to exchange
a few words, and eventually Mistress de Carteret took
her off, ostensibly to give some parting advice but
mostly to indulge in reminiscences of their stay in
London.

'We shall miss you in Sark,' she said ruefully. 'I
suppose your mother half expected you to stay on
here?'

'I think she must have anticipated it,' retorted Judith
quietly. 'She knows my place is with my husband.'

'But that will not prevent her from wishing you
home! I hope she is recovering her strength.'

'So do I. You will give her my love, mistress? Tell
her I shall hope to visit some time soon. After all, my
husband has a brigantine; it should not be too difficult
to persuade him to bring me!'

Margaret laughed. 'And you will be seasick, no
doubt! Poor Judith, you did not enjoy your journey
here!'

'No, but I would endure worse to see my family
again!'

'I'm sure you would, my dear. You will miss them as
much as they will miss you.'

'A little. But I shall have Master Burnett and others
to keep me company.'

Margaret left the subject then, but Judith wished the
Seigneur's wife had not put her own fears into words.
She already did miss the affection of her mother, the
cheery company of Josué and even the slightly bitchy
exchanges with Genette. And she would miss seeing
Sammy grow up. These were the people who had
always been closest to her. Penna and Marie, too. Soon

she would say goodbye to her father. Thomasse would
be her last remaining link with her old life. Thomasse
knew them all, of course, everyone knew everyone else
on the small island. So they would at least be able to
talk about family and friends together, which would be
something.

The afternoon wore on. Oliver seemed occupied in
an interminable conversation with her father. She
wondered that the two men could find so much to say
to each other. Although they had always been on
friendly terms, apart from the short time during which
her father had doubted Oliver's honour, she would not
have expected either man to become so involved in
deep discussion. Unless her father had brought up the
question of the long-delayed marriage settlement. Yes,
mayhap that was it. However, even as she began to
grow restless for her husband's company the two men
parted and Oliver came across to join her and Margaret
de Carteret, where both ladies had taken refuge from
the sun under a canopy.

'Almost there,' he told them cheerfully. 'Have you
enjoyed the sights?'

'Yes,' Judith assured him. 'I did not imagine the
river to be so well used. We must have passed hundreds
of vessels, both large and small. I wonder why the
Seigneur did not have the *St Ouen* sent up to London.'

'His captain is not familiar with our coastal waters,
nor is he used to navigating this river. That, plus a
contrary wind, is why you landed at Plymouth when
you came. The brig has made a slow but safe passage
round the coast over the past week or so.'

'I see. Well, I for one was glad to land when we did!'

He chuckled. 'I gather you were seasick?'

'You gather right! If only the sea were as calm as
the river!'

'It can be, almost. We must choose good weather for your next venture upon the ocean. An you wish to see the world, you must overcome the nausea. Most people do, after a short while.'

'I have escaped the confines of Sark,' mused Judith, 'and am satisfied with being in England. Though London was dreadful.'

'You thought so?' He quirked a mocking eyebrow. 'Did you not enjoy your visit to Court? Many people would give all they possessed for the chance to be received by the Queen.'

For a moment Judith thought he referred to her second visit, with Sir Charles, and her stomach muscles knotted. But his quizzical look held no censure, only amusement.

'It was certainly an experience I shall never forget,' she said with a meaningful grimace. 'And I'm glad to have been, to have seen her. But after Sark the air of London is so smelly, so full of sulphur and other malodorous things. And the filthy streets, with those kennels running with ordure! I cannot believe such things to be healthy.'

'They are not, hence so many people leave the great cities during the hot summer months.' He drew her a little closer. 'I am glad you do not like London, for neither do I. The months I have been forced to spend there were purgatory. I long for the fresh air of Kent. Even more for the salty tang of the sea!'

'This air is fresh enough.' She wished he had not mentioned his longing to be back at sea.

''Tis much better, I agree, and provided you don't look down into the turgid water you can almost image you are out in the Channel. But see, the masts of the ships anchored off Gravesend are already in view in the distance.'

Judith stared where Oliver pointed and sure enough, a small forest of masts and the odd patch of sail could be seen reaching up above an intervening spit of land where the river curved.

They took up their positions at the rail once more, this time with Judith's eyes straining ahead.

'Will there be horses waiting?' she asked. 'I think I must learn to ride. I had no need on Sark!'

'Nor will there be here, angel, if you are content to ride pillion. I have many trusty men who would carry you wherever you wished. Lambert posted ahead last evening and should be waiting for us with the necessary mounts. You will ride pillion with me.'

Judith's pleasure showed in the radiant smile she turned to give him. 'I shall feel safe with you, husband!'

He grinned. 'You would be equally safe with Lambert, I am convinced, yet I will not entrust you to any other today! We are almost home, wife.'

His voice deepened and the expression on his face started her pulses racing all over again. All he had to do was to look at her with those twinkling green eyes and her bones melted!

He placed an arm about her shoulders, as though knowing the effect he had upon her, knowing she needed his support. 'Look.' He nodded ahead. 'The craft are spreading out into two groups now. That's Tilbury on the north bank.'

The river widened as they approached the towns. The traffic on the water seemed even busier than that just below the Tower, where most of the larger vessels bound for London docked. Some ships rested at anchor, others drifted lazily on the breeze, sails filling or flapping as their masters navigated the channel or sought an anchorage or mooring. Their barge began to steer for the south bank and Gravesend.

'There she is!' exclaimed Helier, coming up behind them. 'There is the *St Ouen*!'

Judith eyed the familiar vessel with a sense of nostalgic relief. Had it not been for her seasickness, which had improved after the first few days, though she had never lost the queasiness entirely, she would have thoroughly enjoyed the voyage. She was glad not to have to endure another, at least not yet, and she had no real regrets over remaining behind in England. How could she have? A new and exciting life lay ahead. A life which would include the man she loved.

But the man she loved had become absorbed in his own interests. Less obviously delighted than the Seigneur, nevertheless his eyes had taken on a new sparkle as he gazed with loving pride at a larger vessel anchored a short distance away, out in slightly deeper water. The tide was low, though, and so despite this it lay tipped over on the mud.

'There is my brigantine, the *Mermaid*,' Oliver informed her with assumed carelessness.

His tone did not deceive Judith. He loved that ship. Why, she could not imagine, for it was not sitting square on the bottom as all the other vessels were.

'She looks a fine boat,' she acknowledged, adding doubtfully, 'but it cannot be very comfortable inside. Everything must be at an awkward angle.'

'True, it is when she's anchored in a fathom of water.' He laughed. 'But at sea it is another story.' His voice took on a new enthusiasm. 'It's a modern design, Judith, one which, given a chance, will revolutionise shipping and make our navy the best in the world. Aboard my ship, you will not be tossed about as you were on the *St Ouen*. Why, you may not feel seasick at all!'

'I shall believe that when it happens,' said Judith

sceptically. 'But why do you think she is so much better?'

'Because the bottom is shaped like a fish! Don't you see? It cuts through the water instead of simply floating on it. That not only means a smoother ride, but it travels faster, too. We can overtake almost any other vessel at sea!'

'Given the right wind,' commented Judith drily. 'Are we going aboard today?'

'Don't be so discouraging,' chided Oliver with a twinkle. 'Any galleon or carrack would be subject to the same wind conditions!'

'Do you often wish to overtake such vessels?' asked Judith, becoming ever more curious.

'Of course,' said Oliver airily, but she sensed a certain constraint in his manner. 'The first to port obtains the best mooring!'

'We shall not beat anything today,' she observed wryly. 'Everything is passing us!'

'But these hired barges have special moorings reserved. We shall not lack for a place to land.'

He proved to be right and before long the party and all its baggage was ashore. The Seigneur's seamen were there with the cock boat, waiting to ferry passengers and luggage out to his ship. As predicted, Lambert was waiting with horses for his master. During the ensuing bustle Judith stood entranced, watching her husband issue orders, greet his sea-captain with obvious delight, engage in a brief but convivial conversation with the sturdy, bronzed, salt-encrusted man, and then turn his attention to assisting Helier to organise his departure.

Oliver had not said whether they were to go aboard the *Mermaid*. The brigantine appeared deserted. Mayhap all the seamen had abandoned their ship while it was lying at so strange an angle. But she had to confess that at close quarters it did indeed look a fine vessel. The high poop, though, had few distinguishing features. She would have expected some painting and gilding, some clever carving. It did have several gun ports along the side. She supposed a vessel used to carry valuable merchandise must be able to defend itself against pirates. Oliver had put all his money into the design, wasting none on mere display.

She had quickly discovered that he was not basically a flamboyant man. Away from the Court, where extravagance and show were necessary, he had chosen to wear a leather doublet over padded brown trunk hose, and although the material had a lighter pattern woven into it the overall effect was workmanlike rather than decorative. His shapely limbs were encased in earthy-coloured hose, his feet in sturdy leather. All the sparkle which so attracted her came from his personality. He could wear sackcloth and still command attention.

The ship was typical of him. The main cabin had windows large enough to offer a fine view. The masts, yards and rigging looked well maintained as far as she could see from a distance, and the visible part of the bottom appeared clean, as though it had been careened and scraped recently. She had no doubt at all that the guns hidden in the ports would be in excellent firing order.

Judith fell to dreaming. If Oliver was right about her seasickness disappearing, she could really look forward to returning to Sark to see her family and friends. She would not wish to stay. The island's limitations became daily more evident. England was green and pleasant once you left the cities behind, and held so much of interest. She must learn to ride a horse. . .

Her musings were interrupted by the return of her

husband. He greeted her with his usual smile, one eyebrow raised in interrogation.

'Tired of waiting yet, angel?'

Judith shook her head. 'There is too much going on for me to be bored! And Thomasse has been keeping me company.'

'All the same, my apologies for leaving you alone for so long. But there was much to arrange. The others are just about ready to leave now, so it is time to make our farewells.'

This was the moment Judith had been secretly dreading, for however much she tried to convince herself that she did not mind, the parting would be a wrench. But in the event it was all over quickly. No one wished to prolong the *adieus*. She took affectionate farewell of Margaret, who made Oliver promise to bring her to Sark soon, took a courteous one from the Seigneur and a rather awkward one from her father.

Pierre cleared his throat, which seemed to be clogged with unexpected emotion. He had never been a particularly close or affectionate parent, yet Judith knew he loved his children and had their welfare at heart, even if he did not show it often.

She made her duty curtsy but then, suddenly, manners were forgotten as she flung herself into his arms.

'Goodbye, Papa. I shall miss you all! Please give my love to Maman for me, and give her this.' She handed him a small box she had been carrying in her pouch. 'A remembrance of me,' she muttered. 'I hope she will like it.'

Although it was not expensive, Judith felt sure her mother would appreciate the silver brooch, exquisitely wrought into the shape of an English rose.

Pierre accepted the box with a grunt, gave her a parting squeeze and turned quickly away. Judith stood with Oliver, his arm about her shoulders, and watched the cock boat row out to the *St Ouen*.

As it disappeared behind the hull of the larger ship Oliver stirred, smiling down into Judith's slightly sad face.

'Come, wife,' he murmured. 'Let us go home.'

CHAPTER TWELVE

HOME lay ahead. A new, half-timbered red brick
manor house which Judith eyed with increasing
excitement.

During the two-hour journey from Gravesend she
had rested comfortably against Oliver's stalwart back,
her hand confidingly upon his waist. How different
from the rather edgy ride from Plymouth with Hiou!
She had been afraid to let her body rest against the
lackey's; such contact would have been both distasteful
and dangerous. But with her husband she could relax,
enjoy the intimacy and view the Kentish landscape with
undiluted pleasure.

Lambert accompanied them, as did Blackler, Oliver's
sea-captain. Another man led the hired pack animals —
not one of Oliver's regular servants; he came with the
horses. Thomasse looked comfortable enough up
behind Lambert, thought Judith with a secret grin.
Each had been suspicious of the other at first, afraid of
a husband's or wife's intrusion between master or
mistress and servant. But Lambert, when he wanted
to, could turn on almost as much charm as his master,
and Thomasse had succumbed, though why he had
wanted to engage her woman's interest rather puzzled
Judith. He might, of course, be hoping to win
Thomasse's favours, but Judith rather suspected
Thomasse to be more than a match for him if he did.
Her strict Presbyterian faith would prevent any descent
into immorality.

Oliver's horse, recognising the terrain and eager to

reach his stable, quickened his pace as they passed through quite a thick copse on a track leading from gatehouse to house, which stood proudly at the top of a small rise against a backdrop of fields, oak, beech and ash trees, and distant hills.

'I love the woods here,' murmured Judith. 'There were so few trees on Sark.'

'They've had to pass laws against felling them here,' admitted Oliver. 'The need for timber is so great. It's wanted for building ships and houses and is still used by most people for heating and cooking despite all the coal being mined these days. Added to which, the new ironworks, and the glassworks which have grown up since the Flemish and Huguenot refugees brought their skills here, burn it in their furnaces at a fearsome rate.'

'They should be forced to burn coal.'

'Wood is cheaper and easier to acquire. But because of those laws, now the house is complete I couldn't fell any more trees if I wanted to.'

'But surely you don't?'

He chuckled. 'Don't sound so disapproving, wife! I do not. Those I cut down to make this path some years ago were enough to provide all the timber I needed for the house I wanted to build in place of the ruin I had to pull down, and I have several coppices on the estate to provide all the firewood we need. What do you think of the house?'

They were drawing near now. His tone had been studiously casual, as it had been when pointing out his brig, but Judith sensed he was waiting for her opinion with a certain defiant pride. She drew an excited little breath.

'I love it! What must you have thought of our farmhouse on Sark? This place looks so spacious, and it has an upper storey, too, and windows in the roof! It is beautiful, Oliver; I love the red bricks, and all those tall chimneys! You must have dozens of fireplaces! When did you build it?'

"Twas finished a couple of years since. I have not spent much time here, I fear.'

Was that regret she heard in his voice? It certainly held a rueful note.

'How can you, when the Queen is so demanding?' she wondered aloud.

'I do not spend all my time at Court. I'm abroad a lot.'

'Where abroad?'

'At sea mostly. Or on the Continent. Antwerp, Paris.' He drew his mount to a stop before the entrance porch. 'Here we are.'

Grooms were waiting to take the horses' heads. In an instant Oliver had thrown his leg over his beast's neck and dismounted. He turned to her, his eyes bright in the twilight, his hands lifted in invitation.

'Come, wife. Let me introduce you to your domain.'

Judith reached down to place her hands on his shoulders and allowed him to lift her from the side-saddle pillion. He let her body slide the length of his and held her close for an endless instant before he released her. Then he took her hand and led her towards the door.

An elderly woman waited on the step inside the porch, and behind her, in what looked like a small hall, several indoor servants had gathered. Oliver greeted the neat, steeple-hooded figure with a wide grin.

'How now, Ursula! Is all well?'

She dipped him a respectful curtsy. 'Aye, master. I trust all will be to your lady's liking.'

He smiled at Judith, drawing her forward. 'Mistress Burnett, this is my housekeeper, Dame Ursula Holt.

The house has been in her care while I have been away.'

The woman curtsied again. 'I hope you will be satisfied, Mistress Burnett.'

She was worried, Judith could tell, but whether it was because she had neglected her duty or thought the new wife might dismiss her, she could not decide. She tried to set the woman's mind at rest on the latter point, at least.

'I am certain you have managed the house well, Dame Holt. I shall need all the help you can give me, for I am unused to ordering such an establishment as this. I am certain we shall work well together.'

For a fleeting second, Judith saw relief and another expression cross the housekeeper's face. Disdain. She should not have admitted to being unused to such a household. Her first mistake.

Oliver seemed not to have noticed. He took her in and greeted all the other servants crowded into the small hall, then presented her as their new mistress. Thomasse had by this time followed them, and he introduced her, too.

A convoy of porters was busy carrying their boxes and baskets through into a much larger chamber to the left, and on up a staircase, which was out of sight. The familiar smell of cooking came from the regions off to the right.

Oliver led her through to the large room, impressive both in size and decoration. Several mullioned, glazed windows allowed the last of the daylight to filter in, though many candles had already been lit. A huge carved stone chimneypiece dominated the scene, oak beams supported the floor above and every wall had been covered with oak panelling. A soft rug or two lay between the heavy furniture, and plenty of cushions in the carved chairs promised comfort.

'I call this the Great Chamber,' Oliver announced proudly. 'Come, angel, let me show you the other rooms.' He marched her across to a door on the far side of the chamber and flung it open. 'Here we can eat in privacy and,' leading her quickly to a second door, 'in here we can sit in comfort, especially during the winter, when this smaller sitting-room is warmer than the Great Chamber.'

Judith had no time to do more than register more oak beams, further panelling and mullioned windows, before he was hurrying her back to the staircase. Their baggage having already gone before them, Judith was not surprised to find her boxes piled in the large bedroom at the front of the house to which he led her, where Thomasse was already disgorging their contents on the huge tester bed. Oliver's things were nowhere to be seen.

As though reading her thoughts, Oliver produced his most roguish smile and chuckled. 'Do not distress yourself, angel. Lambert is unpacking my things through there.' He indicated an opening through to a small closet-room off the bedroom. 'There would not be enough space for all our things in here. And next door,' he dragged her exuberantly back into the gallery and along to the neighbouring room, 'is another private sitting-room, which you may call your own, and beyond that in the west wing is my library.'

'You have so many books?' asked Judith, trying to regain her breath and stop her brain from whirling into an uncontrollable spin.

'Not really, but I must keep records and charts and that is as good a place as any to do it. And along in the other direction are the private offices and a couple of guest chambers, with more round in the east wing. I will show you all of that tomorrow, and you may inspect the servants' quarters, too. They are well housed in the attics or over the stables. What do you think?'

He sounded so boyishly eager that Judith could not help a smile. A smile that told him just how pleased and excited she was at this homecoming to a strange house in a strange land.

'I could never have dreamed of anything half so splendid,' she told him sincerely. 'But, Oliver, I am hungry! The aroma from the kitchens. . .'

He laughed. 'Do not remind me! We have not eaten since noon! Ursula will soon have something ready for us. Where would you like to partake? Here, or in the dining-room?'

The housekeeper had been given no chance to accompany their rapid tour of what she must look upon as her territory. Judith hoped the woman would not feel affronted. She must surely be familiar with her master's mercurial temperament by now and prepared to make allowances. 'Whatever you say, husband,' she murmured, 'though perhaps it would be kind in us to eat downstairs, where Dame Holt can demonstrate her housekeeping prowess?'

'Nonsense! 'Tis late, darkness has already fallen. Everyone will be eager to find their beds! We will make ourselves comfortable here; there can be no need to stand on ceremony. Lambert!'

He raised his voice and his lackey came through from the neighbouring room. 'Lambert, send a message to Dame Ursula asking her to prepare a repast to be brought up here. Mistress Burnett is fatigued. We shall retire immediately we have eaten.'

'Aye, sir.'

Lambert cast them a sardonic look as he left the room. 'Fatigued?' he seemed to be saying. 'There are better reasons for early retirement, indeed there are!'

And Judith had no doubt his master shared his sentiments.

She did herself.

She did not know if it was nerves or excitement making her stomach churn. Hunger gnawed at her vitals or she would not have asked for food, but eating it when it came might be difficult. As the moment for bedding with Oliver drew nearer she told herself not to worry, that all would be well, as it had been on their wedding night. But then she had not known he would leave her without so much as a farewell and subsequently ignore her very existence for six long months. His neglect still rankled. A man who could write a tender love poem when he had nothing better to do could surely have found a moment to write a few reassuring lines to a new wife longing to hear from him. He had not mentioned the poem. She did not dare.

'Change into a night-gown,' Oliver suggested softly. 'I will do the same.'

He dropped a brief kiss on her forehead and disappeared into the adjoining chamber. She heard him begin to whistle as the sound of pouring water told her he was preparing to bathe the dust of travel from his skin.

Thomasse smiled. 'Shall I help you off with your gown, mistress? The boy brought hot water just before you arrived. You will feel fresher for a wash.'

By the time Oliver returned, clad in a flowing gown of oriental silk, Judith had cleansed most of her body and donned the gown she had prepared but not used on her wedding night. Thomasse was still teasing out the tangles from her mistress's hair.

'Leave us.' Oliver softened the order with a smile that had Thomasse blushing. 'Go and ask the house-keeper to show you your quarters. You will need to settle in. I will do that.'

Thomasse looked for permission and Judith nodded. No point in putting off the moment when she and Oliver would be alone together. Thomasse curtsied before picking up her small basket of personal things, bidding them a good night and leaving the room.

Oliver grinned widely as he took her by the shoulders. His manner was easy, his green gaze clear.

'So, my angel,' he murmured, and even as he spoke his voice deepened and small sparks of fire flamed in those mesmeric eyes. 'At last we are alone together again.'

'No thanks to you.'

Judith did not know what made those challenging, accusing words come out, but they did. Her resentment must have gone deeper than even she had guessed. But once they were spoken there was no taking them back.

Oliver's hands dropped to his sides. The fire in his gaze died. He studied her heated countenance from beneath coolly lifted brows.

'Methought we had discussed that matter and reached an understanding. You still hold my neglect against me, it seems.'

He sounded insufferably cold and arrogant. Yet Judith detected a note of hurt beneath the mask. At least, thank God, he did not know that he owed his early release to her special pleading, had not thought her remark referred to that. She had not been thinking of that, either. It had been her hurt, romantic heart speaking, not her realistic, practical self. She had

known he did not love her, so why should she feel so
upset because he had not taken the trouble to send her
a letter? Even if he had, it might not have reached her,
and he had been too honest to pretend one had gone
astray.

In the Fleet it had been the circumstances rather
than her emotions which had made her draw back from
intimacy. Here, there could be no possible reason, and
truly she did not want to prevent. . .

She lifted her hands in a gesture of helplessness.
'Forgive me, husband. I do not know what made me
say that. You are right. The past should be forgotten.
We have all our future before us. I would not wish to
spoil that.'

He relaxed at once, and the usual mischievous smile
flitted across his face. 'Well said, generous angel.' He
made a movement, as though he was about to take her
into his arms, but a servant chose that moment to
knock.

Oliver shrugged, a rueful grimace replacing the
expression of moments before. 'Our repast, no doubt,'
he sighed, before calling out, 'Enter!'

A new convoy of servants carried in dish after dish
of food, setting it down on a linen-covered trestle
hurriedly erected by the first entrants. Last but by no
means least, in Judith's opinion, a flagon of wine and
two goblets were placed upon the board.

'How beautiful they are!' she exclaimed as the servants withdrew, dismissed for the night. She touched
the rim of the exquisite glass reverently.

'Made in Venice,' Oliver explained. 'It is still better
than that made here. Will you take some wine?'

'Please.' She had never felt in more need of its
effects. It might bring courage, and a slight deadening
of her senses to see her through the next hours safely.

Because, suddenly, Oliver was a stranger, the place was equally strange, even the familiarity of Thomasse's presence had been denied her, and the new life she had so been looking forward to only hours ago seemed difficult and daunting, full of unknown pitfalls, like Dame Ursula Holt's attitude, and the need to learn so many new things. Sark had at least been familiar and safe.

And you almost hated it! she reminded herself sternly. Was she so lacking in spirit that new surroundings, a new husband and walking forward into the unknown should make her wish to go back? Of course not! Had she not faced the Queen in her own chamber? And come away with what she had asked for? The night ahead must surely be easy by comparison. Especially as the thing she most desired was to be bedded by her husband, to experience again all the delightful sensations only he had the power to evoke. She had come thus far. There could be no turning back now.

Courteously, he seated her at the board before taking his own chair. He sniffed appreciatively at the stew and offered to serve her some.

'Just a little,' she agreed, 'or I shall not have room for all these fish.'

'And that would be a pity.'

He was laughing at her. But Judith did not care. She couldn't help grinning in return. 'Or this fresh bread and golden butter, not to mention those delicious custards and cherries.'

'That's better. You have a lovely smile, my Judith. I prefer it to your frowns!'

He was teasing now, and she responded in kind. 'I keep my smiles for those who deserve them! Make certain that you do, sir!'

His chuckle restored all her good humour and did much to relieve her tension. She found she could eat with relish, though she partook sparingly. She noted that Oliver did the same. Neither were keen to eat more than just enough to relieve their hunger that night.

At last the inevitable moment came when the meal finished. A last draught of wine, and they rose from the board.

'I must congratulate Dame Holt tomorrow,' remarked Judith, suddenly nervous again, looking for something to say.

'She has but done her duty.'

'But done it well. Do you not congratulate Lambert or your sea-captain on a job well done?'

He grinned. 'Of course. And flail them with my tongue when they fail! You must learn to do the same, angel, or service here will soon deteriorate.'

'I shall make my displeasure plain, of course.'

Words. What good were words? She stood like a ninny, unsure what to do. On their wedding night Oliver had taken things in hand from the moment they were alone, but tonight, somehow, he appeared reluctant. Could he possibly be nervous, too?

The thought caused her some amusement. He saw the tiny smile that curved her beautiful mouth and cursed himself for a fool. Why was he restraining himself, suffering untold frustration, because he was afraid to show her just how much he wanted — nay, needed — her? But afraid he was, for if she knew the hold she had over him she would wield her power and he would never be a free man again. Yet she was, after all, his angel. And his wife.

'Something amuses you, angel,' he said. 'Tell me what it is.'

She regarded him steadily, unsure how to respond. Then decided to be honest. 'Nothing, really. But we. . .well, we seem so uneasy together all at once. Yet on Sark. . .'

That was all it took. Next instant she had been swept off her feet and deposited on the huge bed. Oliver did not wait for longer than the instant it took to throw off his robe, but followed her down immediately. His lips found hers and then everything else faded into insignificance.

Her bones liquified. He could do with her exactly as he liked. What he liked was to remove her night-gown, to pull her to him so that soft flesh moulded to hard muscle.

His breath fanned her face, warm and redolent with wine. She felt the feather-light kisses on her lids, her cheeks, her jaw. More than that, she thrilled to the feel of his sensitive hands roving over her inert body, sending signals of exquisite pleasure to rouse it to new and urgent response.

A small, throaty moan escaped her as she ran her hand over his wide shoulder and on down his strong back. Her fingers lovingly traced the furrows where the whip had fallen, the injuries healed now but leaving permanent scars. Her reward came in an answering groan and a sudden breathless urgency.

He murmured something inarticulate as he ran his fingers down her rounded thigh and shifted to sprawl across her, lowering his mouth to her waiting breasts.

She clasped his shoulders fiercely, hugging him to her as his mouth worked merciless miracles on her senses. Oh, how she had longed for this! How readily her body responded to his magical touch! Yet, even as he poised himself above her, intent upon the ultimate joining, a small part of her brain held aloof. Everything was not quite as it should be. He did not love her, and deep down she still felt angry at his neglect. So, pleasurable as it was, she did not experience the same ecstasy as on their first union. And although Oliver collapsed, sated, crushing her under his weight, his release total and evident, she sensed that he, too, had been holding some part of himself back. Vaguely disappointed, she wondered why.

Recovered, Oliver rolled aside and settled her head on his shoulder, brushing strands of hair from her forehead.

'Angel,' he murmured. 'Oh, angel, how I have longed for you these months past!'

'I am certain,' said Judith carefully, 'you managed to find plenty of consolation elsewhere.'

He stirred at that. 'You still believe that?' he demanded angrily. 'Have I not told you otherwise?'

She wanted to believe him, but —— 'Then why —— ?'

Judith bit off the words. She had upbraided him enough for not sending for her. He had had his reasons, valid to him if not to her. And now she had met the Queen she could begin to understand.

The candles still burnt and by their gleam she saw the grim set of his lips as he completed the question for her. 'Why did I not send for you, wife? I thought I had explained, more than once. . .'

'And I do understand, now,' she admitted quickly, already regretting the impulse which had caused his anger. 'Please forgive me. I did not mean to carp.'

'I know it troubles you, but try to believe that I regret the past as much as you do. Ours was a strange marriage, wife, not begun in the best of circumstance, but I believe we can deal well enough together, for all that.'

His anger had gone. Judith snuggled closer and ran

her mouth over the soft scattering of hair on his chest. It was her peace offering and he accepted it as such. His arms tightened.

'Angel, you will make a dignified and efficient mistress of my household, and a loving, capable mother.' He paused a moment, then added lightly, new laughter filling his voice, 'And we do seem to suit well enough in the marriage bed.'

That was undeniable. Whatever her mental reservations, her longing to be wanted for more than her qualities as housekeeper and mother, her body was ready to respond again. She felt him stir against her and her breathing quickened.

'Wanton,' he teased, and now that merry, delightful smile was back on his face. She saw it only for a moment, though, for he sprang from the bed to douse the candles, leaving her longing only for his return.

When he did, he drew the curtains around the bed, not fully, for the night was warm, but enough to ensure them intimate privacy.

'Marry, angel,' he breathed, ''tis small wonder I desired to bed with no other woman!'

'Can that really be true?'

She held her breath waiting for his response. Her remark — it had not been intended as a question — had been indiscreet, born of her need to believe him.

'By the life of God!' She had angered him yet again. 'How many more times must I admit to my damnable weakness?'

He considered his desire a weakness. She would rather not have known. But believe him she must.

'Oh, Oliver! Of course I believe you! How could I not?' The sincerity in her voice cooled his temper immediately. She felt the taut muscles relax against her. 'It is just that I find it so difficult to understand

how you can prefer me above all other women. Me,
Judith Le Grand, a nobody from Sark. When there are
so many beautiful, high-born women for you to choose
from. . .'

'Not one of them possesses your fresh charm,' he
murmured, running his lips over her velvety skin. 'Nor
your simplicity of character, your beguiling, wayward,
stubborn innocence! Believe me, angel, I am not used
to being so bound in a woman's toils and do not find it
a comfortable experience.'

The rueful note was back in his voice again, hiding,
she thought, a real feeling of resentment. To coax him
out of his mood, she ran a light finger down his
breastbone and gave a gurgle of warm laughter. 'I will
see that you do not regret it!'

'Oh, angel!' He was laughing, too.

Now she was enfolded in warm intimacy, swept along
on a tide of grateful, glorious emotion which could lead
to only one end. And this time, needing to recoup his
own resources, Oliver took his time. And because he
wanted to please her he used all his skill. So Judith
rediscovered that first, abandoned joy and was finally
washed up on the strange, elusive shores of
wonderland.

After a while, long after they had both regained the
ability to think, Oliver withdrew. She wanted to keep
him there, sheathed in her warmth, knew that he had
wished to remain, and had done so for as long as
possible.

He grunted, settled her head on his shoulder once
more and said, 'That was better for you, wife.'

Judith was startled. 'How did you know?'

'Oh, innocent one! A man can tell when he pleases
a woman, just as she can tell when she pleases him.

You knew, did you not, that I had found ecstasy in you?'

'Yes.' The admission came shyly.

'We do indeed suit each other, wife. I had long feared a cold, unrewarding marriage bed endured for the sake of heirs. I thank God I found you.'

This was more than she could have expected. She reared up on an elbow and ran soft fingers round his bristly chin. 'And I thank Him, too.' She leaned over and, for the first time, kissed him freely, tenderly on the mouth. 'I had feared being forced to wed with someone I could not——' she almost said love, but stopped herself just in time '—bear to have touch me. We are both fortunate, husband.'

'Destiny,' he murmured, 'is a strange force. Had I not been washed up on your island's shore——'

'Had I not been out watching the last of the storm——'

'We would not have met. Or mayhap we would. Had you accompanied your Seigneur to Court, as you did.'

'You would not have noticed me.'

'Fishing for more compliments, angel?' He sounded indulgent, on the brink of sleep.

'No,' she whispered. 'Just being practical.' And she would be, in future. No more flights into the realms of love and romance, where Oliver could not follow. She kissed him again, a lingering caress which fused their lips together in mutual tenderness. 'God give you good rest, husband,' she whispered. But Oliver was already asleep.

She listened to his steady breathing for some time, thinking. She was indeed blessed. She must keep to her resolution, must not pine for the impossible—his love—but must make the best of what she had. A passionate husband, a beautiful home and, at long last, escape from the confining life on Sark.

When she woke it was to find Oliver leaning on one elbow studying her face in the dawn light filtering through the curtains. His finger trailing along her jaw must have woken her. She smiled sleepily, then thrilled to the look in his green eyes. He did not have to ask. She moved instinctively towards him, her body flowering into new, expectant life.

Half an hour later a loud rap on the door urged Oliver up to sit on the edge of the bed and reach for his gown.

'Who is it?'

'Lambert, master. With hot water.'

Oliver rose, tucked the covers around Judith, giving her a wink the while, then called for Lambert to enter. Thomasse was not far behind him. Oliver and his lackey disappeared into the small adjoining chamber and Judith was free to have Thomasse attend her.

Her first night as true wife to Oliver and mistress of Harvel Manor had come and gone. She could look forward to the future with greater confidence.

CHAPTER THIRTEEN

IT BEING Sunday, they were bound to attend church, and Captain Blackler accompanied them. All the servants went too; if they hadn't Oliver would have been responsible for paying their fines.

Aware that the villagers, including the priest, were eyeing her with unconcealed curiosity, Judith walked sedately by Oliver's side and sat quietly through a service she found somewhat tedious, for it held neither the beauty of those she had attended in Westminster Abbey nor the fire engendered by Pastor Brevint on Sark. But the village lay within the boundaries of Oliver's estate and the people present were therefore his tenants. She studied them with an interest equal to theirs, though not quite so blatantly. It was now her duty to visit them in their homes. They did not look too desperately impoverished, but she must discover more of their circumstances so that she could offer help where it was needed. This was something she really wanted to do.

In the churchyard afterwards the women curtsied and the men touched their woollen hats in respectful acknowledgement of her position. Oliver chatted for a few moments with one or two of the men and their wives, quite at ease with his tenants.

On their return to Harvel Manor Dame Holt immediately sent the servants scurrying about their business before, stiffly formal, she approached Oliver.

'Master Burnett, perhaps your wife would like to

inspect the kitchen and store-rooms now? She can see your meal in preparation.'

Judith spoke up. She had no intention of being ignored.

'Thank you, Dame Ursula.' If Oliver could address the woman so, so could she. 'Nothing would please me more.'

The housekeeper inclined her head. 'This way, mistress.'

Oliver grinned. 'I'll wait for you in the Great Chamber, with Blackler. Don't be long!'

Judith nodded but made no promise, because she was determined to see everything there was to be seen. But if Dame Holt thought to pull any wool over her eyes she had a shock coming!

Dame Ursula quickly dispelled her suspicions on that score, taking her on a detailed inspection of the busy kitchen and the extensive store-rooms before leading her down into the cellar, dug out of the soil beneath part of the east wing to provide a cool place to store the barrels and flasks of ale and wine.

'The manor is extremely well stocked with food and drink,' Judith observed as they returned to the kitchen, where the fires blazed despite the promised heat of the day, for a haunch of venison and several fowl had been left to roast on a spit turned by a red-faced urchin, and a number of kettles hung on cranes above the flames, their bubbling contents giving off enticing aromas which made Judith long for dinner. 'I believe it could withstand a siege!'

'A prudent housekeeper plans for every eventuality,' responded Dame Holt austerely.

'Naturally,' replied Judith calmly. 'Though I do think a siege a trifle unlikely, don't you, Dame Ursula? The remark was intended as a compliment.' She smiled. 'Not to be taken too literally.'

Dame Holt returned a reluctant relaxation of the tightly folded line of her lips. It could scarcely be termed a smile. 'Then I thank you, Mistress Burnett.'

'Excellent. We shall deal well together if you will not always assume that I am criticising, even when my orders go contrary to what has gone before. You have done an excellent job in the past. I appreciate the care you have taken of my husband when he has been here, and of his household when he has not, which I gather has been much of the time.'

'I have done my best, mistress.'

'I know you have, and I'm quite sure you will carry on doing so. And now, I must confess that the walk to church has made me hungry! The food smells delicious. I shall look forward to sampling it at dinner.'

'Thank you, mistress. I am always at your service. If anything is not to your liking you have but to say.' Dame Ursula's tone had softened and she managed to smile. 'The meal will be served in half an hour.'

Judith rejoined Oliver feeling that something had been established with the housekeeper. The mistress of Harvel Manor must ultimately order the household, not the housekeeper, however efficient the latter might be.

They ate in the small dining-room off the Great Chamber. Judith found the presence of so many servants daunting, but Oliver took no notice of them and she soon grew used to their presence.

John Blackler joined them for the meal. The two men discussed all manner of things and Judith listened avidly, content to absorb knowledge. Blackler, it became evident, knew far more of her husband than she did. They talked a lot about the brig and voyages past and to come. Every now and again, though, they exchanged a look and changed the course of their conversation. She felt excluded. Oliver was keeping something from her, but what?

After being so scratchy the previous night she feared to anger him again by asking questions. She must be patient. Already the tensions between them had lessened; she sensed a growing comradeship and treasured it. She must show trust. He would tell her his secrets in good time.

In the cold light of day she wondered at herself for being so difficult last night, questioning and probing when she should have been revelling in her husband's desire. She knew why she had done it, of course. She had felt lost, adrift in an uncertain future with a man she scarcely knew. The prospect had seemed exciting until that final moment when, parted from family and friends, the security of the familiar, without a link other than that provided by Thomasse, she had been faced with the full implication of her hasty marriage. During the frustrations of waiting for her husband to claim her, dreams had kept her sane. Now she had to make them come true.

She knew for certain now that Oliver did still want her. He was taking the trouble to treat her with tenderness and consideration—when he was not absorbed in conversation with Captain Blackler, she acknowledged wryly.

But after dinner Blackler went off about his own business while Oliver took Judith to inspect the formal gardens. Happy to have her husband to herself again, Judith exclaimed her delight at the neat boxwood hedges dividing the beds, at the marigolds, gillyflowers and other blooms providing a riot of geometrical colour. But best of all she liked the roses, blooming against the arches and walls, and the small trees, some already bearing fruit, scattered around the edges of the formal beds to give privacy and shade.

'The garden in Sark should be quite colourful by now,' she remarked. 'I do hope Maman is able to enjoy it. Of course, the trees I planted will not give much shade for a year or two, but oh, how I hope it turns out as well as this one!'

Oliver's arm lay casually about her shoulders. 'You will be able to claim credit for your garden, angel, but I can claim none for this. 'Twas all laid out by the husbandman who works under my bailiff. Between them, they have done an excellent job.'

'Which will afford me great pleasure, husband!'

They strolled on to the vegetable garden. Here Judith recognised beans and peas, carrots, parsnips and turnips. A clump of tall, leafy green things with earth banked up about them defeated her.

'What are they?'

Oliver grinned. 'Leeks. Did you not grow them on Sark? They add good flavour to stews.'

'Oh. No. Oh, look! Strawberries!'

'And here,' announced Oliver triumphantly, 'is a ripe one!' He picked it and fed it to her. Judith opened her mouth and he popped in the tiny berry. 'They should all be ripening soon. We shall be in for a feast!'

'I think the gardens here are wonderful, Oliver. How far do your lands stretch? What crops do you grow?'

'Further than we can walk, angel. We will mount up tomorrow and my bailiff shall accompany us on a tour of the estate. You shall see the wheat growing and the sheep grazing. . .'

His pride could not be hidden. He obviously loved the place, for all he had spent little time there. And he was entitled to his pride, for this was not inherited

wealth he was showing her, but possessions bought
with riches he had worked and suffered to attain.
Mayhap, she thought wistfully, his ideas would alter
now. Mayhap he would be happy to spend more time
in such a lovely house. Now he had a wife to make it
home.

'Will you teach me to ride?' she asked.

'Of course. You shall begin tomorrow! I will have
my marshal of the horses saddle a quiet mare for you
and you shall ride out, on a leading rein for safety. By
the time we return from our inspection you should be
able to manage the beast well enough to amble about
the estate. The finer points of horsemanship can come
later.'

'Thank you! I shall enjoy that so much! I do not
mind riding pillion with you, husband, but I could not
bear always to have to do so. I did not enjoy the
journey from Plymouth, mounted behind my father's
lackey.'

'I don't suppose you did. The Queen will never ride
except when she is on her own horse, and I can
understand the feeling. I should hate to be dependent
on another myself.'

They had wandered back into the flower garden.
'Shall we sit on that bench?' suggested Judith.

The sun beat down on them and Judith was glad to
reach the seat set under an arch of roses. The perfume
from the blooms filled the air. She took a deep breath.

'I would not mind,' she murmured, 'if I never saw
London again!'

Oliver still had his arm about her. He drew a breath,
too, but it was not the scent of roses he sought, but of
her. 'Twas far more heady. Even in an unassuming
gown of brown damask she had stood out in church as
a woman worthy of the position she now held. The

villagers had automatically treated her with all the respect due to the mistress of Harvel. She would have no problem holding her own here. Or anywhere else.

He drew yet another breath. Next moment he had her firmly held in his arms, his mouth seeking hers. He had not even intended to kiss her, yet when he found her lips, soft and pliant under his, instantly his passion rose.

'Angel,' he groaned, 'what are we to do?'

'Retire to the privacy of our bedchamber?' she suggested huskily.

'Marry, wife, but I confess I shall have difficulty in reaching the house!' He laughed breathlessly. 'But I shall try!'

He leapt to his feet, pulling her up with him. Hand in hand they raced across the gardens, in through the porch and on up the stairs, tumbling into their room and on to the bed.

'This,' murmured Oliver between kisses, 'was a splendid idea!'

And in this respect, thought Judith as she let herself sink into rapturous response, Oliver was all she could ask of a husband.

He kept his promise and the following day they rode out to inspect the estate. Both his bailiff, Huddy, and Blackler accompanied them. All three men took it upon themselves to offer their advice on riding, although it was Oliver who kept a firm hold of the leading-rein. Judith enjoyed herself, quickly picking up the essentials of controlling a horse — particularly one which could not possibly bolt! They penetrated deeply into Oliver's domain, inspecting fields of wheat and other crops, flocks of sheep grazing quietly in one grassy field, a herd of cows in another and nearer the

house, in a large paddock, several mares either in foal
or accompanied by their young.

These interested Judith most. 'You breed horses!
How lovely!' she exclaimed.

Oliver chuckled. 'I have little choice, angel.' His
special name for her came out despite the presence of
the other men. 'Since I own a park of more than four
miles in circumference I must keep four breeding mares
of not less than fourteen handfuls high, and they must
be covered by a stallion of at least that size.'

'Why?' asked Judith, who had dismounted to fondle
one of the frisky colts.

'They would be needed in time of war. Small horses
are no good for carrying a man in armour!'

'All this talk of war!' exclaimed Judith as she was
lifted back into the saddle.

'We're already at war with Spain in all but name,'
said Blackler with a shrug. 'Not here on land, perhaps,
but certainly at sea and in the New World.'

'Do you —— ?' began Judith, but was quickly interrupted by Oliver.

'Enough talk of war! 'Tis far too fine a day to worry
our heads over matters which are of no concern to us!
Come, wife, let us see if you can keep your seat at a
canter!'

And soon, exhilarated and happy, Judith had forgotten the Spanish threat in the enjoyment of her first real
taste of fast solo travel on horseback.

The next day Blackler returned to Gravesend to
oversee the readying of the *Mermaid* for another
voyage. There was, apparently, much to do. And when
all was ready, Oliver would sail with her.

This prospect proved to be the only blight on Judith's
happiness over the next two weeks. Even the news that
Norfolk had at last been beheaded could not shake it.

'So Elizabeth finally made up her mind,' mused Oliver. 'He was our last duke. Let us hope that is the end of the Ridolfi affair.'

She dismissed the news from her mind. It did not concern her. Shortly she would have to relinquish her husband's precious company and remain at Harvel on her own. She did not relish the thought. But at least the housekeeper had dropped her antagonism. Judith almost thought of Dame Ursula as a friend, the relationship between them had become so pleasant.

At last the dreaded day arrived. A messenger came from Gravesend to say that the brigantine would be ready to sail on the tide the following afternoon. Oliver immediately transformed from the indulgent husband and astute landowner into the exuberant adventurer she had first known.

Of course she loved him that way just as much as any other, but wished he did not yearn to be off at sea. She did not think trading held much interest for him these days. The vessel was not bound for Antwerp. In fact, London was fast becoming the financial and trading centre of the world now that most of the Flemish bankers had fled the Inquisition and settled there.

'Where are you headed?' she asked him that night. 'Will you be away for long?'

'I have business in various ports,' he responded vaguely. 'I cannot say how long it will take. But never fear, wife, I will send a messenger ahead to warn you of my return.'

'I shall be waiting,' she replied quietly. Remonstrations and pleas would do no good. They would merely stiffen his resolve. And she was not a clinging sort of person. She would survive without him for as long as it took him to return.

But oh, how she would miss the nights spent in his arms! That night should have been one of the best ever, for Oliver appeared almost desperate to possess her. But Judith was unable to respond with her usual abandon. The morrow and separation loomed too close. Why did he have to go?

And Oliver, desperate for her, was equally desperate to escape her bonds. Were he not careful he would lose the will to leave her side, to carry on with the dangerous yet stimulating, rewarding life he had carved out for himself. And that, he swore, he would never do. He would never be chained to any woman, however lovely and desirable. . .however much he enjoyed her lively yet tranquil company. He was a man, free to come and go as he pleased, not some flunkey happy to hang around waiting for tit-bits from his mistress's hand. Or some deranged lover expiring for lack of a kind word from his beloved. He had noticed her slight abstraction, and knew its cause. She did not want him to leave her.

And as he cradled her in his arms, feeling the soft whisper of her breath stir the hairs on his chest, he sighed deeply. He did not want to leave. Yet self-respect dictated that he must.

After her husband's departure the weeks passed on leaden feet. Judith filled in her time with riding lessons, tending the garden, in desultory needlework and in walking. She had always walked on Sark and even riding could not take the place of a brisk stroll about the estate with Thomasse in attendance. When she visited the village she went on foot. She had made a start on calling on the tenants there, and been welcome in most homes. The women in particular seemed happy that someone was taking an interest in them and the children. She scarcely saw any of the men, for they were all out about their duties. But she heard few complaints. Huddy, it seemed, was an excellent bailiff, carrying out Oliver's wishes to the letter. And Oliver had proved to be an unusually considerate landlord.

'Pay the maximum wage allowed, be generous with food and clothing and keep their homes in good repair and you have happy, conscientious husbandmen,' he had said on one occasion when they were discussing the estate.

Judith felt his sentiments did him credit. They echoed hers exactly. But then, so many of their ideas were similar. It was only in temperament they were so different. He so restless, she so content now she had escaped to England. Yet one complemented the other. She recognised that his energy and enthusiasm enlivened her, while feeling pretty sure he found a certain peace in her more measured approach to life.

But she did wish he loved her. That would make everything perfect.

August was striding fast into September before the promised messenger came from Gravesend. Oliver was back!

Even so, the voyage had been short by most standards. Mayhap the promise of equinoctial storms had driven the brig back to port. The weather had become rather unsettled of recent days, and a storm never seemed far off. But that day the sun shone down, warming a stiff breeze. The man arrived shortly after midday. Judith made an instant decision.

'Give the seaman some food and ask him to wait. Have my mare saddled,' she ordered. 'I will ride to Gravesend with the fellow.'

As a lackey hurried away to pass on her order, Thomasse remonstrated.

'Mistress, do you think it wise to place yourself in the charge of a strange man? Should I not come with you? Or one of the men from here?'

'Do not fuss, Thomasse! I shall be quite safe with Oliver's seaman, I am certain. Can you imagine him sending anyone he thought other than trustworthy? Of course not! And I can manage quite well without you for one night, be it spent in an inn or on board the *Mermaid*. I intend to surprise my husband, and do not want a string of servants following me!'

'Mistress, I still do not think —— '

'Enough, Thomasse! I know you have my welfare at heart, that this is not Sark and there are more dangers here, but I must go! I have never seen the *Mermaid* at close quarters, never been aboard. Now is my chance! Come now, pack me a small bundle, a change of gown and just enough for one night.'

It would not be dark for many hours yet. She had plenty of time to ride to Gravesend and find Oliver before the sun set. She could not admit it to Thomasse, of course, but her urgent wish to rush off to meet him stemmed from a desire to make up for her lack of response on their last night together. He must have noticed, and probably thought she was sulking, though he had not accused her of it. He had just appeared even more anxious to be off the next morning, leaving long before he had real need. She wanted above all things to put matters right between them.

The seaman answered to the name of Rufus, probably because of the colour of his hair. Tough, youngish and armed with a useful-looking cutlass, he looked more than capable of defending her from all but the

most vicious attack. She found him not best pleased at
having to escort her to the ship.

'The master said nowt about any such thing,' he
grumbled. 'What if he don't agree?'

'Then I must take the blame!' Judith treated him to
one of her rare, beguiling smiles. 'Come, man, let us
not waste time! Or must I order one of the grooms to
accompany me, and tell my husband of your reluctance
to serve me?'

'Nay, mistress, 'tis not that, 'tis just that I do not
know the master's mind——'

'Then let us go and find it out!'

She gave him another smile and he succumbed.

Six miles was further than she had ridden beyond the
estate before, but Judith knew her horsemanship to be
sound. She had had an excellent teacher. Her mare
was slow, reluctant to move at more than a walk, but
otherwise they made good time, unburdened by anything other than her bundle, strapped to the back of
Rufus's saddle. His horse had already travelled the
road once and was not unwilling to drop his pace to
match the mare's, though Judith could see impatience
written all over Rufus's ruddy face. Still, he proved a
solicitous escort, warning her of dangers she might not
have noticed — deep pot-holes and overhanging
branches being the main hazards on that road, not a
busy one. As they approached Gravesend, the forest
of masts signalling its location long before the buildings
came into view, the shadows had lengthened considerably. She estimated she still had a couple of hours
before the sun set.

'I must return this here beast to its livery stable,'
Rufus pointed out as they entered the town. 'You'd
best leave your animal there, too, mistress. The walk
down to the quayside bain't no distance at all.'

'Very well. Is there an inn where we can obtain refreshment?'

'At the livery. You could take a room there. The master often uses it.'

Judith hid a smile. Rufus had guessed her reason for wishing to stop at an inn. The ride had made her hot and untidy, in no fit state to greet a returning husband!

'A good idea,' was all she said. But the room would serve as a refuge should she not be welcome aboard the *Mermaid*. The brigantine would probably be crowded with rough seamen, and Oliver might prefer her not to spend long aboard. He might not allow her on board at all. But that possibility she refused to contemplate.

Rufus went off with the horses while Judith ventured inside the inn. It was not a place she would normally visit unescorted, but Rufus assured her the landlord was well acquainted with Master Burnett and would do his best to make the master's wife comfortable. After he'd stabled the animals he'd wait for her in the courtyard.

Judith was shown to a small, private chamber tucked under the eaves. It appeared clean and modestly comfortable.

'Master Burnett often uses this room, mistress, when he's ashore,' puffed the innkeeper's wife. 'He finds it comfortable enough.'

'Thank you, I'm sure I shall too. Can you have a can of hot water brought up to me?'

'In less than five shakes, mistress. 'Tis always kept on the fire. Is there anything else you need?'

'Nothing, thank you.'

Judith washed her face and hands, changed into the new gown she had brought with her and set the matching high-crowned hat on her head over the linen cap protecting her curls. The dark green suited her. She hoped Oliver would like it.

He had left her with more than enough money to meet the cost of a new wardrobe and any household expense she might incur or need to meet. Dame Ursula had relinquished the dispensation of housekeeping funds reluctantly but with good grace.

Harvel Manor lacked for little. Some of the things there had come from faraway places, brought back after long and hazardous voyages. Other things had been fashioned by local craftsmen to Oliver's exacting demands. She had appreciated the elegance and luxury of the place more with every week that passed, for most of the treasures it contained were locked away, seen only when the gold or silver needed cleaning or the jewellery was required for adornment. The Venetian glass which had so impressed her on her arrival had proved to be only one example of the beautiful things Oliver had collected over the years.

What had he brought back this time? she wondered. And where from? Had he sailed as far as the Mediterranean Sea? Pirates posed a danger there. But then, they did in the Channel, too. The Sea Beggars were not particular which ships they plundered. No wonder the brig carried guns!

She reached the foot of the narrow stairs and began the journey along a dark passage to the door. Arrested by the sound of men's voices, she paused before passing a door which had just been opened, fearing a collison with whoever emerged. A Spanish voice said something about *Dios* and an English voice replied.

'God will be with me, never fear. I have waited these months to take my revenge. She killed my master. She will not be long in following him to the grave.'

'You are certain the woman is at Nonesuch?' asked a third voice.

'I have it from one of the servants there. If the Court has moved on, I shall follow. All I have waited for was the Church's blessing. Now you have given it, Father, I can go about my task with a clear conscience.'

'You may indeed.' The accented voice must belong to the Spaniard. 'The Pope himself has blessed the enterprise. The Duke of Norfolk was a devoted Catholic. His murder should be revenged.'

'Then I will depart immediately. Farewell, sirs.'

Judith stood transfixed. Three months had passed since Norfolk's execution. Yet here were men still talking of revenge for his death.

There was nowhere for her to go, even had she had the wit. The men emerged from the room to find her standing there. That she had heard at least part of their conversation was evident from the shock mirrored on her face. The leader, the owner of the third voice, a noble by his dress, reacted instantly.

He took Judith's arm in a cruel grip and a strong hand covered her mouth.

'Who is she?' hissed the man who must be a Spanish Jesuit, though he was dressed in ordinary garb, for members of that Order were considered traitors in England.

'How should I know?' The man holding her shook her arm roughly. 'Do not scream, or you will die instantly.' The threat looked real enough, for Norfolk's erstwhile servant had a dagger in his hand. 'Tell me who you are, what is your business here?'

Judith, thoroughly terrified, kept enough wit to realise that she did not want to draw Oliver into danger. 'Judith,' she muttered. 'I am a traveller, no more, staying at the inn.'

The man with the dagger spoke sharply. 'We can't let her go. She heard too much. I should never reach Nonesuch and you would find yourself in the Tower, my lord.'

'There is only one thing for it,' said his lordship after a moment. They had hustled Judith into the room they had come from. 'You must put her aboard your ship, Father. Take her to sea. . .'

'She must be cleansed of heresy before she dies!'

'Then cleanse her! 'Tis your duty, Father. Ours is to see that the heretic Elizabeth pays for her crimes!'

'Very well. But you, my lord, must help me to get her aboard. As for you, Stalker, you had best be on your way. 'Twill be nightfall soon, and the more distant you are from here by then the better.'

'My horse is already saddled. *Adieu*, sirs. I rely on you to see that no harm befalls our plan.'

The assassin opened the door, peered carefully into the passage, and disappeared. By this time a dagger had appeared in His Lordship's hand. He pressed the tip against Judith's ribs.

'Walk quietly with us,' he hissed, 'and you will prolong your life.'

'You have no need to die at all, my dear,' offered the Jesuit. 'Repent and take an oath of silence and you may live.'

'How do you know I am a heretic?' gasped Judith. 'I could be a good Catholic——'

'I think not, my dear. A good Catholic would have rejoiced in our plan, not stood rigid with shocked disbelief. Come, let us make for the ship.'

She had little choice. Rufus should be waiting for her. Would he come to her aid?

There turned out to be little hope of that. As they passed the taproom the Jesuit called in and several men

rose to join them as they left the building. Four husky
seamen. Rufus would be able to do nothing. Except
mayhap follow. . .

She must not draw their attention to him.

Rufus was there. He started forward, surprise on his
face, Judith looked him straight in the eye without a
trace of recognition. The lord still had hold of her arm,
still had the dagger, hidden by his cloak, pressed
against her ribs. She shook her arm, as though to throw
off his hold. He merely tightened his grip.

'Be sensible,' he hissed.

But from the corner of her eye Judith could see the
dawning of anxiety on Rufus's face, and was satisfied.

She left the courtyard of the inn convinced Oliver's
man was close behind.

CHAPTER FOURTEEN

THEY hustled Judith through the streets and to the waterfront. There a small cock boat waited, drawn up on the mud. One of the seamen picked her up, carried her out and literally threw her into the bilge-water sloshing about in the bottom while the two conspirators climbed aboard. The crew pushed off, clambered in and began to row.

Only then did the lord pull her up to sit on a thwart beside him, her bottom wet and her new skirts dripping water.

'Sensible wench,' he commented languidly. Now the immediate danger of her drawing attention to them as they walked to the quayside had receded, he was inclined to be more relaxed, even indulgent.

Judith ignored him. Her eyes were fixed on the receding shore, where Rufus lounged against a barrel. What was the man doing? Why didn't he rush off to find Oliver? She seethed inside until the truth dawned. As the cock boat drew purposefully near to a small vessel lying at anchor in shallow water and a line was thrown down from it, he straightened and began to stride away. He had been waiting to discover her destination. Oliver's man was no fool!

But where was the *Mermaid*? She scanned the nearby ships anxiously, but saw none that resembled her husband's brigantine. It must be moored in a distant part of the anchorage.

The journey out had not taken long. Almost before she knew it she was being bundled up a rope-ladder

and hauled over the gunwale to end up sprawled on
the deck. Again, the lord helped her up, this time to
her feet. She shook his hand off, straightened her hat
and rubbed at her bruises.

'Don't touch me!'

He laughed. 'And who is to prevent me? But do not
fear. I have no interest in your charms. Of course, the
sailors might be glad of the chance to sample your
wares, for although there are more willing wenches to
be had in Gravesend they will soon be left behind. . .'

He trailed the sentence off, an unfinished threat.

So they would be sailing soon. On the tide, she
supposed. It had looked to be rising. Activity on deck
had already begun.

She quaked inside, but would not let him see her
fear. It was the Jesuit who terrified her, with his hints
at 'persuasion' and his Order's reputation. So far he
had ignored her, but how long would that last? And
when he did begin to question her, what chance would
she have of withstanding his torture? Look what just
such a one had done to Oliver! He might not flog her,
but the Order had other means of persuading women
to recant. And of extracting oaths sworn on the Bible.
She wouldn't be able to withstand the pain, she knew,
and afterwards, although she would not have meant
what she confessed or swore, she would still feel bound,
for one could not challenge the authority of God's
Holy Word, in whatever translation and under however
much duress. . .

'Dear God,' she prayed silently, 'please let him
come!'

That Oliver would fly to her rescue she had not the
slightest doubt. The danger would appeal to him. And
he had a ship's crew at his command. If only Rufus
could reach him quickly!

She cast another desperate glance at the neighbouring vessels. All appeared deserted apart from a guard or two left aboard while the remaining members of their crews enjoyed the delights of Gravesend. No one she could see took any notice of what was happening on board this vessel. Even when she was once more grabbed and hustled across the deck as a preliminary to being taken down and thrust into the hold, no one evinced the slightest interest. A recalcitrant female being manhandled was no unusual sight in a port full of rough men.

The hold. A dark, stinking hole where rats scratched about in the detritus left by successive cargoes.

'You cannot leave me here,' she wavered, her courage almost evaporating as the men prepared to climb back to the deck above. How could she endure being shut down in this awful place? They did not know of her fear. . .

The lord's face appeared in the hatchway. 'Just until they've sailed, my dear. They will leave you the lantern. Then Father Jerome will come down to speak with you. I shall be going ashore, so I will bid you farewell. I advise you to continue to be sensible.'

The sailors comprised a mixed crew of mainly Spanish with a couple of Englishmen thrown in, as far as she could tell. Those who had hustled her down evacuated the hold after their masters and replaced the hatch. She heard a bolt shoot home.

'Oh, Oliver! Please come soon!' she whimpered into the looming shadows.

Time seemed to stand still, but it must have passed, for the lantern began to flicker. Panic choked Judith's throat at the threat of being left in complete darkness. The sounds from above had taken on a new urgency. The ship must be almost ready to sail. A slight swaying

of the deck beneath her told her the tide had already
lifted its bottom from the mud.

The misery compounded of wet garments, bruises,
fear of confined spaces and terrifying anxiety grew as
the light began to fade and the rats got bolder. She
shooed them away, glad the men had left her free, not
tied up in a helpless bundle.

All kinds of desperate measures flitted through her
brain. If she started a fire with the lantern they would
smell the smoke and have to come down and release
her! But the risk was too great. They might simply
evacuate the ship and leave her to her fate. Or she
might be smothered by the smoke before they realised
what was happening. The chilling prospect of being
burned alive put paid to that idea.

And then it dawned upon her that somewhere in this
devilish place she might find something that would
suffice as a weapon. She scrambled to her feet and
began a frantic search among the rubbish littering the
boards.

In one dark corner she found a baulk of wood. She
could not grip it properly in one hand, would have to
use both to swing it but it was good and heavy and
should knock a man down, if not out. If only the Jesuit
came on his own. . .but that would be unlikely. He was
bound to bring an assistant or two with him if only to
hold her down. All the same, she clutched the piece of
wood to her like a lifeline as she found an empty chest
to sit on and drew it forward beneath the dimming pool
of light.

The sounds from above had been no more than a
background noise until, suddenly, alarmed shouts,
stamping feet and something that sounded suspiciously
like fighting made her catch her breath. Oliver
had come!

She listened anxiously for sounds of shots, but heard none. The Spaniards had been unprepared for attack, so perhaps their firearms had not been primed. But she would have expected Oliver to use a musket, if only to fire a warning ball. . .unless he wanted a silent attack. . . But it was no use trying to imagine what was happening overhead. Instead she began to pray.

A few moments later the hatch lifted. She looked up in anxious hope, but it was not Oliver who appeared on the ladder. The lord came down, so he hadn't gone ashore yet, followed by the Jesuit, who replaced the hatch before descending himself.

They had brought another lantern. But the added light meant they saw the piece of wood, which was too cumbersome to hide.

'Put it down, my dear, and don't make a noise,' instructed the lord in a resigned voice, but he held a threatening, unsheathed sword in his hand, and waved it at her. 'Those pirates will not discover us down here.'

Pirates. He thought the attackers were pirates. She would not disillusion him. She swallowed hard to find her voice. 'Won't they be looking for cargo?' she suggested croakily. 'Where else should they look but in the hold?'

'By the life of God, I know not what they seek! To attack in port is dangerous for them, and they must see by the way we ride in the water that we carry no merchandise!'

'Mayhap 'tis the wench they seek.' The Jesuit father spoke abruptly. Judith's mouth formed an expectant *oh*. He smiled benignly. 'Do not raise your hopes, my child. God will preserve us and leave you in my merciful care.' He crossed himself piously.

Judith snorted. Her heart hammered in her breast, excitement had almost taken over from fear. If Oliver came she must somehow divert those men's attention. She hadn't put the piece of wood down. Both she and the lord knew it was useless as a weapon. But as a diversion, maybe. . .

The sounds from above came nearer. A final thump, and the hatch flew back. The two men at the foot of the ladder stepped aside, the lord waiting with unsheathed sword to challenge whoever tried to descend.

But the man in black who appeared in the hatchway leapt straight for the lord, knocking him over as he landed, and wrenched the naked blade from his adversary's hand as they briefly struggled together on the deck.

Judith clutched the piece of wood, ready to swing it at the Jesuit should he attempt to interfere. But the intruder was back on his feet in an instant. A mask covered his face.

The lord took longer to recover, for the breath had been knocked from his body. Two more men, with colourful scarves tied to cover their faces, followed the man in black down, using the more normal means of the ladder. Standing with cutlasses drawn they presented a threatening backdrop to the tableau which met Judith's fascinated gaze.

Oliver — she was certain it was he despite the mask — had barely glanced in her direction. Instead, he was eyeing the empty hold, the priest and the lord with some amusement.

'So, my lord Scarlton. You are ferrying no treasure back to Spain?'

Scarlton's face paled, his gaze fixed in fascinated horror on the outline of a swooping bird embroidered on the other's broad chest. 'The Sea Hawk!' he gasped

hoarsely. And added in a shocked voice, 'You know
me?'

'Of course.' Oliver's tone echoed the boredom of
Scarlton's earlier manner. It did not sound like him at
all. And what did the lord mean, calling him the Sea
Hawk? She was certain it was Oliver. The lithe movements of his body, a glimpse of brilliant green eyes—
they were enough to convince her. Besides, she always
seemed to know the moment he entered a room. He
radiated some power her body recognised and
responded to. Yes, it was Oliver. But for reasons not
at that moment clear, he did not seem anxious to claim
knowledge of her. Quite the reverse.

'Unless, of course,' he went on indifferently, 'your
treasure lies in a woman's charms? What is the wench
doing here?'

'She is a heretic,' put in the priest defiantly. 'I have
been called to save her immortal soul!'

'Huh,' responded Oliver dismissively. 'I think we
will leave that to God's good grace. She will come with
me.'

'You go too far, pirate,' muttered Scarlton, 'attacking law-abiding ships in harbour! I shall complain to
the Queen.'

'I think not. She would not be pleased to learn that
you consort with Spanish Jesuits, my lord. And a
Spanish ship is fair game anywhere, especially when it
fails to advertise its nationality in an English port. I
hold a licence from the Prince of Orange. As you well
know, the Sea Hawk is no pirate, but a privateer.'

A privateer! Oliver, a privateer? The news stunned
Judith, but she had no time to dwell on this new aspect
of her husband's character. The others were still
talking.

'It comes to the same thing,' asserted Father Jerome

acidly. One thing Judith allowed him: he showed no
fear. 'Were you caught, you would be hanged for one!'

'Unlawfully, of course. But when did the Holy
Inquisition ever abide by any law but its own infamous
precepts?'

The question was rhetorical and no one expected or
gave an answer, though Jerome bridled with fury.

'Come, wench,' said Oliver briskly, 'I will take you
ashore.'

'No!'

Scarlton stepped forward, desperation in his manner.
Well he might be desperate, thought Judith smugly.
Just wait until she told her tale!

'He is a traitor!' she accused, loudly but calmly.
'They have hatched a plot to assassinate the Queen! I
heard them talking; that is why they brought me here!'

'Ah! I thought it strange for them to snatch a woman
from an English port. Now had we been in Antwerp
'twould have been no surprise. . .' His eyes gleamed
devilish green sparks. 'In that case, you are both under
arrest. My men will remain on board to make certain
you do not escape before the constable comes for you.
Come, wench, let us depart.'

Giving the lord and the priest a wide berth, Judith
walked towards him, her eyes fixed on his, but his gaze
remained impersonal. When she came near enough he
took the baulk of timber from her then grasped her
hand, his grip firm, the pressure reassuring.

'Up you go, my girl,' he ordered, almost roughly.
'My men will help you.'

Arms reached down to lift her up. She recognised
red hair fringing the woollen cap above a colourful
scarf. She gave Rufus a grateful smile as he helped her
to reach the upper deck. He merely scowled back.
Everyone seemed quite determined not to know her.

Then Oliver was by her side. 'Well done, angel,' he breathed into her ear, while pretending to hustle her to the next ladder. 'Keep it up until we're away from here.'

She did not even have time to murmur her thanks before she was scrambling up the ladder, at the top of which more eager hands reached out to assist her. Here, on the open deck, all the original ship's crew had been assembled. She ignored them as Oliver led her to the side, helped her over the gunwale and held her firmly while she found her footing on the rope ladder. He had men in the Spanish ship's cock boat ready to receive her. A larger boat drifted at the end of a line, awaiting the departure of Blackler—she had vaguely recognised him in charge on deck—and the rest of his seamen.

The Spanish vessel soon disappeared from sight, as other, ghostly ships slid in and out of view in the gathering darkness, silent and undisturbed by what had been happening near by. Only then did Oliver rip off his mask and turn to give her his irrepressible smile.

'So,' he murmured, 'the Sea Hawk rescues his lady!'

She threw herself against him, feeling the reassuring strength of his arms close about her. 'You never told me! Oh, Oliver, thank God Rufus found you and you came in time!'

His lips, warm on hers, took her breath. She shut her eyes, drinking in the sheer sensual joy of his nearness.

'They did not harm you, sweeting?'

Anxiety laced his tone. Judith shook her head. 'Not much. Some discomfort, a few bruises and the threat of inquisition—but I am fine, really.'

'They shall pay for their misdeeds,' he promised grimly. 'But that experience,' he suggested, stroking

her untidy hair from her face, 'should make you less
inclined to wander the countryside without adequate
escort, wife. Angel, you should not have
ventured——'

'I wanted to surprise you!'

'You achieved that, wench!'

'And I'm glad I did,' she defended swiftly. 'Else I
would not have discovered the plot to kill the Queen!
An assassin called Stalker is riding to Nonesuch Palace
this very instant! You must stop him, Oliver!'

Oliver stiffened. Tension and sudden energy radiated
from him. 'I had not realised. I will set out the moment
you are safely aboard. Return to Harvel on the morrow
and await me there, angel.'

'Let me accompany you, please!' Now she was with
him once more it seemed urgent to Judith that she did
not lose sight of him again so quickly! 'I want to see
this through. And I think I should recognise the man!'

'But you cannot accuse him to his face. 'Twould be
dangerous for the Spaniards to know your identity.
They would not rest until you had paid the price for
this defeat. You would be easy prey. For that reason I
pretended not to recognise you aboard the ship. And
neither can the Sea Hawk be the accuser, for he must
remain incognito. Should his identity be revealed
'twould be most unfortunate.'

'You knew Lord Scarlton. Does he not know you?'
she wondered anxiously.

'We have met, but I am convinced that he did not
recognise me. I disguised my voice.'

'I thought it sounded odd! Oh, Oliver, my rash
action put your safety at risk! Can you forgive me?'

'I was but repaying a debt, angel.'

She had forgotten. 'There was no debt,' she
whispered.

'The score is even now. And without your impulsive journey we would not know of the Queen's danger.'

He might not think the score even were he to hear of her visit to Elizabeth. She changed the subject quickly. 'You fight for the Prince of Orange. Why, Oliver?'

'Because he would grant me a licence. Elizabeth would not, for we are not at war with Spain. Drake, of course, goes his own way, plundering the Spanish galleons without official authority from anyone, though she helps to finance his voyages and takes her share of the profits. Substantial ones from his latest raid on Nombre de Dios, I hear. But I prefer to work nearer to home and finance myself, though I give her gifts to keep her sweet. Besides, the Flemish cause is a just one, and is always short of funds.'

'Elizabeth knows what you do?'

'Aye.'

'Who else?'

'Burghley, Sir Charles, you and the crew,' he said succinctly.

The dip of oars ceased as the boat drifted against the side of the *Mermaid*. But as she gained its deck to be greeted by a relieved Lambert, she heard another, larger boat approaching. The brig's longboat, with the remainder of the crew aboard.

A tough, motley-looking gang, she thought, as she watched them embark. Blackler exchanged a nod with Oliver as he came aboard.

'All done?'

'Aye, sir. All done.'

'What does that mean?' demanded Judith. 'Have they been arrested?'

'We could scarcely call the constable without revealing our identity. Blackler has locked the entire crew down in the hold. They'll escape in due course and set sail for Spain with all speed, no doubt. We left them no boat in which to row ashore.'

'But Lord Scarlton? He will not wish to sail to Spain. He will get ashore somehow and follow Stalker to Nonesuch to warn him!'

'Neither he nor the Jesuit will be going anywhere,' said Blackler brutally.

Judith frowned. He could mean but one thing. 'They are dead?'

'They were not fit to live.'

He was quite dismissive. Judith turned her head to meet Oliver's eyes. 'You ordered them killed?'

He shrugged, his gaze steady, the tiniest of smiles lifting the corner of his mobile mouth. 'I had no need. John knew as well as I that we could not call on the law. 'Twas a kinder death than even the block, certainly better than hanging, drawing and quartering or the fire. Do not pity them, angel.'

'I do not.' Judith firmly suppressed a feeling that they should not have taken the law into their own hands. Yet not to have done so would have meant that the two conspirators escaped, and Oliver's life—and the lives of his crew—would have been in jeopardy. On the whole, they had had no choice.

'You will kill Stalker, too.' It was a statement.

'An we can find him before he does his dastardly deed.'

She drew herself up. 'I am still coming with you. But I shall need my change of clothes. My riding costume is at the inn.'

'Your things should be here by now. Rufus told me you had left them there and Lambert went to collect them.'

'I may come?' she demanded. 'I could not bear to be sent home like a child!'

Oliver's face broke into one of his merriest smiles. 'I have been thinking. We will sail up the Thames, take a barge from London Bridge and horses from Kingston. Yes, you may come! But now, let me show you our quarters.'

Our quarters. How reassuring that sounded! Not that they would occupy them for long, though the journey up the Thames must take some hours. But they would be travelling by night, while Stalker slept. God willing they would reach Nonesuch before he did.

Her eyes showed her happiness as Oliver led her to the master cabin, set behind the mizzen mast under the quarterdeck. Lambert, hovering in the cabin's dimness, was thanked for his good work in collecting her clothes and dismissed.

Oliver drew back the curtains concealing a box bed built into one corner. It looked quite large enough for two.

'Remove your wet clothes and lie down there,' he said, using his tinder-box to light the lantern hanging from a beam above. 'I'm sorry to have to leave you, angel, but I must go back on deck. John will need all his skill to navigate the river safely in darkness, and I must be there to see that all goes well. Try to sleep.'

Disappointed that he could not stay with her, Judith nodded dutifully. But her curiosity had become so great that a question burst from her as he turned to go.

'Oliver, when you escaped that carrack off Sark — were they flogging you because you were a privateer? Did they know?'

'No, angel. They caught me in Antwerp, as I told you, and took me for a spy.'

Her eyes widened. 'They said they were looking for a spy. And were you?'

He grinned suddenly and his merry laugh rang out. 'My, wife, but you do ask the most difficult questions! Tell me, would you consider carrying back information regarding an assassination plot against the Queen spying?'

'No. That is what we are doing now, is it not?'

'Aye. Then, I had gained knowledge of the Ridolfi plot from Walsingham, in Paris. I was travelling as a merchant, of course. 'Twas urgent that I reached England speedily.'

'They knew you had this information?'

'They suspected as much, though they could not prove it. Not without flogging the truth from me.'

'But they knew who you were?'

He shook his head. 'I was travelling under false papers.'

'So as Oliver Burnett you are in no danger from the Spaniards?'

The reckless smile played about his lips as he declared, 'No, I am safe enough unless they capture the Sea Hawk!'

'Why did you not tell me all this?' she whispered, hurt that he had not trusted her.

'Angel—I did not want you or anyone else on Sark involved more than was necessary. You had had trouble enough, due to my presence. Supposing the Spaniards had returned? 'Twas better you knew nothing.'

'Then, mayhap. But since I came to England? Could you not trust me?'

He sighed, a trifle impatiently. 'Must I tell you everything, wife? I went to sea to carry on my business. That was sufficient information, in my view. Besides,' he added more reasonably, 'I thought you might be dismayed. And you are.' He tilted her chin so that he could better examine her eyes.

'Only because of the danger you run!'

'I know. But you must not fear for me. And I kept my secret still because the same thing applied. What you did not know could not be forced from you.'

'I see. I have become a danger to you.'

He heard the quiver in her voice and answered it by drawing her close. 'Don't worry about it, angel. I can look after us both.' His lips touched her forehead. 'I'm glad you know now. Mayhap you can better understand my abrupt departure from your island. And why I could not return. Elizabeth kept me at Court by threatening to expose me as the Sea Hawk. She knew I could not risk that if I wished to carry on as a privateer. But I must not linger. Blackler needs my help. Try to sleep.'

He kissed her again, this time on the lips. A hard, possessive caress, but brief.

Left alone, shaken by that fierce kiss, Judith looked around the cabin for evidence of her husband's occupation. He had spared himself no luxury here. The glow from the lantern illuminated fine furniture, superior panelling and splendid windows, but because of the darkness outside Judith could see little through the last.

The brig was already on the move, creeping almost silently out into the main stream and then using the incoming tide and a favourable wind to carry it towards London.

Judith divested herself of her damp garments and replaced them with the riding habit. She had no intention of undressing to go to bed. She needed to be ready for any emergency that might arise. The

Mermaid could collide with another vessel, though not many chose to navigate the river by night.

Instead of lying down, she began to investigate the chest where he had thrust his mask and the thin, black garment carrying the insignia of the Sea Hawk. He had stripped that off the moment he entered the cabin to reveal a stout leather jerkin capable of deflecting most sword thrusts, she thought. She opened the drawer, curious still and wanting to touch the emblems of her husband's other life. She supposed she should have guessed. In truth, she had not been particularly aston-ished or aghast once the first shock of discovery had passed. 'Twas his adventurous, mercurial, dauntless spirit which had first appealed to her.

But could she endure to wait patiently at home, knowing the dangers he ran whenever he went to sea? She would have to, she knew, hard as it would be. She could not chain the Sea Hawk, the way a bird of prey could be chained to a perch. No, she would have to make the best of the time he was content to spend with her, not pine for the impossible.

CHAPTER FIFTEEN

BEFORE long, tiredness overcame Judith. Oliver had not returned, nor did she expect him to. She did not like to intrude on the quarterdeck, for fear he thought her a nuisance. But, looking through the windows, she could, at times when the patchy cloud lifted, see the banks of the Thames clearly visible in the moonlight. On some stretches, where the river wound, Blackler had to tack back and forth across the stream, but that was not often. On most reaches the wind came from their starboard quarter and the ship drove straight ahead, making excellent progress.

Deciding there was no longer any point in fighting her weariness, Judith eventually lay down on the bunk, still fully clothed, to discover that the pillow and coverings held traces of Oliver's distinctive odour. She settled down with a deep sigh of content, and was soon asleep.

The transfer to a barge, just below London Bridge, made necessary because the masts of the *Mermaid* would not pass under the bridge's arches, took place around dawn. At Oliver's insistence the trip upriver to Kingston was achieved speedily, the bargees resorting to oars when the wind failed. Blackler, Lambert, Rufus and three other men accompanied Oliver and herself, the remainder of the crew being left behind on the brig. Soon Richmond was behind them and Elizabeth's beautiful palace on the banks of the Thames no more than a collection of towers and pinnacles etched on the horizon. Horses were readily available at Kingston, and before long the party was on the road.

Judith knew that neither Oliver nor Blackler had slept during the night, and doubted whether any of the other men had, either, except perhaps Lambert, who might have snatched a little rest. Yet they evinced little sign of tiredness. She marvelled at their stamina. As for herself, the sleep had renewed her energy and she enjoyed the ride through the Surrey countryside with Oliver beside her.

'Your horsemanship has improved, angel,' he remarked as they slowed the animals to a walk after a brisk canter. 'You are able to manage that strange beast without apparent trouble.'

Pleased by his compliment, Judith smiled. 'I have taken instruction every day. I enjoy riding. The horse marshal has been most patient with me. I knew I could easily make the journey into Gravesend, despite the warnings everyone gave me! And I can this one too.'

He chuckled. 'Undoubtedly. And you will not delay us by more than an hour.'

'I cannot see that I shall delay you at all! None of the beasts is fast; we cannot push them any harder than we are!'

Her indignant protest brought an angry flush to her cheeks. Oliver could be so infuriating! Now he was laughing at her!

'I did but jest, angel.'

His eyes twinkled into hers and her stiffened features collapsed into a reluctant smile. She should be used to his teasing by now!

Meanwhile they had topped the slight rise and, with an encouraging whoop, Oliver spurred his horse forward. Judith followed, the knowledge that he hadn't meant what he said and the exhilaration of the ride filling her with exuberant joy until she remembered the object of the journey. Please God they arrived in time to save the Queen!

At Ewell, Oliver stopped to take what accommodation he could for themselves and his men. The small town was pretty full, with the Queen in residence not far away, and they found themselves lodging in three different establishments.

'All the better,' observed Oliver when they had gathered together again. 'We are spread about the town, and shall have a better chance of spotting this Stalker when he arrives. I would wager the first thing he will do is look for a lodging. I want one man to remain in each of the inns to look out for him, with you, Rufus, ready to ride after me should he turn up. The rest of us will make for Nonesuch. I must contact Sir Charles.'

'Will you seek to speak with the Queen?' asked Judith as they, accompanied by Blackler and Lambert, resumed their journey mounted on fresh horses.

'I think I will pass on the warning through Sir Charles. 'Tis safest for us if no one else knows from whence it came.'

'The guards must be warned to look out for a stranger.'

Oliver gave a derisive laugh. 'Strangers abound, and the Queen allows anyone to approach her when she is out. She refuses to take proper care of her person. No, we must try to catch him before he reaches her.'

'He cannot have arrived yet.'

''Tis unlikely, certainly. See, there is the palace, ahead.'

It rose above the sweeping Surrey countryside, a magnificent building, all towers and crenellations, the dream palace of Elizabeth's sire but belonging now to the Earl of Arundel, for Mary had sold it.

They rode along the avenue of trees towards the gatehouse. Several men were engaged in a game of bowls on the green before it. Oliver abruptly brought his mount to a halt. The others quickly reined in too, all the horses protesting at the sudden pull on their bits.

'Marry! Fortune is with us! Do you not see Sir Charles yonder? We shall have no need to convince the gatekeeper of our credentials!'

He leapt from his horse and strode across the green. Sir Charles looked up from watching a rival's ball trail the jack away from his own, and gave an exclamation of surprise.

'Oliver! What do you here? Has the Queen called you back?'

'I am certain you would be one of the first to know if she had! Nay, Charles, I am come without invitation, but with a purpose. I need your help. Can you leave the game?'

'Assuredly.'

He exchanged a few words with the other players, who greeted Oliver before excusing Sir Charles. The two friends walked back to the waiting horses.

'Mistress Judith! My greetings. What a pleasure to see you here!' Charles swept her a bow. Still in her saddle, Judith inclined her head, giving him a warm smile in return. She liked Sir Charles and was pleased to see him again. After all, he was one of the few friends she had in England.

Soon he had escorted them through the gatehouse into the vast, busy courtyard. There they dismounted, handing their horses to waiting grooms.

'We need somewhere private to talk,' said Oliver.

'Come with me.'

He led them to a secluded corner of an inner yard. 'This should do.'

Oliver nodded. Charles's face grew grim as Oliver told him what Judith had discovered, and of her capture and rescue.

'Her Grace must be told at once,' he declared. 'Do you wish me to convey the message? Or will you seek an audience yourself?'

'The former, I think. I do not wish to advertise my involvement to anyone but Her Grace. As far as others are concerned, let the warning appear to come anonymously. But make certain it is heeded. If necessary you may say it came from the Sea Hawk. That should convince them.'

'Very well. What do you intend?'

'I intend to be in any crowd that forms about her, in case my other arrangements fail and the man manages to get close.'

'You will be forgiven after this, my friend. But I agree. 'Twould be best for me to approach her, or you and Mistress Judith may never feel safe again. If I cannot gain audience, have I your permission to tell Leicester?'

'Aye, he will take the threat seriously, on your assurance that the warning comes from the Sea Hawk. Is she leaving the palace today?'

'This afternoon there is to be a pageant in the open air, presented by the local populace. Everyone from miles around will come.'

Oliver groaned. 'Just as I feared! Well, she will be safe until then. Our man cannot yet have arrived. Methinks we should return to our inns and snatch some sleep.'

'Use my lodging,' offered Charles. 'I share with

others, but no one will require a bed at this hour. Let me take you there.'

'My thanks, friend. 'Twill save us the double journey. One of my men, Rufus, will bring news if Stalker arrives. I told him to ask for you if I was not in evidence.'

'I will make sure to be on hand.'

So it was arranged. He led them to his allocated room, temporarily turned into a dormitory. One large bed had been surrounded by truckle beds imported for the occasion. Their usual occupants being absent, Oliver joined Judith on the big bed while Blackler and Lambert stretched out on a couple of the truckles. The men were all asleep almost before they had lain themselves down. Judith, having rested the previous night, was not quite so exhausted, so lay for a while on her side, contemplating the relaxed, beautiful face of her husband.

In sleep it lost the animation which went with merry eyes and a mischievous smile. Lost the subtle ambience of leadership, of stern authority. Instead it looked younger, heart-stoppingly vulnerable. Those long black lashes sweeping his cheeks made him look like an innocent child, though the beard outlining his strong jaw belied that illusion. His firm lips had softened, not into a smile but into a slightly parted, peaceful line that tugged at her heart. She longed to kiss them, but dared not in case she woke him. So she just went on studying him with yearning eyes until at last she, too, fell asleep.

They were woken at around midday by the advent of Sir Charles accompanied by menials bearing food.

'Thought you'd be hungry,' he explained, waving the food forward to a waiting table. 'I have passed your warning on. Her Grace appeared unperturbed, and will leave the palace in an hour.'

Oliver sat up and yawned, though his eyes were already fully alert. 'There has been no messsage from Ewell?'

Charles shook his head. 'I've made enquiries at the gatehouse, in case your man Rufus came and could not find either of us. But no one has enquired.'

'The devil take it,' muttered Oliver. 'Stalker cannot have travelled as hard as I imagined. He should have reached Dartford last night, and 'tis no more than five and twenty miles from there. He should be here by now. Mayhap I misread his intentions. He may have come straight here. We can take no risks. We must make haste to attend the pageant.'

'Tomorrow,' Charles informed them grimly, 'she goes hunting in the park.'

'I wonder whether he knows,' mused Oliver. ''Twould be a better opportunity than today's entertainment.'

'A stray arrow,' agreed Charles sombrely.

Judith shuddered. She might not be over-fond of the Queen as a person, but Elizabeth represented England's only hope of continued freedom from the Spanish and, with it, the Papal yoke.

Having eaten, they joined the throng gathering to watch the pageant. Judith searched with anxious gaze, but saw no one resembling the man she had seen so briefly in Gravesend.

'I do not think he is here,' she told Oliver, whose hawkish green eyes never stopped scanning the crowd, alert to any unexpected movement, any hint of danger to his Sovereign.

When Elizabeth appeared, a great shout went up. As Oliver had predicted, common people from miles around had come to view the spectacle. Some bold admirer rushed forward to kiss her hand. Judith gasped, and felt Oliver tense beside her.

''Tis not him,' she whispered.

Leicester had swiftly interposed himself between his Queen and danger, but, seeing no weapon and sensing no threat, stood aside. The Queen graciously accepted the man's homage, exchanging a few words with him before moving to her seat, set on a dais under a protective tree.

Judith barely saw the performance, for Oliver had already pointed out that Stalker's identity could easily be hidden behind the mask of a performer. Accompanied by music from itinerant musicians, each scene was short. The first depicted some story from Greek mythology, the next from the Bible, extolling the virtues of Protestantism. Concealing draperies and beasts with huge false heads abounded. Charity and Virtue appeared, and odes were recited lauding the Virgin Queen.

At last it was safely over. Elizabeth retired to the security of the palace. At least, as Oliver observed wryly, he hoped it was safe. Leicester and the guards had been alerted and he himself could do no more.

The sun was sinking fast as they returned to Ewell. Oliver made a round of all the inns enquiring after Stalker and looking in on all the taprooms, Judith at his elbow. The man they sought had not yet put in an appearance.

'He must be lodging elsewhere,' he muttered.

'Mayhap he will choose to sleep under a hedge,' commented Blackler. 'He will not be traced afterwards, should he escape capture.'

'True. Well, then, let us sup and sleep. Tomorrow will be an anxious day.'

Privacy was unobtainable in that crowded town. Oliver had been forced to agree to sharing a room with another couple. His men had all been squeezed into corners, but they were used to such conditions.

Judith accepted her fate philosophically. There could be no true reconciliation with Oliver that night, no enjoyment of their mutual passion. They would have to wait until this emergency was over and they could return to Harvel before finally settling their differences. They were, after all, not so great. And for the first time she was part of his other life, a partner in his current enterprise to save the Queen. Nothing, except failure, which she would not contemplate, could disturb her deep content at that.

The other couple had no inhibitions. Behind the scanty privacy of the bed curtains the man took his wife with short, sharp ferocity. She made no sound, seeming to Judith to endure rather than enjoy. Thankfully, Oliver had the knack of drifting off the moment his head touched the pillow, unless he had more pleasurable activities in mind. To her the performance had been depressing, though it was probably no more and no less than most wives expected of the marriage bed. But it might have stirred him into demanding something similar of her, and that, after discovering so much pleasure with him, she would have found it difficult to endure.

So Judith lay, feeling his warmth beside her, longing for his body to join with hers, but not in the dispassionate way their fellow lodgers had mated. No, she longed for the delicious way Oliver had of exciting her every response before completing his possession. It was some time before her body stopped demanding fulfilment and she drifted off to sleep.

* * *

All eight of them gathered early and were on the road by dawn. Oliver had seen no sense in leaving men in Ewell when they could be of more use helping him to scour the park for the assassin.

Oliver led his contingent straight into the park. A bower had been prepared for Elizabeth's reception. The butler had already set off with a train of carts and pack-mules carrying breakfast to the point of assembly. The hunters were out stalking deer, picking up droppings for the Queen's inspection, so that she might select the quarry. To locate Stalker would be difficult, if not impossible among all this activity. But Oliver set his men to scour the route Elizabeth would take.

They had not gone far before they met a detail of guards, who challenged their right to be there. Fortunately the officer knew Oliver of old. The two men exchanged greetings and the soldier waved them on. He would be keeping a close guard over the Queen once she set out.

Oliver and Judith rode side by side for a while, but then a deer sprang from a nearby clump of trees with a huntsman in pursuit and for a moment they became parted. The copse had to be searched and Oliver jumped a recently fallen tree to enter it while Judith prudently made her way round the obstruction in order to follow him in.

The spreading branches had not yet been cut off and foliage still clung, shrivelled, to the stems. Behind this screen she came face to face with Stalker, standing stock-still beside his mount.

He recognised her at once, despite her change of attire. She had no doubt it was him. She tried to call Oliver, but her voice would not come. Stalker appeared as shocked as she.

But he recovered first. He had a bow in his hands

and in one smooth movement he had an arrow aimed at her heart. Judith knew what he intended. Her voice returned in an aching scream. 'Oliver!'

As she called out the man loosed the arrow. Her horse, sensing her panic, panicked too, tossing its head and sidling skittishly to one side. The arrow hissed harmlessly by as the sound of thundering hooves told her Oliver had come.

Heart pumping, hands shaking, Judith managed to bring her mount under control. As it was an elderly hack, its skittishness had been born of fear, not high spirits. As her panic subsided, knowing rescue was at hand, so did his.

She looked up and quickly closed her eyes. Stalker lay on the sward, a knife sticking from his chest.

Oliver leapt from his saddle and came across to her.

'Judith, angel, are you all right?'

She opened her eyes to find his face, whiter than she had ever seen it before, turned anxiously up to hers, an expression in his eyes she had longed to see. She nodded, unhooked her leg from the pommel and slid down into his arms.

Oh, the comfort! But he was trembling as much as she. White and shaken, he held her as though he would never let her go, his head bent so that his cheek rested against hers.

'To think I allowed you to walk into such danger,' he groaned.

'But the Queen is safe.'

As though to prove the truth of her words, a commanding woman's voice rang out.

'Is this the knave? Have his carcass removed!'

Reluctantly, Oliver slackened his grip on his wife and turned to greet his Sovereign. He dropped to one knee; Judith curtsied deeply.

'So, sirrah!' Elizabeth greeted him abruptly. 'You
may rise. I don't know what the devil you are doing
here, but it seems I have once again to thank you for
your loyalty. Were it not for your timely intervention,
I might yet be lying victim to an assassin's shaft. My
thanks. Are others concerned in this affair?'

'I think not, ma'am. Sir Charles told me his information was that 'twas planned out of personal revenge
for the execution of Norfolk, the fellow's master.'

Elizabeth's lips twitched at this reply. After all, she
knew the identity of the Sea Hawk. But amusement
turned into a sigh as she dismounted. 'I had no wish to
see that fool dead. But in matters of State personal
feelings must take second place. My council urged the
earl's execution. Give me your sword.'

The command took Oliver by surprise. Judith saw
the shock on his face replaced by understanding as he
did as bidden.

'Kneel,' ordered the Queen.

Oliver dropped to one knee again. The sword
descended to touch each of his shoulders in turn.

'Arise, Sir Oliver.'

Oliver rose to his feet, only to bow low again before
the woman who held the fate of England in her
beautiful hands.

'Serve me well in the future, Sir Oliver. You may
return to Court if you wish, remain here with us. We
will be glad to have you once more among those who
serve us.'

'Madam.' Oliver put all the respect in the world into
that one word. But his next utterance courted the
Queen's displeasure. 'An you will give me leave, I
should prefer to return with my wife to my manor at
Harvel. Others may serve you here in great felicity,

but I think Your Grace knows that the life of a courtier does not suit me. I prefer to serve you in other ways.'

For a moment Elizabeth's petulance showed, but it swiftly passed. She snorted a derisive laugh.

''Tis good to see that you love your wife, I vow! 'Twas a touching scene I interrupted! Having made them, too many are careless of their marriage vows. Very well, sirrah. You have our leave to depart. Go home and get your wife pregnant, if she is not already so. Found your dynasty. I trust your offspring will inherit your brilliant spirit and her gift of advocacy.'

'Gift of advocacy?'

Oliver's puzzled expression reminded the Queen of her vow of silence. 'Oh, gracious lord!' she exclaimed. 'Does he not yet know? I shall say no more. Come, let us proceed! Breakfast and the hunt await us!'

In a few hectic moments the Queen's entourage had gone, leaving Oliver alone with his wife and small band of followers.

Judith had still not recovered from that embarrassing speech of the Queen. Get her pregnant indeed! 'Twas her own great sadness that she was not already great with Oliver's child. But to have the Queen. . .and then for her to mention their secret. . . She wanted to sink through the ground.

The soldiers had already taken Stalker's body away. There was nothing left for Oliver but to do as he had requested, return to Harvel.

Everything fell a little flat. Oliver had been distinguished by a knighthood, but had refused a place at Court. Judith supposed she should be happy about that, but she was far too anxious about the Queen's slip. What must Oliver be thinking? Would he question her when they were alone? Almost certainly, she decided, trembling.

'Come,' said Oliver briskly, the beginnings of his
quirky smile playing about his lips. 'After so signal an
honour it seems a little tame to return to Ewell to settle
our accounts and proceed back from whence we
came—but that is what we shall do. Celebrations will
be in order once we are back aboard the *Sea Hawk*.'

'The *Sea Hawk*?' wondered Judith, momentarily
jolted from her depressing thoughts.

Oliver grinned. 'The *Mermaid*'s alter ego, when she
becomes a privateer.'

'I see.' She forced a smile. 'So both you and your
ship take on a new identity, the same one.'

'Precisely.'

Her face sobered and small lines of concern
reappeared between her eyes. 'We are not to travel
direct to Harvel?' she asked, disappointed yet also
relieved.

'You have done enough riding for one day, angel,
and there are still a few miles to be covered before we
reach Kingston. The journey will be easier by river.
We will be home on the morrow. When, my love, I
shall expect to discover what secret lies between your
sweet self and our Queen.'

CHAPTER SIXTEEN

JUDITH might have enjoyed the journey back and the
subsequent celebration aboard the brig had she not
been dreading the confrontation Oliver had threatened. It had marred her farewell to Sir Charles, who
had made a point of remaining behind to congratulate
Oliver on his new honour. He had, of course, overheard the Queen's indiscretion, and sought to comfort
her.

'His pride will be hurt for a while, but knowing my
friend he will soon recover,' he had tried to reassure
her. 'You mean too much to him now, Lady Burnett.'
His grin spread as she blushed at being addressed by
her new title. 'He may not realise it yet, but he loves
you, Judith. And I know full well that you love him. I
wish you both happy.'

The Queen had said he loved her, too, but how
could Elizabeth know? If he did love her, surely he
would forgive her for interfering in his affairs? But if
he did not, and she doubted it despite the genuine
emotion he had displayed at finding her in such immediate danger, the fragile relationship which had begun
to strengthen and blossom during their weeks at Harvel
might be wrecked. So although she joined in the
celebrations, drinking more sack than she should to
cheer her spirits, a cloud hung heavy over her head.

Oliver acted as though without a care in the world.
But he had withdrawn from her, treating her little
differently from one of his crew. She wondered
whether he actually remembered his ominous words as

the evening wore on and the level of drunkenness grew. He did not share the incapable, noisy inebriation of most, but he had imbibed far more than she had seen him drink before. In the end she knew her presence had been forgotten and crept away, to lie alone in the cabin, listening to the noise and wishing Oliver had not been knighted if it meant the celebrations kept him from her.

When she woke the following morning he lay on the bed beside her, snoring gently, one arm flung carelessly across her ribs. He really had drunk too much, she thought indulgently. Her own head ached, and she feared to think what his would be like. Still, the ride to Harvel should cure them both.

She carefully removed his arm and climbed over him, trying not to disturb his sleep. But as she began to pour water from the ewer to bathe her face the tenor of his breathing changed. He emitted a snort and she knew he had woken.

'Good morn, Sir Oliver,' she greeted him softly.

He stretched and groaned. 'Good? What is good about it, pray? Alack-a-day, but my head feels fit to burst!'

'I imagine all the crew are suffering so. Mine is none too clear,' she offered in consolation.

He sat up suddenly, then clutched at his brow, looking as though he wished he hadn't. 'God! What a celebration!'

Aye, what a celebration, he thought sourly. His own excessive drinking had been in part born of jubilation, but mostly of a desire not to face the truth. He could have taken her straight home to Harvel. But it had seemed suddenly attractive to put off the moment when he could continue to deceive himself no longer.

Marry! But did he truly love the wench? Had

Elizabeth the right of it? Had the emotion crept up on him, a thief in the night, to steal away his independence, his freedom to please himself and no other? And what of this secret shared between the Queen and his wife? He had to know what it was, yet was more than willing even yet to delay the discovery of an answer he might not like.

She stood there, her hair in a tangle, her face glistening with water. Like him, she had slept in her clothes. Yet beauty shone from her. And the way she was looking at him. Indulgently. Lovingly.

She knew exactly what he was now. And the knowledge had not turned her from him. But still. She had a secret.

He rose reluctantly to his feet and answered a knock on the cabin door with an irritable, 'Come in!'

Lambert had a cup in his hand. He briefly acknowledged Judith before addressing his master. 'For your head, Sir Oliver.'

'Marry, but you're not intending to address me so all the time, are you, man?' Oliver lifted a hand to his forehead and gave one of his wryest grins.

'Not if you do not wish it, master.'

'I do not. But that draught is welcome. I cannot remember when I last woke with such a head.'

'Nor I, master,' remarked Lambert drily, handing him the cup. 'Are we leaving for Harvel soon? Do you wish me to go ahead and order horses?'

Oliver quaffed his potion, pulled a face and handed back the cup. 'An excellent idea. We should be ready to leave within the hour.'

'Lambert!' Judith's voice stopped the lackey at the door.

'Yes, my lady?'

'Do you have more of that remedy? I fear my head is a little thick this morning, too.'

'Wife, I apologise! How thoughtless of me! Lambert, bring Mistress Judith a cup at once!'

'Aye, sir.'

Lambert departed hiding a grin. He returned almost immediately.

Judith drank the draught down, trying not to taste it. But even so it left a bitter dryness in her mouth. 'Whatever have you put in it?' she demanded, pulling a face.

Lambert gave a small bow. 'My secret, mistress. I will row ashore, recover your mare and order the other horses.'

Oliver seemed to have lost all his merry sparkle. He set about making ready to depart minus his usual cheerful chatter. He must be feeling bad, thought Judith.

The *Mermaid* had anchored in much the same spot as it had occupied before the dash to London. The Spanish ship had disappeared. Oliver pointed this out as they were ferried ashore. Blackler was to remain with the brig, the crew too. The ship would not be sailing again immediately. Its departure would depend upon the weather as much as anything. Autumn gales could prevent it from leaving for many weeks.

Thomasse greeted Judith's return with genuine relief. Even Dame Ursula seemed quite glad to welcome her back, Judith found, especially when told of the adventures that had befallen her mistress. No mention was made of his being the Sea Hawk. In the version Oliver gave, he had been acting as himself throughout. The housekeeper was not privy to his secret.

She expressed herself delighted to be serving a man

who had been knighted by the Queen, and seemed to find no difficulty in addressing Judith by her new title. She made a great fuss of seeing the food served.

Afterwards they wandered about the garden, and still Oliver did not broach the subject of the Queen's remark. He must be waiting until they retired to their bedchamber, Judith surmised. But at least her head had recovered. She hoped Oliver's had, too.

'Well, wife,' he began, the moment a fussing Thomasse and phlegmatic Lambert had left them. 'What is this secret you have not seen fit to share with me, pray?'

Judith swallowed. 'I did not wish to incur your displeasure, husband. But I could not allow you to languish in the Fleet for marrying me without attempting to explain to Her Grace the circumstances under which you were forced to wed.'

Oliver's chin lifted. 'You knew I had refused to plead.'

'Aye, husband. But understand it from my point of view. I had to make the Queen understand and release you. Otherwise I should always have felt guilty. Supposing you had died in that evil place? I could never have forgiven myself.'

'What did you tell her?'

'The truth. That you had not ravished me. That you were pressured into the marriage. That you would never have wed me had Sieur Perrier not seen you comforting me and construed the circumstances wrongly.'

Oliver had begun pacing. Now he stopped. 'And what did she say?' he demanded abruptly.

'That since it seemed you could not help your disobedience she would see to your release.'

Judith stood, trembling, helpless to do more to make him understand.

'Was my release so important to you? Had I died, as you feared, you would have been free to wed where you chose.'

His unemotional words took her by surprise. No angry recriminations. No prideful denial of her action. Instead, it seemed, a genuine desire to discover her true feelings.

In that moment she knew she could hide them no longer. Whether he loved her or not, he must know that she loved him.

She crossed the chamber to where he stood, gravely awaiting her reply. Lifted her hands to his shoulders. Looked straight into green eyes bright as emeralds.

'I love you, Oliver,' she declared. At his sharply indrawn breath she smiled, that slow, warm smile that so entranced him. 'I think I have loved you from the moment I set eyes on you, half dead and bloody as you were. My life is nothing without you to share it with. I want no freedom to wed elsewhere.'

Devil take it, it was true. The Queen was right, curse her. He did love the wench. And suddenly freedom, the kind of freedom he had always sought, mattered not one jot. The chains of false values dropped away. He was free to revel in his love.

He drew her close. Her arms encircled his neck. Her lush body pressed against his, eager, yielding.

'Angel, I love you,' he admitted huskily. 'I have tried to deny it to myself, for I found it difficult enough to leave you when duty called me elsewhere. But I cannot do so any longer. I love you,' he repeated again, and lowered his mouth to claim her eager lips.

In a dizzying state of euphoria, Judith responded with all the ardour of her passionate nature. The kiss was long, searching, each seeming to draw the very soul from the other. At length Oliver lifted his head, looking down with adoring green eyes, his cheeks flushed with passion. But the smile was back at the corners of his mouth.

'Why are we standing here?' he murmured. 'The bed would be so much more convenient.'

Judith's throaty chuckle was answer enough. The bed accepted them into its dark privacy.

Oliver refused to hurry. He wanted to prove his deep love. A hasty coupling would not do, however urgently his body demanded it. Her pleasure always rewarded his care, his own ravishment his prize, but this time, with love declared between them, he wanted her to reach the highest pinnacles of delight.

Judith thought she might die as the ripples of sheer ecstasy swept over her. Her arms tightened, she held him to her with all her strength, willing him to fill her with himself, and if she died thus she would surely go to paradise.

Oliver knew she had peaked and allowed his body release. As he died his little death he wondered why he had so stubbornly denied his love. This love would not fetter him, but release his spirit to soar into new realms of achievement. Not perhaps in the way he had always dreamed, but. . .

A kiss on his neck came, warm and clinging. 'Oliver?'

'Aye, my love?'

'Thank you for loving me.'

'How could I help it? And never think I wed you against my will. I was quite capable of standing up to every man on Sark! But I do believe that, deep down, I loved you even then. The thought of never seeing you again did not appeal.'

'But you were not over-anxious to renew the acquaintance,' she reminded him. But this time there was no accusation, no resentment in her voice, merely gentle, humorous chiding.

'I was too afraid of becoming your slave,' he confessed wryly. 'But now I am become your willing bondsman for life.'

'Oh, no,' protested Judith, 'I want no slave! Just a dashing, merry, devil-may-care husband and father who will sometimes jerk me out of my rather prudish, practical ways.'

'You must remain prudish if I ever demand too much — as in the Fleet. And I would like an heir one day, my love, if God so wills. Whether I shall make a good father remains to be seen. I have had few dealings with infants.'

'You will make your children laugh,' predicted Judith. 'You will be stern but just. Oh, Oliver,' she added, worried, 'I do hope we can obey the Queen's command! I wish I were pregnant already.'

'There is plenty of time, sweetheart. 'Twill be my pleasure to do my best, of course, but I confess I am in no hurry to lose my wife to a family. In that, as in all else, we must accept God's will. The lack of offspring will make no difference to our love.'

Judith hoped that might be so. But children were important, especially now Oliver had a title to pass on. She prayed she would not let him down.

His thoughts had strayed to other matters.

'You have not met my family as yet. We must travel to Plymouth when the weather permits. Mayhap a voyage round the coast in the spring. From thence we will continue on to Sark. Possibly we can be there for the anniversary of your birth.'

'The tenth day of May. This year I missed any

celebrations, for we had just arrived in London. That was celebration enough, and Papa bought me that exquisite gown. To spend my natal day on Sark next year would be wonderful.'

'You are not reluctant to return?'

He sounded offhandedly anxious over her reply so she chose her words carefully, while speaking the absolute truth.

'No. It is a beautiful island and I confess I miss the people, for they were all my friends. But I would not wish to return for good. I prefer living here, with you, my husband.'

That, of course, deserved a kiss. And then another. 'Twas almost dawn before either of them found any sleep that night.

In the brilliant sunshine of early May Sark looked quite beautiful. The voyage had been enjoyable. The *Mermaid* did cut through the water as Oliver had said, and Judith had hardly felt queasy at all. Her dislike of the sea had faded fast.

Blackler did not round the Bec de Nez to reach the Seigneur's new harbour, but sailed on south, turning in to anchor off Le Grand Bay, below Beauregard.

'I thought I would like to land at the same spot I first arrived on your island,' Oliver explained to Judith, who was eyeing the towering cliffs and secluded shore with unconcealed pleasure.

'But not naked and half drowned this time,' she laughed. 'Oh, Oliver, how glad I am I saw you. Just imagine! I might have been wed to Simon Perrier by now!'

'And I would most probably have been dead. Destiny, my love. I escaped death, and you an impossible

marriage. But come, let us get into the boat so that
they can row us ashore.'

'You did let Papa know we were coming?' asked
Judith. Oliver had been strangely reticent about their
forthcoming return, telling her little of his plans beyond
the fact of when they were to sail. They had spent a
month in Plymouth beforehand, staying with his
parents, who had welcomed him as a prodigal, and her
with a warmth which had grown into affection. She had
been sad to leave, but was looking forward to seeing
her own family again.

'He knows. But he will not be here to welcome us,
angel.'

'Not here?'

'No, angel. But see, Josué is coming to meet us.'

Judith scanned the rapidly approaching shore and
saw a group of figures descending the path to meet
them. Josué, Penna and Jasper and two small figures
who must be Elie and Bess.

'Has something happened to Papa and Maman?' she
demanded, her voice quivering.

Oliver hastened to put her mind at rest. 'Of course
not, angel! You would surely have heard! I apologise,
I did not seek to make you anxious! But I have a
surprise for you. Rest assured your parents are well
and happy. But they are no longer on Sark.'

'Then where are they?' Judith spoke sharply. For
eight long months they had lived in perfect harmony.
Oliver had remained at Harvel, channelling his restless
energy into improving the estate while she had used
her home-making talents on the house, and in equip-
ping a nursery. To their joy, a baby was due in
September. She had not imagined anything could disturb their amity, but he was testing her patience to
the limit!

'Back in Jersey,' he answered with a brilliant grin.

'Then why have we come here?'

'Do you not wish to see your brother?' he enquired mildly. 'And the house, and all the other people you left behind?'

'Of course, but I thought we were visiting my parents!'

'And so we shall be! Patience, my angel. I have brought you here to present you with your birthday gift.'

'Oh.' Deflated, Judith met her husband's twinkling gaze. 'You have a surprise for me?'

'Aye, my beautiful wife. I trust you will like it.'

Reassured as to the health of her parents, Judith felt her curiosity begin to stir. Whatever could Oliver have bought for her that merited a visit to Sark when her parents were no longer here?

She had to wait to find out. They landed, climbed up to the cliff plateau and were exuberantly greeted by the small party waiting there to welcome them. Together, they all ascended the path along which Edward and Josué had carried the half-dead Oliver. Memories did not seem to trouble him, but they haunted Judith, though part of her mind still puzzled over her surprise gift. As they approached the top, an inkling began to dawn.

Behind the farmhouse she had known as home a new, two-storey building had risen. And away to the left, another, smaller dwelling had sprung from the ground.

'My home,' Josué told her proudly, pointing. 'I own Le Petit Beauregard now.'

'Papa gave it to you?'

'Aye. When he sold the remainder of his tenements. I wished to remain on Sark.'

'He sold them? To whom?'

Josué grinned. 'You had better ask your husband.'

Oliver had been walking quietly a pace behind the brother and sister talking with Jasper, while Penna, Thomasse and Lambert brought up the rear. Judith stopped and turned.

'Oliver?' Her voice held breathless incredulity.

He came up beside her and Josué dropped back. The children ran on ahead and made straight for the door to her old home. Penna did not call them back.

'Oliver?' she repeated. She felt as though she were walking in a dream. She had guessed the answer. But why had he done it?

'Aye, angel. I bought it. Are you pleased? 'Tis yours.'

'My birthday gift?' she breathed.

He nodded. 'The house, yes. The tenement is yours as part of the marriage settlement. I retain the rights your father held over all the tenements Helier gave him. Shall we go and inspect our new home?'

The others thoughtfully left them to proceed alone. Penna followed her children into the old farmhouse, inviting the others to accompany her. Judith noted that the temporary building which had been the Sidney's home a year since had disappeared.

Josué, his arm about the shoulders of a pretty young girl, the daughter of one of the Seigneur's relatives living on the island, strolled off towards his own home. So that was how the wind blew! Young Margaret would make him a fine wife, thought Judith happily.

The house was not as large or as sumptuous as Harvel, of course, but generous quantities of stone and timber had been imported to build a home worthy of Sir Oliver, Le Sieur Burnett, after the Seigneur, the most important man on Sark.

He took her on a tour of the place, pointing out its features, which included a splendid kitchen, separate from the room where they would live. Servants were already installed and some she knew of old. They greeted her with happy smiles.

'Your mother pined for Jersey,' Oliver explained. 'Your father told me how unhappy she was when we spoke during that trip downriver to Gravesend, and how he feared for her health if she remained on Sark for much longer. He himself had lost the will to remain after Edward's death. And then there was Genette. He had to see her well wed, and that will be easier on Jersey.'

'Twould have been easier for me, too, thought Judith, but said nothing. Genette had always been her father's favourite. She bore neither of them any grudge, for had she not found Oliver?

'We came to a tentative agreement then,' Oliver went on, 'which was sealed when I returned last July.'

'You were here last July and did not tell me?'

'Aye, my sweet. Forgive me, but I wanted to keep the secret. I appointed an architect and made all my wishes known. I had not seen the building until today. I think it has turned out well, don't you?'

'But why, Oliver?' She could not believe he could have known of her secret longing to retain some ties with Sark. 'I had told you often how much I wanted to escape the confines of the island!'

'But I knew that deep down you loved the place, angel. You were just restless, that was all. And in future you will have two homes to chose from. We will divide our time between them. Either are equally convenient for privateering — Blackler can sail from here as easily as from Gravesend, and be nearer to Spain. He will quickly become familiar with these waters. He navigated them well enough when he was chasing that carrack trying to rescue me.'

'That was the *Mermaid*? I've often wondered.'

'Aye. Operating as the *Sea Hawk*, of course. It ran the Spanish ship aground soon after she sailed from here but found I was not aboard. The Spanish told them I was dead. So you can imagine the surprise when I turned up in England again — better late than never! The message I carried for the Queen was no longer of moment. The Ridolfi plot had already been foiled. Blackler pretended to be delighted by my return, but it meant he had not inherited the ship.'

'I think he must have rejoiced to find you safe.'

Oliver grinned, confident in the regard of his captain. 'At least it meant he did not have to search for a sponsor!'

Judith went up to her husband and wound her arms around his neck. 'You have sent Blackler out without you these last months. Will you ever sail with the *Sea Hawk* again, Oliver?'

He touched her cheek, his eyes serious for once as they met her clear grey gaze. 'Would it distress you if I did, angel?'

'I should worry about you.' Her arms tightened. 'But I should not try to prevent you. Such sport is in your blood.'

The lines deepened between his eyes. 'It was. But I have found such content these last months. My love of privateering has taken second place to love of my wife. And when our son is born. . .'

He left the sentence unfinished. Judith drew his lips down to hers. 'I am glad. And should you wish to settle on Sark I should raise no objection. My happiness lies with you, not in a place, wherever it may be.'

'So,' he breathed. 'We are content in each other. Long may this satisfactory state of affairs last.'

'You think it will not?'

He shook his head, the merry twinkle back in his eyes, the mischievous smile on his lips.

'I cannot imagine it. I could not live without you, my angel. You are all I want.'

'And you I. I love you,' breathed Judith.

The ravishing kiss threatened to last forever, but Oliver suddenly drew back his head. 'Marry! But I had forgotten, Blackler was to sail almost immediately! He will return in two weeks to take us to Jersey. Meanwhile, he will seek a prize in these waters. We must go and wave him God speed.'

He grasped her hand and hurried her from the house, leading her out to Longue Pointe, the headland overlooking the bay so poignant with memories. Judith was not yet heavy with child, in fact her bulge was slight, so she kept up with him effortlessly.

The *Mermaid* had just upped anchor. As the sails filled, Oliver doffed his cap and waved it in sweeping arcs. Judith took off hers, too, and lifted the white linen high into the wind, flying it like a flag. Another memory surfaced. The last time she had done this Oliver had been sailing away from her. She laughed her jubilation as a blast on a horn acknowledged their farewell.

Soon the brig was out past the Ile des Marchands, disappearing towards the distant horizon. Judith rested back against her husband's warm body. His arms about her waist held her fast. Solid, comforting, there. Where she needed him to be.

And Oliver, removing his eyes from the distant blur, found he had no regrets at being left behind. Burying his nose in her hair, he murmured, 'Your father made a good start, angel. But we will make this the most prosperous tenement on Sark.'

Judith twisted in his arms to face him. 'You will do it, husband. And you will do it with all the daring, all the energy you bring to every task. But I will help you.'

'And our sons will have both Harvel and Beauregard to inherit. Maybe more land, who knows? As the Queen said, we must found a dynasty.'

'Well,' rejoined Judith practically. 'We have made a start.'

The old mischievous smile curved his lips. 'And we have our lives before us in which to complete the task!'

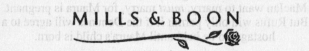

LEGACY *of* LOVE

Coming next month

SERENA
Sylvia Andrew
Regency (West Indies/England)

Miss Serena Calvert, owner of Anse Chatelet on the West Indian island of St. Just, was determined to give her young niece Lucy a London Season, whatever the financial privations. But their aunt's health would not permit her to launch Lucy, and Serena was forced to go too, as chaperon.

Once in England, Serena met a delightful gentleman in slightly scandalous circumstances, and both looked forward to meeting again more formally in London. But that meeting resulted in a massively public snub for Serena, and only then did she become aware that *she* was the target of revenge...

HOSTAGE OF LOVE
Valentina Luellen
Scotland 1740

Rufus MacIan and Alistair Denune have feuded for years, but now their children are grown. Michael Denune and Maura MacIan want to marry, *must* marry, for Maura is pregnant. But Rufus will only permit it if the Denunes will agree to a hostage, to be held until Maura's child is born.

How can Cassandra refuse, when she loves her brother—even if this does bring her into contact with Rufus's adopted son, Adam MacIan? He, at least, seems to be civilised...until Cassandra realises the feud hasn't died.

LEGACY _of_ LOVE

Coming next month

THE RELUCTANT BRIDE
Barbara Bretton
Delaware 1887

The Pemberton Arms would have long since crumbled but for the optimism of Molly Hughes. She dreamed of a chance to restore the old seaside hotel, the only home she'd ever known. That chance was suddenly within her reach—depending on how she handled Nicholas St George, the Englishman who had just inherited her beloved "Pem"— and meant to sell it off! Nicholas had been appalled when he'd set eyes on the ramshackle nightmare he'd inherited. Nothing could save it. Not even the charm of Molly Hughes…

Before he weakened any further, he'd conclude his business and sail home—post-haste! Molly had a surprise in store for Nicholas…

WICKED STRANGER
Louisa Rawlings
France/New York 1817

Elizabeth Babcock had always been "just plain Bessie", overshadowed by her socialite sisters. Few suitors looked beyond her razor-sharp repartee—and temper to match—before leaving for less challenging opportunities. Until, that was, a night in Paris, when she crossed rapier wits with Noel Bouchard…

A gambler, a soldier, a man of the world, Noel Bouchard prayed never to be saddled with a dull domestic life. Marriage, if entered into at _all_, should be an adventure—tempestuous and lusty. He needed a woman with verve and spirit. With passion and wit. A woman like Elizabeth Babcock…

FOUR
HISTORICAL
ROMANCES
&
TWO
FREE GIFTS!